THE GALLERY

A Detective Nula Ryan Murder Mystery

John Wheatley

Independent

Copyright © 2024 John Wheatley

All rights reserved

The characters and events portrayed in this book are fictitious. Any similarity to real persons, living or dead, is coincidental and not intended by the author.

No part of this book may be reproduced, or stored in a retrieval system, or transmitted in any form or by any means, electronic, mechanical, photocopying, recording, or otherwise, without express written permission of the publisher.

ISBN-13: 979886052347

CONTENTS

Title Page
Copyright
THE GALLERY   1
Prologue : August   2
Chapter 1   3
Part 1 - July   6
Chapter 2   7
Chapter 3   17
Chapter 4   31
Chapter 5   41
Chapter 6   51
Chapter 7   55
Chapter 8   58
Chapter 9   64
Chapter 10   66
Chapter 11   71
Chapter 12   73
Chapter 13   77
Chapter 14   82
Chapter 15   88
Chapter 16   94

Chapter 17	100
Chapter 18	102
Chapter 19	106
Chapter 20	110
Chapter 21	112
Chapter 22	117
Chapter 23	126
Chapter 24	130
Chapter 25	138
Part 2 : August	152
Chapter 26	153
Chapter 27	156
Chapter 28	163
Chapter 29	167
Chapter 30	183
Chapter 31	192
Chapter 32	200
Chapter 33	204
Chapter 34	209
Chapter 35	220
Chapter 36	223
Chapter 37	246
Afterword	249
Chapter 38	250
Chapter 1	253
Chapter 2	257

THE GALLERY

PROLOGUE : AUGUST

CHAPTER 1

I could have done without an unexplained dead body incident on that day of all days.

I was driving into Divisional HQ when I got the call. Directions to go to a section of the canal locks at Milthwaite. Body discovered by an early morning cyclist.

It was my first day back on duty after maternity leave. Not my maternity leave, directly, but that of my girlfriend, Wendy. I had taken two weeks leave to be around. Wendy had been home with the gorgeous little Phoebe for a week, and what an amazing week it had been! But neither of us had realised how exhausting it would be. I guess I was just hoping for an easy day.

Frank was there to meet me.

'Hiya Nula,' he said. 'Y'all right? Nice to see you back.'

'Hi Frank. What is it then?'

'Body in the drink. Female. Caught up in the sluice on the other side of the lock.'

'Cyclist found her?'

'Yes. Over there. I've taken a statement. Photographer's done his stuff.'

'Any ID?'

'Don't know yet. Forensics in there now.'

The area had been cordoned off, guarded by a couple of uniform, and a white tent stood on the bank of the canal. A few locals were watching from a distance. I put on SOCO gear and popped my head inside the tent. The medic was Dawn Wilson. We'd met on a couple of cases before. She was just zipping up the body bag.

'Hi Nula.'

'Hi Dawn. Any ID?'

'Nope.'

'Cause of?' I asked, speculatively.

She shook her head. 'Not obvious. I've done all I can here. Need to get her back to the office. Is the wagon here yet?'

'What do you think then Nula?' asked Frank.

'Could be accidental. People fall in and drown. Drunks.'

'Festival yesterday. No shortage of drunks.'

'Did you get much of a look?'

'Not really.' He shrugged his shoulders. 'Semi-naked. Not been there long, I'd say.'

We phoned it in, requesting information about anybody reported missing, then instructed uniform to secure the site and close off the canal towpath in both directions. Ten minutes later, the ambulance appeared at the canal bridge, fifty yards off, and they brought a stretcher trolley down for her. Once the ambulance had gone the curiosity dissipated and the locals drifted off. A little later, a press guy turned up wanting details, but we could only tell him there'd be a statement in due course. Frank and I paced round the area, getting a picture of the lie of the land, just in case. The state of undress was obviously a suspicious circumstance, but until we got the report from the lab there wasn't much we could do.

It was midday before we got away. Frank had come out with the uniform, so I gave him a lift back.

'So, going all right then, is it? The kid I mean.'

'Tiring.'

'Tell me about it. We've had three.'

'Tell me it gets easier.'

'It doesn't.'

Relaxing now, Frank dropped into his more jocular chummy vein. 'What about when she goes to school?'

'How do you mean?'

'Well, like, when they do the 'all-about-my family' thing. Will she have to say she's got two mummies?'

With anyone else, you might think they were trying it on, but not with Frank.

'I suppose so, yes. What's wrong with that?'

'Nothing, really, I guess. Just might be awkward, I thought.'

'Kids have all sorts of odd family set-ups these days, Frank. It's not all mum, dad and 2.4 children.'

Frank laughed. 'No, I suppose not. Most coppers' kids think they come from a single-parent family anyway.'

When I got into the station, there was a stack of desk work waiting for me. I buried myself in it for what I hoped would be an uninterrupted remainder of the day. At about three I got a message through that no missing persons had been reported in the Milthwaite area. Then, just after four, the relative peace and calm of the office was broken by Frank bearing down on me with great purpose. 'Briefing Room, with Inspector Renwick, now,' he announced. 'Preliminary pathology report back. Looks like we've got a murder on our hands.'

PART 1 - JULY

CHAPTER 2

A compact gallery space in a small, trendy town in a picturesque Pennine valley. The gallery, with its fresh light walls and dark blue calico screens, runs on a shoestring, relying on meagre local authority support and tiny Arts Council grants to supplement its income from classes in painting, sculpture and jewellery-making for both children and adults. It also puts on regular exhibitions of the work of local artists. On this particular Saturday morning, the meeting is to commemorate the local watercolourist, Duncan Tomlinson, who died in the early spring, with an exhibition of his work curated- ex gratia - by Ralph Anderson, local resident and Lecturer in Art History at the University of Leeds.

He is present with his wife Barbara, and their daughter Natalie, recently returned from completing her degree in History at Nottingham. He is slightly edgy because, at any moment, he is to be called upon to make a short speech, which is difficult because the truth is that he didn't really think that much of Duncan's work, and only took on the task of putting the exhibition together as a means of displaying his own prestige in the local community,

The space is crowded. This is because Duncan was, without doubt, a colourful local character. As well as the considerable output of his own work, he contributed, down the years, some memorable sets and backdrops for the Milthwaite Players, and took a hand in communal festivities and events too numerous to mention.

Besides Ralph Anderson and his family, a number of local artists are present, together with some of Duncan's relatives and drinking companions. There is a handful of the pupils who have benefitted, recently, from the gallery's painting classes, members of the Players, Julie Brown who is the gallery's main teacher and organiser, and a chap from the local press who is also his own photographer. They all want to give Duncan a jolly send-off.

A cork pops and the buzz of conversation is heightened by a moment of merriment as Julie, the cork popper, lets out an unintended nervous giggle before beginning to pour prosecco into plastic wine flutes.

'Who is that man over there in the corner?' asks Natalie, leaning in towards her father. The man she is alluding to has a distinctive, rather crumpled raffish appearance, with a dark beard sprinkled with grey, rugged features and a slightly sour expression.

'Adam Mitchell,' replies Ralph, without great interest.

'Adam Mitchell, the poet?'

'Yes, well, writer of trashy novels anyway.'

He steps forward to take a glass of prosecco, and gives one to Barbara. Natalie takes one for herself. Barbara now turns away to talk to Beverley Reddish from the church committee, and he takes the opportunity to glance over to Magda Bentley and their eyes meet for a moment in secret knowledge.

He considers Magda Bentley to be the most innovative of the local artists; the rest he tends to think of as hacks churning out mediocre watercolours of the same cliched topics. Magda is thirty-five. She is wearing a red jumper which amplifies pleasingly the shapeliness of her bosom, and underneath she is wearing a short dress with pleats at the hem, giving her legs, tantalisingly, an almost schoolgirlish appearance.

The moment passes, but the irritation of making a speech about Duncan, which he wishes he had planned a little more, has been at least briefly offset by pleasanter thoughts.

He turns to make sure that Barbara has not noticed anything. She is still talking to Beverley who obviously has something which she thinks worth the telling for at a certain moment she forms her mouth into a meme of shock/surprise: a practised pose which she holds fixed for a full three seconds. Probably, he suspects, something about Paul, the gay vicar, who has been exercising the patience of the church committee since his arrival eighteen months ago.

Julie now tries to silence the assembly so that the formal side of things can start. She is not very good at this and simpers a little nervously with embarrassment, but a few sympathetic coughs and grunts serve to bring about the desired effect. She thanks everyone for coming and hopes everyone has managed to get some prosecco or orange juice and some crisps or salted peanuts, and then, after the briefest of introductions, hands over to Ralph.

'Thank you, Julie,' he says, and then after a purposeful clearing of the throat, 'Duncan Tomlinson. How can I possibly begin to do adequate justice to dear old Duncan? A truly colourful local personality if ever there was one...' Bit by bit, it falls into place; he jumps nimbly from one stepping stone to another and five minutes later, he hears the ripple of polite applause that confirms he has finished without blundering.

A toast is raised to Duncan and the gathering begins to mingle and to glance at the works of his last exhibition. Julie waits, smiling, at the counter, just in case anyone should decide to make the ultimate compliment of buying.

It is at this point that Natalie sidles over to Adam Mitchell and, with the easy confidence of youth, begins a conversation with him.

'Did you know him very well? Duncan, I mean.'

'No,' he says, tersely.

'Not at all?' she queries.

He narrows his eyes slightly, as if caught between her impudence and her charm. 'Knew of him, of course. May have downed a few pints in his company from time to time,' he adds, the gravelly texture of his voice perhaps suggesting derision.

'I just wondered why you'd come here, being a poet, sort of thing.'

'Local arts. I try to show my face when I can.'

'I studied some of your poems at school,' she says suddenly, taking him by surprise.

'Really? A level?'

'No, sorry. GCSE.'

'Oh Christ!'

'Yes, I know. Sorry. It was in an anthology too, which I suppose makes it worse, but I did like them.'

'Well, I am flattered,' he says with an edge of sarcasm.

'I hope you got some royalties.'

The conversation is interrupted at this point by Magda who says hello to Natalie, giving Adam the opportunity to back off.

'I came to a class you did here once,' says Natalie. 'It was with school. Quite a while ago.'

'Did you do art?' asks Magda.

'At uni I did history, but I've always been interested in art.'

'You should come up to my studio if you like. Have a look round.'

'Yes, I will,' says Natalie, smiling.

Having edged slowly towards the door saying a few brief hellos along the way, Adam Mitchell eventually and gratefully reaches the point at which he feels he can leave without appearing rude.

He makes his way down towards the village centre and decides that, even though his hangover from the previous night had been at least in part responsible for his bad mood of the morning, a pint at the White Hart is something to which he is being drawn, like iron filings to a magnet. A pint became two, and he chatted happily to Moggy Morton, the plumber, who always had a good tale to tell, even though he seemed to carry with him a vague aroma of drains and unwashed clothes so that you didn't get too close. Then, reflecting on the morning over a final half, he regretted that most of his rudeness had been visited on the young woman who had seemed to think that her having read his poems for O-level, or whatever they called it these days, might be a matter of interest to him. Not even a collection, for God's sake, but an anthology with God knows who else the exam board thought worthy of study.

But now, mellowed, he regretted his bluntness. And he retained the image of her apparent ingenuousness and youthful charm, together with a certain sexual glamour that belongs to the young.

In a pub, in the middle of the afternoon, such things took on a softened and disproportionate significance.

Go on, then, the other half…

Sexual glamour, he repeated from the private lexicon of his favoured phrases. Christ! Don't get me started on that!

The sun was still eye-startlingly bright as he made his way home.

He made a cup of coffee which he knew he probably wouldn't drink, and then lay down on his bed.

Magda Bentley made her way back to her studio, well aware that a particular pair of eyes had followed her round the gallery seeking the moment for a discreet eye-to-eye. It was the kind of attention she was used to, and it rarely displeased her. In this case, the fact that it was Ralph Anderson whose interest was thus revealed, had more than one layer of significance.

The studio to which she now returned was half a mile from the centre of the village in premises which had once been part of a woollen mill - now partly dismantled - which she shared , across a cobbled yard, with a carpet and upholstery wholesaler. In her own corner of this once rambling edifice, the ground floor served as her studio. It was signposted from the road outside, and occasionally passers-by would heed the invitation to enter and browse, and occasionally too, she would make a sale. From the studio, an open and precarious-looking wooden staircase led to the upper storey where her living quarters were. These comprised a single large room with a bed, a cooker and fridge, a sink with drainer, and a shower and toilet which could be screened off for privacy.

The studio was rented, privately, and at pretty much a

peppercorn rent – and in this the first layer of Ralph Anderson's significance - for the owner of the building was, in fact, Ralph's wife, Barbara. Magda had been the tenant for six years, and whether she had actually met Ralph when she first took it on, she could not remember. In recent months, however, he had been prompted – she suspected by his wife – to open up discussions about increasing the rent to something closer to a market rate, and it was out of these amicable discussions, accompanied by the bottle of wine he happened to have with him, that her affair with him had started.

It was not, on her part, entirely from cynical motives that these two things had come to co-exist. She did find him attractive. Her taste in men veered between those older than herself, usually by at least ten years, and those younger: boys of eighteen or nineteen. Men in between tended to be too inclined to be possessive, to want to marry her and to set out a life plan together. Older men, or some of them at least, had that worldly wisdom and detachment which she liked, and which left her free. The young, of both sexes, had the sexual imagination and crazy vitality of adolescence, which she found exciting.

Ralph Anderson was a man of forty-five, she guessed - maybe a little more - tall and still retaining something of an athletic build. It was obviously his daughter who had been with him at the gallery this morning, and she, who, he told her, had just returned from completing her university degree, must be twenty-one or twenty-two, and some of her looks obviously came from him.

Magda had, occasionally, with the bottle of wine still on the go, sketched him. He had strong regular features, a firm jaw, and with thick hair, confidently combed straight back from the brow, dark but with a photogenic streak of pure premature white. His growing old, she suspected, would be, for him certainly, a matter of ever-increasing vanity.

He was also, it had to be said, an enthusiastic lover – though perhaps not quite such a virtuoso as he thought himself - and that counted for something. For the time being at least.

THE GALLERY

The other interesting thing about the gathering at the gallery was that Adam Mitchell had been there. He was not one who usually graced such meetings with his presence, and had looked distinctly out of countenance to be there, but then Duncan Tomlinson had been such a favourite local celebrity, that deliberate absence from his farewell might well have earned one a black mark in the estimation of the local arts fraternity. Or - and the thought gave her a moment's amusement - perhaps Adam was beginning to mellow with age.

From the window of his little office in the carpet warehouse just opposite her studio, Rob Jenkins had seen Magda Bentley arriving back home in the early afternoon, and had muttered to himself one of the concise epithets he had for women who he found sexually attractive. It had been a slack day, a slack week in fact, but the overall situation was not bad. People still wanted carpets, or other floor coverings, even in hard times, and there were plenty of renovations going on. People came to him because he ran a low-cost operation and could supply decent quality stuff and decent fitters at a very competitive rate. He had inherited the carpet business from an uncle and had been in carpets since he left school, which was twelve years ago. He had hated it at first, still hated it in many ways, but no other way of earning his living ever having presented itself, he had stuck with it, and it was now his way of life.

He had been married for a short time in his late teens but it had not lasted. His wife had moved back to Leeds, and he had gone back to live with his mother, now disabled, in the terraced house behind the station where he had been brought up.

He kept an eye on the comings and goings of the artist lady who had moved in across the way. He had been friendly and tried to show an interest in her stuff at first, and she had shown him round. He had suggested that they could go out for a drink together, if she fancied it, but when, without saying it in so many words, she declined, he had backed off. But he remained curious. From his office, he could also see directly across to the window of the upstairs room where the artist lady lived. Usually the curtain was closed, but she was not always careful, the artist lady, he had seen enough to know that. A grandstand view he had had, more than once, albeit fleetingly, of those impressive boobs, and glimpses too of her visitors, including, most recently Anderson, the landlord, though he was by no means the only one.

Bit of a slutty, actually, he said to himself, with a kind of moral disapprobation that amounted to approval.

You think yourself above the likes of me, don't you, but a bit of a slutty, aren't you, really?

By four o'clock, he had packed up for the afternoon, and was on his way home, a five-minute journey in his Hilux. His mother, in her wheelchair, had managed to wheel herself out into the yard at the back to get some sunshine.

'Very nice,' said Rob. 'You're getting very proficient.'

'I couldn't get back in though,' she said with a laugh. 'I'm dying for the loo.'

'Come on, then,' he said, wheeling the chair round and pushing it back up the ramp. 'I'll see to you.'

He was quite used to dealing with his mother's needs of one sort or another, from dressing to bathing, and she often said to him, 'I don't know what I'd do without you.' 'I don't know what I'd do without him,' she often said to the neighbours. 'I'd be in a right mess.'

'Have you finished up there for the day then?' she asked.

'I'll have a walk back up later, finish some paperwork.'

'You should have stopped a bit and finished off.'

'I thought I'd get back and see you were all right.'

'Going back up there on a Saturday night, I don't know!'

'Good job I did pop back too, eh?'

She laughed. 'You should be going out, having a bit of fun on a Saturday night.'

'It'll not take me long. I'll pop along for a pint when I've done.'

'That's more like it.'

'What do you want for your tea then, ma?'
'Have we still got some of that pork pie?'
'Aye, I think so.'
'Well, I'll have some of that, then. With a few oven chips. You can pop a tomato on as well if you like. Are you having some?'
'Might as well. Do you want the telly on?'
'You can put it on later. When you go. Just wheel me outside for a bit while you're doing.'
'Been nice again, hasn't it, ma? Maybe we're set for a heatwave.'
'Don't say that. You'll put the 'fluence on it.'

Going back into the kitchen, he switched on the oven to warm up, took the remainder of the pork pie out of the fridge and cut it into two slices. Then he put the oven chips onto a tray, put them in the oven, and whilst they were doing, went for a quick shower and shave to freshen up. The house had been adapted significantly since his mother had become wheelchair bound, with a stair-lift and a walk-in shower room, as well as the toilet downstairs which was wide enough for the wheelchair. The council had been sluggish at first, but he had chased them up, insisting on his mother's rights at every turn, quite prepared to make an unpleasant nuisance of himself if he had to.

There is a photograph of Rob on the sideboard, one taken a couple of years ago, looking more or less the same as he does now: short sandy crew-cut, angular face, hollow cheeks, pale blue eyes; and another, a school photo of when he was twelve, the same features still evident on a much younger face, though the face has now lost the hint of a cheeky grin it had then.

'Proper little boy, weren't you?' his mum often says, looking at this photo.'

'Do you want the telly on with it?' he asked, when he's pushed her back in for her meal.
'Not if you want to sit at the table.'
'No, you're all right. I'll have mine on my knee.'

He gave her the tray which sat over the arms of the wheelchair and then switched on the television, flicking to TV Gold, which was her favourite channel. It was an episode of *Only Fools and Horses*.

'Here you are, mam. Cup of tea to go with it.'

'You know what I wonder, son?' she asked as they settled into their meal, and as the programme went into the commercial break.

'What's that ma?'

'I wonder why they don't make television programmes like this anymore. It's just the thing to give you a lift.'

'Well, I reckon you're right there, ma. Pity about all the adverts though.'

'Well, I like those too. I think they're quite good. Funny sometimes, too.'

CHAPTER 3

Ralph Anderson was correct in thinking that the conversation between his wife and Beverley Reddish had had as its main topic Paul, the gay vicar. Beverley thinks of herself as a good Christian woman but also as a sensible one, and, in the balance, she is firmly of the opinion that having a gay vicar is not ideally what one would want. Barbara does not really share this opinion, but there are certain strands of local village discourse where she feels it tactful not to argue too strongly.

'It isn't really that he's homosexual,' Barbara is explaining, with some awkwardness, to Natalie, later in the day. 'The thing is that he can be rather geeky and embarrassing.'

'I'm sure there are plenty of straight vicars who are geeky and embarrassing,' suggests Natalie who does not particularly bother herself with church things generally.

'For example,' says Barbara, as she begins to relate the tale which Beverley Reddish was telling her earlier at the gallery, 'if, for example, you bump into him in the supermarket, he is loud and laughs with a horsey snort that makes you wish the ground would open up to swallow you – if not him.'

'I suppose he's just trying to be friendly,' argues Natalie who has a young person's dislike of prejudice and narrow-mindedness.

'Yes, I'm sure you're right, darling.'

'Don't tell me you've been affected by all this LGBT stuff that's going round at university,' chips in Ralph, with some amusement.

'You make it sound like a disease.'

Ralph laughs, as if not displeased by this characterisation.

'I just think it's wrong to automatically dislike someone because they are gay,' says Natalie.

'I'm not saying I dislike people who are gay,' says Barbara, hoping that she will not be called on to be a peacemaker between Ralph and Natalie. Things have been on an even keel since Natalie returned from Nottingham, but she is always on the lookout for a potential flashpoint.

'You did that play last year *Run for Your Wife*. Everyone was hooting at the gay chap in that – you didn't mind that.'

'You're right, dear. I'm sure there are a lot of double standards about, but anyway I've got to get on. And so have you.'

Barbara has an extra-ordinary committee meeting at the theatre to attend. It is unusual to have meetings on Saturday nights but this one has been called to discuss, most importantly, the arrangements for the food and drink festival in two weeks' time, where the Players are organising a gin stall. Also on the agenda is the approval of the selection of plays for next season. Natalie, who is due to go to Teacher Training College in September, has just acquired a job waiting on at the White Hart. Tonight is her first shift.

'Don't you think that top is a little revealing?' asks Barbara, as Natalie prepares to set out for her shift. 'Don't want to give the wrong impression on your first day.'

'I thought that was rather the point about being a barmaid,' says Ralph.

'Don't be coarse, Ralph,' says Barbara.

'Course not,' replies Natalie, giving an amused laugh as she turns to the mirror to view herself.

'Right. I'll drop you off if you're ready then. Have you told your dad when to pick you up?'

'I can walk. It's only fifteen minutes.'

'You will NOT walk,' says Barbara, as if some atrocity has been suggested. 'Ralph!'

Ralph lowers the newspaper he is reading. 'Mmm?'

'Do you know what time to pick her up?'

'Natalie?'

'Shift supposed to finish at eleven, but I expect there'll be some clearing up to do.'

'Don't let them put upon you,' says Barbara.

'About quarter past, then?' suggests Ralph. 'What time will you be back, Barbara?'

'Well, you know what these committee meetings are like. Should be back by ten. Half past at the latest.'

For Ralph Anderson, the fact that both Barbara and Natalie are out for the evening is quite convenient. For the ten years she has been a member of the Players, he has actively encouraged her participation. His view of the Players is pretty similar to his view of the local watercolourists – people who commute up to town to be bankers and solicitors during the week and then play at being *luvvies* at the weekend but it has filled a gap in Barbara`s life. It means that, especially on the run-up to a play and during the week of performance, she is sometimes out for several nights together, and if he is honest with himself, he encourages her participation precisely for this reason. But to be fair, he has her interests at heart. After the children started at secondary school – Natalie's elder brother is now doing articles as a solicitor in London – there was a period when Barbara had seemed rather lost and miserable. Joining the Players had helped her along the way towards finding a sense of purpose, and she hadn't looked back.

Personally, he enjoys the sense of freedom in the house when Barbara is busy; he reads, he does The Times crossword, he listens to music, he does his university work when there is anything to do, and occasionally, he goes out for an evening walk and calls in at the pub for a couple of pints.

On this particular evening the convenience of both Natalie and Barbara being out of the house is that it allows him to go out without anyone asking where he is going. What he intends to do, on this particular evening, is to walk over and pay a visit to Magda Bentley at her studio, to continue – he smiles to himself – the business of reviewing the rent. Barbara herself, who inherited the 'ruin' as it was called in the family, had no interest at all in the rent, but the 'review' provides a convenient pretext, should he need one, for going there.

There is no guarantee that Magda will be in, of course, and no guarantee either that if she is in, she will be amenable to his design. She is very much her own creature, and can be capricious, which is possibly part of the attraction. It is worth a try, however, and the thought of it has had his mind simmering with a slow-burning excitement all through the afternoon. He takes a bottle of wine that has been chilling in the fridge since he placed it there at two o'clock, puts it into a carrier bag, and lets himself out. The house is in a quiet close, and with little chance that the immediate neighbours will notice the fact that he is choosing a route away from the direction of his usual 'local', he makes his way towards the old cobbled track which, in the old days, led down to the mill.

There is nothing he feels compelled to do to counter his lust for Magda; it is a natural and powerful feeling, and that it has been reciprocated on a number of occasions adds to its strength. Nor does he feel any guilt about his adultery. There are certain ways in which the world works, and he conforms to them. Down the years, there have been a number of discreet liaisons in Leeds, usually postgraduates who have drifted into his sphere, some of them just brief encounters, some which have trailed on for weeks, even months. Leeds, of course, is at a safe distance. This is closer to home but he feels safe with Magda as she is a free spirit, operating outside the fixed gridlines of Milthwaite social ethics. And the slight element of risk does add, he admits, a certain frisson of excitement.

But the bottom line is that he does not want Barbara to suspect, or worse, find out about Magda. Though their own marital relations have dwindled, over a period of years, to a point where they might be said hardly to exist at all, he feels certain that an open discovery of adultery would provoke a strong, if purely conventional, reaction from Barbara that would be very unpleasant. He can see absolutely no point in disturbing the peaceful external surface of her life, or of his own.

It isn't strictly true that Rob Jenkins' *walking back up* is to do, as he said to his mother, with the completion of paperwork relating to the sale of carpets. The computer which he uses for his accounts is also quite serviceable, out of hours, for viewing porn, and visiting dating sites without fear of interruption.

At this moment, he is in conversation, on an Asian site, with a Chinese girl in Cambodia who has said she will send him intimate photographs if he will commit to helping her escape from her own country to England. He has no intention of helping her, but it is interesting to see how far he can push it.

His usual method is to persuade the girls on the dating sites to hook up with him online but outside the dating site itself. This is strictly against the advice that both parties are recommended, for their own security, to follow, but it is usually not very difficult to persuade the girls that the opposite is true, i.e., that they are being exploited by the site, and that therein lies the danger. The advantage of this is that he can avoid some of the safeguards that the sites tend to put in place – the reputable ones anyway, and he avoids the dodgy ones because those are the ones where you are most likely to get scammed.

Just send me one photo, so I know you are genuine.
I am a good girl. Clean.
Ok. I know. But just one photo.
OK. I do screen shot.

It came through. It was disappointing. She was nice-looking, but though she had taken off her vest, she was still in her underwear.

He went off-screen and waited three minutes.
Are you still there? she asks.
Yes.
You like picture?
Yes, I've been looking. It's lovely. but take off your thing off, let me see you, properly.

He waits another minute. No photo comes through. He clicks

21

out. There are plenty of girls like her. And in the end, they just want money to fund their escape. Sweet talk and sexy talk they are prepared to indulge, but in the end – it always came round to it - just money.

He has sometimes toyed with the idea of going to Thailand, say for a month, to see if it is all true what people say about how easy it is to get girls there. There was a guy at the pub, Brian, a builder, who said he had bought a house there from the settlement when his wife had bought him out, he said. Kept a girl there too, he said. Take that with a pinch of salt, Rob had thought to himself, must be in his sixties at least, what would a girl see in Brian? Though to be fair there might be some truth in it, what with the things people will do to escape from poverty. Witness the girls he sometimes talked to on the internet. You didn't come across any there who were happy with their lot and wanted to stay put. For his own part, he had quite a penchant for Asian girls, slim ones anyway, with nice faces, not those who wore the full nun's outfit. Asian girls, maybe more from Thailand and Malaysia rather than India or Pakistan, could be quite sexy. Vietnamese, Chinese too. Though it was Thailand and Cambodia the poorer countries that you tended to hear about. A month in Bangkok, or maybe one of those coastal places, might be just the job. Though obviously, anything like that would have to wait until after his mother had passed. And she was in no hurry for that to happen, and neither, for that matter, was he, really.

Looking down from his window to the cobbled courtyard below, he sees Ralph Anderson arriving at the door of Magda Bentley's studio. The bag he is carrying, Rob supposes from its shape, contains a bottle of wine.

A bottle of wine. Ralph Anderson is nothing if not predictable. Fair exchange is no robbery, perhaps that's how he sees it?

He wonders if it will be dark enough for him to see the light going on in the room above, assuming, as he does, that, in due course, it will.

Wouldn't mind being a fly on that wall, he mutters to himself.

It is Natalie's first night. She is slightly nervous, as is to be expected, especially at those points in the evening when there has been a rush at the bar, but she hasn't made any dreadful mistakes, at least she thinks not. And there has been the indulgence of the clientele, not exclusively but mainly middle-aged men, with an eye for a pretty barmaid and a line in flattery with which they can, with impunity, titillate themselves.

Martin, the guy she has had a couple of dates with is there but she has not had any time to talk to him, and he has been in conversation with a couple of his mates from the Labour Party who she recognises from the meeting he took her to.

Adam Mitchell, the poet – or trashy novelist, whoever you believed - is also there, and it is only as she is halfway through pulling his pint that he recognises her as the person he spoke to at the gallery earlier in the day.

'So, you did my poems for your exam, then?'

'Some of them. There were about six,' she says, watching the head on top of the beer as it comes to the top of the glass.

'Six. Well, I hope they were good ones.'

'My teacher was very keen. Miss Holden. Helen Holden. She said you were the best in the collection.'

He hands over a ten-pound note. 'And yours…' she hears, for the umpteenth time in the evening.

'Thanks,' she says, and hands him his change, putting 20p in the jar, as she has been instructed.

At about twenty past ten, in a lull after some of the younger customers have set out for the livelier nightlife of Leeds or Huddersfield, Martin comes to the bar.

'How's it going?'

'Fine,' she says, though her legs are beginning to feel like water.

'Just a half please,' he says.

She reaches for a glass.

'How do you fancy going out for a meal, Wednesday maybe, dinner at Marmaduke's? I hear it's pretty good.'

She shrugs her shoulders agreeably. 'OK.' After all, it is not the time or place to say, *can I think about it?* 'OK.'

'Great. Meet me in here, perhaps, sevenish… or I can pick you up…'

'No, here's fine.'

'Seven then. I'll book for eight.'

'What do you think of the new girl, then?'

Adam looks up to see Moggy Morton, dressed up for the night, but somehow with the same drainy odour. Moggy sits down next to him.

'Bit tasty?'

'Bugger off,' says Adam. It is sometimes necessary to cut Moggy off before he gets started.

'Please yourself, fuckwit,' says Moggy, getting up and taking his drink towards other company.

Adam looks up to Natalie, and imagines her as a fifteen- or sixteen-year-old, the time when she had his poems served up for her English exam.

But Helen Holden, her teacher. Miss Holden as she had referred to her. That was an episode he didn't care to be reminded of.

Had Rob Jenkins been a fly on the wall in Magda Bentley's studio, as he would have liked to have been, he would have been privy to the following scene.

Magda is sitting at her easel, working on an abstract design which has been floating through her head for several days, inspired by something she saw in a book about Chinese architecture. Having opened the door for Ralph, she has returned directly to what she was doing and has not looked in his direction since. Ralph remains standing, leaning against a full-size cupboard which contains some of Magda's materials. He waits.

'Have you come for any particular reason?' she asks, archly.

He gives a little laugh. 'I'll give you three guesses.'

'I never rely on guesswork,' she says.

'You'd get it in one,' he jokes, 'nor would it be guesswork.'

'I spoke to your daughter, at the gallery this morning,' she says, changing the subject.

'Yes.'

'She's very pretty. I'd like to draw her. Paint her perhaps. Do you think she would sit for me?'

'Not a good idea, I'd say.'

'Oh dear. Why not?'

'You'd be a bad influence.'

'Yes, I probably would.'

He waits patiently for another five minutes. There is no sign that Magda's concentration is in any way diminished by his presence.

'Are you going to be working all night?' he asks at last.

'Hard to say,' she replies, dropping a dead bat on it.

'Only I've got a bottle of decent white wine here. Getting warmer by the minute though.'

'How well you know me. Or should I say how well you think you know me.'

'Don't I?'

'You don't really know anything about me.'

'I know you like sex.'

'Good job for you I do.'

'Absolutely.'

'Go on then,' she says, swivelling round on her stool, 'pour me a glass.'

Walking home along the canal towpath forty minutes later, Ralph flatters himself that, certainly as far as Magda Bentley is concerned, he very definitely still has the knack. Her standoffishness at the start, a classic feminine ploy perhaps, was quite easily overcome, and a single glass of wine had been sufficient to prompt a decisive move to the bedroom. And it was not disappointing. Some of its details play back now, as he walks along, pausing the replay here and there, to dwell a little, before fastforwarding to the categorical satisfaction of those emphatic final moments.

Reaching home, he is glad to see that Barbara is not yet back. Looking at his watch, he decides to give it twenty minutes – which should be enough to complete the rest of the crossword – before setting out to pick up Natalie.

Committee meetings at the theatre are often protracted and tedious. There are some people, Barbara often thinks, who simply like the sound of their own voices. It goes with the territory, perhaps. Though in fact, the worst offenders tend to be those who are organisers rather than performers. It is frequently the case that a decision almost reached, and with a generally happy consensus, is thrown back on itself by some scruple or quiddity dug out, it might seem , for the very purpose of engendering delay. Stronger chairmanship, it is occasionally whispered, is what is really needed, but Celia has been Chair now for six years and would possibly be upset if anyone were to challenge her, and besides, it is an office which no-one else particularly wants to occupy.

Finally, however, the plays for next season have been selected and approved, and Barbara as Secretary has noted down the details for circulation to the membership. Eleanor Vance has agreed to co-ordinate the gin bar purchases and a rota, and Richard Loose has agreed to be on hand to set up the table and sell the tokens. Unless someone suddenly discovers a potential pitfall or qualm hitherto overlooked – quite possible – the meeting seems to be heading for its close. Thankfully, because it is an extraordinary committee meeting, Celia does not ask if there is any other business and to a collective sigh of relief the meeting is declared closed.

'Will you lock up, Barbara?'

'Yes,' says Barbara who is arranging her papers and putting them away neatly in her briefcase.

'Anyone coming to the pub? Cyril?'

'I'll just help Barbara put the chairs away. May join you in a bit.'

Apart from the two of them, the room begins to empty.

Within two minutes, the chairs have been stacked and slid neatly away in their alcove, and Barbara is ready to click shut her briefcase when she feels the light touch of a hand on the small of her back.

'Cyril?' she murmurs, and though it is framed as a question really it is not one. She reaches behind, and touches his fingers with her own.

'Barbara,' he whispers.

How many meetings had they contrived to end in precisely this manner over the last few years. She stands and slips into his arms, and their lips brush momentarily in a kiss.

'How was the send-off for old Duncan then?' he asks.

'Oh, you know. As you'd expect. Usual people. Plus Adam Mitchell.'

'Adam was there, was he? Not seen him for ages.'

'Didn't know you knew him.'

'Used to work at his publishers. We sometimes found ourselves on the same train up to Manchester. You may not believe this, but I once tried to get him to write a play for the society. Said he'd think about it, but nothing ever came of it.'

'Perhaps as well from what they say about him.'

Cyril laughs and they kiss again.

'I was looking in an old diary,' he says at last. 'Next week will be the sixth anniversary of the weekend we spent in Whitby.'

'Make sure nobody finds that diary!'

'It's in code. Impenetrable. I assure you.'

'Good.'

'Do you remember it though?'

'Of course. We spent almost the whole weekend in the apartment. Hardly went out at all. Well, the weather was pretty miserable.'

'Oh, was that the reason? I don't think I noticed the weather.'

'I do still remember it,' she says, squeezing his hand. 'Of course I do.'

Adam Mitchell leaves the pub at ten past eleven, glancing back to catch a last glimpse of the new girl, Natalie, who is now collecting glasses and wiping tables. He then begins the twenty-minute trudge up the hill to his home, a two-bedroom stone cottage just at the top of the village. He now feels doubly sorry that he was brusque with her at the gallery earlier in the day. One is brusque with what one cannot have, he reflects; perhaps that is what was at the root of it.

It is a beautiful summer night: the air soft, still retaining some of the benign warmth of the day but with nocturnal scents. There was a time when he would have walked on, on such a night as this, through the woods and up onto the top of the moor. A chance to be truly alone, to be at one with oneself. In fact, he had once taken such excursions in all kinds of weather and at all seasons: lying on a rock with the frost all about like sugar, looking up at the myriad stars of a January night, wrapped up in an old oilcloth whilst the rain tumbled over his face. Getting close to it – whatever it was. He didn't do such things now. He regarded that kind of antic in others as an affectation, probably had been no more than an affectation in his own case. The affectation of a fresher more hopeful mind.

He lets himself in, opens the window, for a slightly moist fetid smell has accumulated during the day, and takes out the bottle of whisky. It is probably not a good idea, he reflects, in fact it is definitely not a good idea, but what the hell! A small one.

In his thirties, when he first came here, he had had something to say. In his poetry, that is. His insights and perceptions, as someone said in The Times, or The Guardian – one of them – were razor sharp and original, and words came to him easily, flowing like oil from the olive press. His two volumes of poetry *Rules of Proximity* and *The Angels' Share* had marked him, they said, as one of the rising poets of his generation, but it was barely enough, even with the readings and signings from which to make a living. And he had grown tired of all the travelling involved. That was when he had started on the novels, and from them he had derived a fair income.

Regan's Yard, the first in the series of novels featuring the Detective Phil Regan, had some decent stuff, and he had taken a long time over it, but his publisher, Duncan, had insisted on upping the commercial potential in the follow up, *The Teahouse Mannequin,* which had basically meant taking it downmarket. Dumbing it down.

'Don't look on it as dumbing down,' Duncan had said, 'look on it as making it accessible to a wider audience.'

They had given him an editor, Emma, who had basically rewritten it in shorter sentences and words of no more than three syllables, and had told him to include more sex scenes, and more detailed descriptions of Lydia's designer underwear - Lydia being Regan's girlfriend. When he had returned the email, saying that in fact he knew very little about ladies' designer underwear, Emma had more or less taken on the task herself. He had formed the picture of Emma as a thin-faced martinet with secretary glasses and a sex-starved imagination, but when he finally met her, at a literary luncheon promoted by his publisher, Emma turned out to be not only smart but highly attractive, an Oxford graduate with obvious ambition. Briefly, he had fantasised a seduction – after all they had shared the same sex scenes and slinky lingerie – until he had noticed the sparkling engagement rock and wedding band which she flashed much too obviously for anyone to be under any misunderstanding. But the novels were not good, he was the first to admit it. In fact, he had come to despise them. If he had anything to say, it was in the poetry of those two volumes.

A sudden unsettling image presented itself to his memory. It was the image of Helen Holden standing here in this room, by the mantlepiece, not two yards from where he was now sitting, reading – no, reciting, for she had learned it by heart – the title poem of 'Rules of Proximity'. Helen Holden, Miss Holden to the girl in the gallery, to the girl behind the bar in the pub. The teacher. He closed his eyes and waited for the vision to dissipate.

He had exploited the opportunity of Helen Holden's adulation to seduce her – she was a very willing collaborator in the seduction – and for several weekends when she was free from her teaching duties, they had been lovers. Friday night and Saturday night were hers, before - with promises of fidelity and commitment - she went back to her weekday world. Meantime, with Magda Bentley, who had introduced them to each other, he had begun a weekday affair that in many ways had trumped his weekends with Helen.

Rules of Proximity - that, almost certainly, would have been one of the poems they put in the anthology for exam study. It was a good poem, possibly the best of the lot, but as far as his writing now was concerned, well, he knew he had not said anything worth saying for ten years and more.

But what about the new girl, Ralph Anderson's daughter, Natalie? Releasing his imagination now onto a much more agreeable plane of contemplation, he admitted what a strong impression she had made on him. What was it about her that kept drawing his attention like a magnet? It was nothing so obvious as the kind of thing he took Moggy to be alluding to in his choice of the word 'tasty'. So, what then was it, besides youth, that refreshing ordinariness, that was so tantalising? Was it that she somehow managed, without being conscious of it, to tread a fine line, poised between innocent charm and sexual allure, the illusion of a virtuous temptress?

What deep nerve did it touch in him for him to be unearthing such age-old stereotypes?

Once upon a time, he would have been able to spin a fine web of words to capture it in nuanced paradoxes and subtle contradictions.

But not these days.

His speculation sounded pretentious, even to himself.

Moggy was probably closer to the mark.

CHAPTER 4

A quiet Sunday morning and, though initially reluctant, Natalie is now quite glad that she allowed her mum to persuade her to accompany her to church. It is not for any spiritual purpose for Natalie has been drifting, for quite a few years now, into that intellectual territory where most of the arguments for God, Christianity and religion come apart, when tested, like cotton wool. But the churchyard, especially the sections with the old, lichened gravestones, brings back pleasant recollections of games of hide-and-seek with childhood friends. It also backs onto the wall of the junior school playground, which again invokes a host of memories. She is interested, too, though for no other reason than curiosity at her mum mentioning him, to see Paul, the vicar, to see if he lives up to his reputation.

The church itself is pleasant. White walls, with leaded windows above on each side of the nave, combine with the stained-glass window behind the altar to capture and soften the light from outside, creating a feeling of peacefulness. The sound of the reed organ which greets the congregation as it enters also lends a homely charm. The church is about a third full, maybe forty people, and Barbara says that this is considered quite a good turnout these days, though of course it's always better when, like today, there is a bit of sunshine. Natalie watches the vicar, Paul, as he leads the way through the service. He is perhaps rather more jokey than you might expect and tends to giggle somewhat at his own jokes; he is maybe just a tiny bit geeky because of his slightly protuberant front teeth, but he is not at all outrageous or embarrassing, and at the main points and prayers, he is as solemn and decorous as anyone could wish: certainly better than the bombastic Reverend Slade who she recalls from her early teenage years, or the one before—Old Potts they called him—who tried to sing the hymns as if he were an opera singer, making all the children choke with suppressed laughter.

Outside, after the service, she stops to talk to him, introducing herself.

'Ah,' he says, nodding towards Barbara who has moved on to talk to another chap on the church forecourt, 'and are you a thespian too?'

'No,' she says emphatically, widening her eyes with comic disavowal.

He grins. 'And you're back from university, your mum, er, Barbara tells me?'

'Yes.'

'What did you read?'

'History.'

'History. Excellent. I'm a history lover myself. Intending to write a book about the early history of Milthwaite actually.'

'Wow! That's brilliant!'

'Well, when I get round to it anyway,' he quips and allows himself a sudden chortle which he then quickly swallows. 'And what are your, your, er, plans, Natalie?'

'I've got a place at teacher training college in September.'

'Marvellous! Well, in the meantime, enjoy the summer.'

'I intend to,' she says and seeing one or two others hovering to speak to him, decides it's time to move on.

'Who was that?' she asks Barbara as they make their way through the gate and along the church approach.

'Who?'

'The man you were talking to just now.'

'Oh, just someone from the theatre group.'

'Does he have a name?'

'Why do you ask?'

'Is it so odd to ask a person's name?'

'Cyril, if you must know.'

'You're blushing, mother!'

'Don't be silly, darling,' says Barbara in her most deadpan practical voice.

'Well, it's quite warm. Must be that. I'll let you off.'

'Anyway, what do you think of our vicar?'

'Seems like a nice man. I like him.:

'Yes, I thought you might.'

'Listen,' says Ralph after Sunday lunch which comprises some ham and salad: a cold collation as he always calls it with an inference of disappointment, as if Barbara could have done better if she'd tried harder, 'I've been thinking, Natalie...' he says, pausing slightly to allow a significance to be registered, 'I've been thinking, why a teacher training qualification, for heaven's sake, when you could do so much better?'

'Well, it's what I want to do.'

'But isn't that just a default. I mean: a teacher training year - isn't that what people do just because they can't be bothered thinking of anything better?'

'Ralph,' says Barbara. 'Leave her alone. She's said it's what she wants to do.'

'Thank you, mum,' says Natalie, not sure that her mum's direct support is what she wants.

Ralph sits back in his chair in a slightly lordly pose. 'I'm just saying, you have a great degree...'

'I've got a 2:2, dad. That's a good degree, not a great degree.'

'It's a good degree, Nattie,' he says, using the soubriquet he favours when he treats her as a little girl, 'there are other things you could do with it.'

'Like what?'

'I don't know. In business, in banking, accountancy, in IT, any number of things, but teaching, Nattie...mmm?'

'I want to be a teacher,' she says, quietly, but between clenched teeth.

'Well, at least promise me you'll go for a decent private school, something with a bit of class, for heaven's sake.'

'Would anybody like some fresh pineapple?' says Barbara, 'or maybe some coffee?'

After lunch, Natalie fished her old bike out of the garage and set off up the lane towards Old Lansley, near the top of the moor. It was good to get out of the house. After the grind of finals, the prospect of coming home for a completely free summer had been like a dream—and in truth the first few weeks had lived up to all the promise—but now the gloss was beginning to wear off. Sundays, she recalled, had always been the day when things might kick off at home, the day when the oppression gathered like a storm and when flashpoints could easily be reached. It was usually between her dad and her elder brother, Gavin; though when mum joined in, usually to defend Gavin, she too would become the target of her dad's ill temper and get drawn into the fray. It had been a bit like that today. That was often the way things started: with her father taking a line over something, with some implied criticism, and provoking people. Gavin was always too ready to take the bait rather than chilling and letting it pass over his head, as they had tried to do today.

'I fucking hate this house!' Gavin had said to her often. 'I can't wait to get away. I just can't wait!'

And true to form, Gavin had chosen the most distant university, down on the south coast, and after graduating had moved up to London and had barely been seen since. Now, she too was beginning to look forward to going up to Huddersfield to find a flat before the new term began. Honley perhaps, where one of her school friends had lived, somewhere near the Jacob's Well pub which she had been introduced to on a visit in her first year.

The lanes up the hillside seemed much steeper than she remembered. Had she really cruised so easily up them all those years ago? In the lanes, especially the sunken ones or those with tall hedgerows to the side, there was hardly a breath of air.

She stopped and turned to look back at all the old familiar sights along the valley: the church tower sticking up through the treetops, the stack that used to belong to Fixby Mill with its red iron hoops, the trees spreading into woodland which concealed the course of the canal and river. Then, on the far side, the secondary school with its new sports complex and playing fields, the enormous mill which was now a spa hotel, and, far in the distance, the railway viaduct in Slackbridge.

She reached a flat section and caught her breath, then approached another steep curve which she determined to climb without stepping down from the pedals. She had just rounded the bend when a man ahead, seeing her, stepped back from the road.

'Thanks,' she called, as if grateful for a service he had performed, and a moment later, she recognised Adam Mitchell, the writer.

'Ha!' he said, affably. 'You again. I think you must be stalking me.'

Natalie laughed, not sure of what to say but conscious that she must looked dishevelled, not to say hot-faced. 'I just thought I'd try a bike ride,' she said. 'Not as easy as I thought.'

'No. Not in these parts. I had a motorbike once when I first came here. But now it's Shanks' pony. As you see, I'm out on my Sunday walk.'

'Have you walked far?'

'My cottage is at the bottom of the lane, about a mile.'

'I must have passed it.'

'Just on this side of the canal bridge.'

'I think maybe I should stick to walking after this!'

'Still, there's the ride back down. I expect that will be exhilarating.'

'Yes,' she said, laughing again.

'And what else have you been up to on your day off then?'

'Oh, nothing much. I went to church with my mum this morning.'

'Ah, yes, the peace and quiet of St Wilfred's.'

'Do you go there?'

'Used to. Not when services were on though. I liked to sit there and reflect, in a purely non-religious way.'

'I know what you mean, I think. I'm not religious either.'
'Right. Well, I'd better let you get on then.'
'OK. Nice to see you. Bye!'
'Goodbye.'

He watched her pedalling slowly away for a moment and then, with a barely audible sigh, turned to walk on.

Twenty minutes later, Natalie reached the reservoir above Old Lansley. Here there was a breeze which rippled the surface of the water slightly: refreshing after the sultry heat of the lanes. A few families were having picnics on the benches and a regular flow of dogwalkers passed by. Over in the far corner and against the visible warnings of danger, a group of boys was splashing and swimming. She rested her bike against a bench to sit for a few moments and reflected on her meeting with Adam Mitchell. He had definitely been grumpy at their first meeting in the gallery but since then he had seemed quite affable. She decided she quite liked him.

She chose a circular route home and it was—as Adam Mitchell had predicted—a lot easier going down, with the wind in her face and blowing out her hair. Passing at last under a railway bridge, she came out on Scar Lane just above the canal and the river, and recognised—a couple of hundred yards along—the remains of the old factory where Magda Bentley had her studio.

She paused for a moment and then decided to knock on the door. There was no answer for a time and she was about to go, supposing Magda to be out somewhere, when she heard a voice approaching the door: 'Hang on, hang on. Be with you in a tick!' and a moment later, Magda was in the doorway.

'Oh, it's you!' she exclaimed, evidently both surprised and pleased.

'I went for a ride and came out just up the road, so I thought I'd see if you were in.'

'I nearly didn't answer,' Magda quipped, 'thought you might be someone else.'

'Hope you're not in the middle of anything.'

'No, no, not at all. Come in. You can leave your bike there, it'll be all right, or bring it in if you like.'

'Wow!' said Natalie, looking round the studio.

It is a big space, full of canvasses, both finished and unfinished, and an atmosphere of vividly coloured chaos. The pipes of the old mill still run through overhead and there are some bits of rusting machinery, cogs and springs and some ironwork lying about, though whether they belong with the mill or Magda has brought them here as specimens to draw is not clear. There is a very large oak table in the middle, covered in another chaos of papers, sketches, electricity bills, notes and a swivel chair whose upholstery is much the worse for wear.

'Welcome to my studio!' says Magda with a flourish.

'It's fantastic,' says Natalie, now noticing a tall cabinet with open shelves on which stand candles of all shapes and sizes with cascades of coloured wax which has melted from them and then solidified in weird overlapping ropes and strands.

'I can sit watching candles for hours,' says Magda, seeing the direction of Natalie's gaze. 'It's like just setting something free to happen and then seeing what it comes up with. I like that.'

'Fantastic,' Natalie repeats.

'This is what I'm working on at the moment,' Magda explains, pointing to a canvas which is a wash of pale blue with various architectural motifs and stylised animals floating across it.

'It's just a set of ideas really. I don't really know what I'm going to do with it yet. Maybe nothing.'

'Does that often happen? I mean, starting something and then abandoning it?'

'Oh, all the time. My boredom threshold is quite low really. Come on, I'll show you where I hang out when I'm not working.'

They go up a somewhat rickety staircase and through what seems to be a trapdoor into the upper space. Here there is Magda's bed, unmade, a clothes rail loaded with skirts and tops, and two chests of drawers—with most of the drawers half open —again containing clothes, sweaters, jeans, underwear. There is also a blue settee and two differently styled upright chairs, a full body female shop mannequin wearing a black cocktail dress and a hat with feathers, and a dressing table with a white porcelain bust of someone who might be a classical composer.

'And here is my little bathroom,' says Magda, pulling the screen aside. 'Cute, isn't it?'

Natalie smiles. There is something about the whole arrangement that is slightly mad and anarchic, and she likes it.

'Let's have a cup of tea,' says Magda, putting an old iron kettle on a gas ring. 'So what have you been up to then, apart from riding up and down the country lanes.'

'Actually,' says Natalie, 'I started a new job last night, waiting on at the White Hart.'

'Oh, poor you.'

'It's only a couple of nights and I quite enjoyed it really.'

'The White Hart, isn't that Adam Mitchell's preferred tippling house?'

'Yes, I saw him there.'

Magda nods, with a wry expression.

'He was a bit, you know, grumpy with me at the Gallery yesterday but last night he was quite nice.'

'That would be the drink.'

'I was telling him I did some of his poems at GCSE. I thought he might be interested but he wasn't.'

'I'm afraid he's lost his way a bit has our Adam.'

'Really?'

'Mmm. He's like someone who nearly got to the top of a mountain but didn't quite make it.'

'Dad said he writes trashy novels.'

'I wouldn't know,' says Magda, pouring the tea. 'Haven't read any of them. But anyway, look, sit down here.'

Natalie accepts the mug of tea and sits down, as directed, on the blue settee.

'So, Natalie, any boyfriends on the scene? Do you mind me asking that?'

'No, not really. And not really to the first question too. Two *no, not reallys*.'

They both laugh.

'Do you mind if I sketch you while we're talking?' asks Magda.
'Me?'
'Yes, why not?' Natalie shrugs her shoulders.
'I'm a fidget,' says Magda. 'Can't relax unless I'm doing something with my hands.'

She reaches for a pad, flips it over to a new page and begins sketching with swift light strokes of the pencil.

To Natalie, it feels strange, sitting there seeing Magda's eyes looking up to her and then down to the sketch as she draws. She thinks she should make conversation but doesn't really know what to say.

'Actually,' she says at last, 'I've been seeing a guy called Martin since I came back. He took me to a couple of Labour Party meetings. He's going to stand as a councillor.'

'Oh yes, Martin. Yes, I know who he is. Labour councillor. Pillar of the community. Grab hold of him. Could be Prime Minister one day, who knows?'

'Well actually, I don't feel too grabby just at the moment.'

'Good for you. There,' she says handing the sketch pad to Natalie.

'That was quick.'

'It's just a sketch. You're easy to draw. Nice facial bones. Soft lines.'

'Thank you,' Natalie says, as if not expecting a compliment, though looking at the sketch and knowing she is blushing slightly, she knows quite well why it is that people think she is pretty.

'You can keep it if you like.'

'Really?'

'Yes, why not?' says Magda, taking the pad and tearing out the sheet. 'Actually, if you're not busy, you could come and sit for me. A proper painting.'

'Oh,' says Natalie, a little flummoxed. 'Well, I mean yes, if you think I'd be any good.'

'You'd be perfect.'

'Well ok then. When's best though?'

'Whenever you're free. I'm here most of the time.'
'OK.'
'Come about four. The light gets softer then.'

At the door, Natalie says, 'Actually, can I leave the sketch here? I'm on my bike, it might get crumpled.'

'Course you can,' says Magda. 'It'll be here for you. Whenever.'

CHAPTER 5

Barbara was glad that Ralph had not made a point of pursuing his lunchtime conversation about Natalie choosing a different career path, for had he done so, he would quite probably have reached the point of becoming angry. She had made a broccoli bake for tea. Ralph didn't eat much of it but he didn't complain. It had been a long time since he had complimented her on any aspect of her cooking. After tea, he went to his den—his study—saying he had things to prepare for a lecture he was doing the following month in Manchester.

Natalie, after returning from her bike ride, now seemed happy. They watched television together for a while and then Natalie said she was tired and was going to bed. All was quiet in the house. Barbara kept the television on but switched the sound down because, in truth, she was neither watching nor listening though she wanted to keep up the pretence of doing both. If she is watching TV, nobody minds her.

Once, before they were married, she remembers, Ralph had accused her of flirting with another chap in a restaurant and had become angry. She had been shocked, partly because it was the first time she had ever seen him in a temper, but mainly because he was simply not the sort of man you would think of as ever being jealous. Later, holding his face between her hands and looking into his eyes, she had reassured him, saying, 'I will never, ever be unfaithful to you.'

She was remembering this now because of the other memory she had affirmed the previous night, alone in the committee room with Cyril.

I do remember it. Of course I do.

In fact, that period was as vivid in her memory as if it were yesterday.

Cyril North lived on the other side of the village, about half a mile past the little theatre, in a row of cottages with long gardens backing onto the canal towpath. He worked for a publishing company in Manchester, commuting from Milthwaite by train each day, and had been made a widower in his early forties. He was a longstanding member of the Players and was regarded as quite a decent actor and, in a context where men were usually in short supply, this made him a precious commodity. Since his wife's death, which at the time Barbara first met him had been a period of five years, he had taken on more roles. They had had no children. It was, he said, as good a way of putting in his time as any.

Not long after she had joined, they had been involved in a play together: an Ayckbourn, she recalled. He was playing one of the leads. She was on props. New to the society, she was quite nervously still finding her way. She watched from the wings, anticipating all the laughs, and felt all the magic. After the last night, when she was still down on the stage gathering the props, he had come down from the dressing room and had taken her hand lightly in his own in a simple affectionate way. 'Thanks,' he had said. 'You were great. Coming to the party?' 'No,' she replied, 'I think I'd better get off home when I've finished this.' He lingered a moment, as if he might say something else, but then just said, 'OK, see you around.' And then he turned to go. The place where he had touched her hand still tingled with alarm and pleasure, almost like an electric shock.

She regretted saying she was not going to the party. She had in fact intended to go, but the question coming from him had thrown her off balance and now she felt she couldn't go lest he should think she had changed her mind because of him.

'How did it go?' asked Ralph when she came home.

'Fine. All over now. Can get back to real life again.'

Real life was not so easy to get back to. She missed the play. Post-play blues, they called it, a well-recognised ailment.

But that night—and many nights after—she lay awake, thinking about it all, and when the post-play blues faded, she found she was actually still thinking about Cyril.

Three weeks later, she had a telephone call from Marjorie Slight, one of the committee members and a regular director. 'Look, Barbara, we're in a bit of a fix. Dorothy Blaise has cried off. Playing Mrs Bradman in *Blithe Spirit*. It's not a huge part, I'm sure you could have it down in no time. Do you think you could possibly give it a go?' 'But I haven't actually been on the stage since I was at school!' Barbara had replied.

Despite her protests, she had agreed to do it.

A bag of nerves, she had turned up for her first rehearsal clutching the script—marked up by Dorothy—which Marjorie had delivered an hour after the phone call. The first person to greet her as she entered the theatre was a smiling Cyril. It seemed like fate.

There were four weeks of rehearsal remaining, then a week of performance. She treated the pangs of infatuation as she would a summer cold or a heat rash: something that had to be endured but that would go away in its own time. These things happened, it was a well-known behaviour pattern in AmDram: close proximity over a short and intensive period, teamwork, interdependence and then feelings spilling over into a messy concoction of romantic angst. One simply had to be sensible about it.

All went to plan.

And then, on the fourth night, she helped him out when he was struggling for a line.

'You absolutely saved my life,' he said afterwards. 'Like a pro. My mind had gone completely blank.'

And with that he threw his arms around her and the matey hug transformed gradually, and with alarming mutual assent, into a soft and dangerous kiss.

She was as shocked as she was exhilarated.

'I'm sorry,' he said, stepping back at last. 'That shouldn't have happened.'

'It's all right,' she said, hurriedly shaking her head as if nothing had happened. She gathered her things quickly and left.

'How did it go?' asked Ralph when she reached home.

'Fine. I'll be glad when it's over, really.'

'You'll miss it!'

That night she lay for a long time with her eyes open, staring upwards, hardly daring to move, as sleepless hour passed into sleepless hour, lest Ralph should awaken and know exactly what she was thinking.

She had been fairly sure at one time that Ralph had affairs with people at the university up in Leeds. She had once found a receipt he had carelessly left on the bedside table for a double room at a hotel in Sheffield. The conference accommodation was overbooked, he explained, and Premier Inn did not do single rooms. Although she suspected he was lying, she had no way of proving it one way or the other and she was smitten with jealousy. Sometimes she had looked through his bank statements to see if there was any further evidence that might be incriminating, and more than once—when he was showering —she had checked his phone messages, but if anything was going on, he was careful to cover his tracks and gradually she had learned to live with the possibility.

Now, however, as she lay awake, it was not Ralph's infidelity that troubled her but the possibility of her own.

The rest of the play week passed by without event; between herself and Cyril, there was just a kind of wariness between them, an avoidance of eye contact.

On the Saturday night, Ralph came to the play and stayed for the drinks and thank you speeches afterwards. Across the room she saw Cyril and their eyes met for a moment, his seeming to question hers, to be weighing her up; or perhaps he was weighing up what a couple they made, she and Ralph. She was glad he didn't come over to talk, to introduce himself to Ralph. That would have been too much of an ordeal.

A couple of times over the following months, she caught a glimpse of him in church, but he was not a regular attender and within that context it was easy to avoid anything other than a passing nod of acquaintance. Life, it seemed, had granted her one brief moment of illicit excitement and had now reverted to the slow and unexceptional trudge of its ordinary path.

What was changing—or had already changed perhaps—she realised, was that she no longer cared about her marriage in any essential way. Sex, already infrequent, had ceased to be of any vital relevance, and gone were the days when she had read his bank statements and checked his phone messages. It was not, she suspected, an unusual state of affairs.

The following spring, she agreed to be the prompt for another production and, having thought herself cured, was surprised at the strength of her disappointment that Cyril was not involved. On the Friday night, he was in the audience and popped his head round the door of the dressing room to pass on the customary congratulations to fellow thespians, and though she had not intended to, she went to the bar afterwards, hoping he might be there. He was. They sat together at a table and chatted.

'Is Ralph coming to this one?' he asked.

'No,' she replied. 'It was hard enough to drag him here when I was in a play, but when I'm just prompting…'

Cyril smiled.

'Besides,' she went on, 'he's away at a conference in Birmingham until tomorrow – or at least that's where he says he is,' she added, knowing even as she said it that she was dropping this little titbit squarely on the path ahead for him to retrieve if he so chose.

'I'd better be off,' she said at last.

'I'll walk with you to the car park,' he said.

'I parked up the road,' she said as they left the theatre. 'It was nearly full when I got here.'

'Well, it's on my way,' he said.

They walked on.

'Here I am,' she said after they walked on a short distance, clicking to unlock the car.

'You've parked just outside my house,' he laughed.

'Oh dear! Is there a charge?'

'Well actually it's just a little further on. I don't suppose you fancy a coffee, do you?'

'I shouldn't really,' she said, looking at her watch.

'No? Ok, then. Well, really nice to see you again.'

'Oh, what the hell! Why not. A coffee. Yes, please.'

She clicked the car shut.

They went into the kitchen and Cyril showed her the view down the garden towards the canal.

'It looks very pretty,' she said.

'Nice to sit out in on a summer day,' he replied.

He put on the kettle but before it could boil, they were in each other's arms, and fifteen minutes later they were in the bedroom having sex.

The trip to Whitby came three months later. Three agonising months of nagging passion and nagging anxiety: an intensity which drained her nerves. If she felt partly guilty for deceiving Ralph, she felt more guilty because of the kids and the veneer of secrecy with which, without them knowing it, she was making them live.

Every step seemed riddled with danger and yet she couldn't help herself. Once, after a trip to the supermarket, she called on him and they had sex for a second time. The third time was on a Sunday morning after the church service. Another time, she pretended an additional rehearsal had been called. 'This is like madness,' she said to herself, carried along on a wave she could not resist, almost wishing someone would find out and break the scandal.

'I just feel so guilty,' said Cyril when their affair was in its third month. 'You have children, you have a settled life.'

She put her finger to his lips. Though she thought about these very things all the time when she was away from him, when she was with him she simply couldn't bear talking about it.

'I do want this,' she said. 'I do want this so much.'

'Then we should go away together,' he said. It was the first time this idea had been mentioned and, because it was so momentous, they shied away from talking about it until the same cycle of thoughts came round again.

'We need to get away,' he said, 'get a chance to be together properly. This is driving us both crazy.'

'I just don't see how I can,' she replied. 'It's just not possible. I mean, it's not just Ralph.'

'I know.'

'I've got two teenage kids, for heaven's sake!'

They were going round the same circle.

'Isn't there anyone else you could say you were going away with?'

'Well, there's my sister. But I'd have to take her into my confidence and I'm not sure about that at all. I'm really not.'

'I suppose we could try to organise something through the theatre: you know, a trip to the National Theatre or something.'

'But other people would want to come too, and if they didn't, tongues would certainly wag if it was just you and me.'

'How about if you organise a trip and I don't go on it. Not officially. We just find a way of meeting up. Maybe spend a night together at least.'

'I don't think it would be that easy. Honestly. It would end up being more clandestine than here.'

More weeks passed by.

The solution came finally and unexpectedly in the form of a phone call from Alison Marks.

'Alison who?' asked Ralph.

'Alison Marks. We shared in my third year at York. I don't think you ever met her.'

'Right. And what did she have to say?'

'Oh, just updating me really. She's just got a new job in Scarborough.'

'Very nice.'

'Actually, she asked me to go over and spend a weekend with her. I told her it was impossible, of course.'

Ralph thought about this.

'Why so?'

'Well, I didn't mean it literally, just that it would be awkward was what I meant.'

'Not necessarily.'

'What about the kids?'

'Well, I'm sure I can keep an eye on them for one weekend.'

'Besides, I'm not sure I really want to. Such a faff.'

'You should go. Do you good to get away for a weekend. Good theatre there, they say,'

'Wouldn't you mind?'

'Why should I?'

'I don't know, I just thought you might.'

'I was actually thinking of going down to Silverstone with Max Jones later in the summer. You wouldn't object to that, would you?'

'No, I suppose not.'

'I mean, we're not joined at the hip, are we?'

'No,' she replied, seeing that now the way was clear and that she just needed to plot her steps carefully. 'So you think I should go then?'

'If you want to, yes.'

'I'm not that sure I do really. Maybe I'll give her a call back.'

And so it happened. In her mind, she did not question whether Ralph's plan of Max and Silverstone was, like her own, a subterfuge. A quick call to Alison secured the deception. Cyril organised an apartment for the weekend in Whitby. She booked a return ticket to Scarborough. He would drive and pick her up there. For three weeks she lived on the edge of an almost unsustainable excitement. Keeping up an appearance of normality, without overdoing it, was an enormous strain. It seemed it would never be over.

And then she was on the train, not quite believing it, at the very beginning of that fairy-tale weekend. For nearly forty-eight hours she managed to insulate herself entirely from the reality of her own life. They walked along the beach hand in hand, they floated in the loveliness of each other's company as if on honeymoon. For the first time they had sex which wasn't rushed or hedged about with anxiety, luxuriating in each other's bodies, indulging themselves with an almost childlike simplicity.

'We should have met years ago.'
'We deserve a chance to be together.'
'Wouldn't it be wonderful. To be just like this.'
'If only we didn't have to go back.'

'Will you be all right?' he asked as he drove her back to catch the train in Scarborough.

'Yes,' she said, still floating, albeit now in a mood tinged with melancholy. 'What will become of us?'

'I guess we have to be sensible,' he said in a voice of quiet resignation.

On the train back, she invented the details of her weekend with Alison Marks, preparing for the return to normality. In the event, Ralph was not especially interested.

The next week was predictably awful and the sense of emptiness and depression faded only to be replaced by the fear, growing day by day, that she might be pregnant. Cyril had brought some condoms to Whitby but they hadn't used them. She didn't want him to. She was thirty-eight. She had somehow thought she couldn't get pregnant. What folly that seemed now as she counted the passing days contemplating a world thrown into absolute turmoil, until finally, thankfully, gratefully, her period started. Immense relief was tempered with sober reflection. How could she have been so selfish: ignoring the devastating effect this would have on her children, if not on Ralph?

Cyril had been understanding. It couldn't go on. Neither the stolen Sunday mornings, nor weekends away. All of it had to go.

'I still think about it,' she had said this very morning outside the church while Natalie was talking to Paul, the vicar.

'So do I. I sometimes wonder if it would have lasted if we'd got together.'

'Maybe that's why our feelings have stayed so strong. A

combination of abstinence and the memory of our own little bit of paradise.'

For a tiny moment, they had squeezed hands. Then Natalie was approaching, and Barbara knew that she was probably blushing.

CHAPTER 6

It was in town a couple of days later when Natalie happened to bump into her old English teacher, Helen Holden: Miss Holden as they had known her then or HH, which seemed cool. She had called in at the university to look at the noticeboards to see if there were any flat shares being offered and had come away with a couple of contacts. They had also given her a link where she could search online. The university precinct was, she thought, quite impressive and potentially vibrant—there were very few students around now during the vacation—but the town itself seemed somehow down-at-heels. Shops where she had bought clothes just a few years ago were closed, everything seemed a bit drab and depressed.

At first, she hardly recognised Miss Holden and thought she might have made a mistake, but drawing closer—it was in Boots the Chemist—there was no doubt that it was the same person.

'Hello,' she called as Miss Holden finished paying and came away from the desk.

The woman looked up with a hint of suspicion at being addressed in a public place. It was clear that she did not immediately recognise Natalie.

'Miss Holden,' she said. 'It's Natalie Anderson. I don't suppose you remember me.'

'Natalie Anderson,' said Miss Holden as if she were trying the words out for size.

'You taught me in Y10 and 11. It's quite a while ago now.'

'Ah yes,' said Miss Holden, still in a guarded, defensive manner. 'I think I remember who you are.'

Natalie found herself noticing that Miss Holden was wearing

a raincoat which was belted up tightly and buttoned up to the neck even though it was a warm day, and remembered that the teacher had had some time off, when Natalie was doing her A-levels, with some kind of nervous trouble, so they said.

'I was thinking of you just the other day,' said Natalie, trying to sound bright and breezy. 'I was at a thing at a gallery in Milthwaite last weekend and one of the poets we did with you for GCSE happened to be there too. Adam Mitchell. Do you remember? I remembered that you were keen on his poems.'

Miss Holden narrowed her eyes slightly. 'Adam Mitchell,' she said as if it was another memory that needed to be tested before it could be confirmed. 'Mmm. Is he still living in Milthwaite then?'

'Yes. I mean, I didn't know he lived there back then. I would probably have gone round and asked for his autograph or something. I expect that's why you didn't tell us.'

'I don't recall,' said Miss Holden vaguely, and Natalie sensed that the meeting and the conversation were not particularly welcome to her. There was a tight look about her lips, a sense of unease.

'Well,' said Natalie, trying to maintain the mood of a bright and breezy chance encounter, 'it's been really nice to see you again.'

This gave Miss Holden the cue to end the conversation and move away, a cue which she duly took.

It was a little bit sad, Natalie reflected on the bus home, that her old teacher had been so reluctant to engage, so seemingly withdrawn. Perhaps she had had some kind of nervous breakdown during the months she had been on sick leave. Natalie had then moved into the sixth form, with different teachers, and so had not really had much contact with her. Before that, however, when she and her friends were at their feisty and prurient adolescent best, Miss Holden had seemed to be one of those young female teachers who had romantic possibilities, and her enthusiasm for the poetry of Adam Mitchell had fitted into that image. 'Do you think she has sex fantasies about him?' they had speculated amidst titters and giggles. It was all a sorry contrast with the spinsterish and rather grey personality she now presented.

Then, at the bus stop in Milthwaite and as if it was a day for renewing old acquaintances, she bumped into Nathan, a boy she had been at school with all the way through from Primary to A-levels. He was getting on the bus just as she was getting off.

'Nathan!'

'Hi Natalie.'

'God, Nathan, not seen you for ages!'

'No. You back then. Finished at uni?'

'Yeah. Been back a few weeks.'

He was hovering on the platform of the bus. 'I think it's about to go.'

'Oh, OK. Well, look, why don't we meet up for a drink or something?'

'Yeah. Suppose so. If you want.'

'What about tomorrow. The White Hart?'

'Yeah, OK.'

'About, what, seven?'

'OK.'

'I saw Nathan,' she said to her mum later.

'Oh, really. How did he seem?'

'How do you mean?' she asked, detecting something quietly odd in her mum's tone.

'Oh, nothing. I spoke to his mum, Linda, well, ages ago actually, probably just after you started at uni. She said something, well, that he'd been having a hard time, some kind of mental health problem I think she was getting at.'

'Why didn't you tell me? I would have gone to see him.'

'I really can't remember, darling. It was ages ago. Are you sure I didn't mention it?'

'I'd remember if you did.'

'Well anyway, he seems OK now, does he, I take it?'

'I said I'd meet him for a drink.'

'Well that's nice, anyway.'

Afterwards, Natalie thought about the impression Nathan had made on her in the afternoon. Was she making it up retrospectively or had she noticed that he looked a bit gaunt? Possibly he did, though it was maybe just the way people change over three years or so, as their adult form settles. Insofar as she had thought of it at all, at the time, that was how she had seen it.

They had actually known each other since the first day of Infants and it was a friendship compounded by the fact that their birthdays were on the same day – so there were shared parties and all that sort of thing. Once, in Y10, they had had a date, getting the train up to Huddersfield to see a film, but really they were better as mates than as boyfriend/girlfriend. Nathan was different from other boys in their class. He was creative, funny, poetic; some of the teachers really liked him because in class he was whimsical and full of amusing quips, but other teachers got wound up by his lack of organisation and forgetfulness. During the A-level season, she recalled, amongst all the other crazy stuff that was going on, he had had some kind of bad patch. There was one exam he didn't turn up to, she remembered, and—not unsurprisingly—he didn't get the grades he needed for his place at uni. There had been a big party after the results came out and he had been there, very drunk—as were many, she had been pretty tipsy herself—and he had told her, in the one lucid memory of a conversation with him that she had, that he was going to stay on for a year to resit his A-levels.

She was sorry now that she had not taken more interest, had not made a point of going to see him during the vacs when she was back from uni herself. But it was good that she was meeting up with him for a drink. It would be a good chance to catch up.

CHAPTER 7

Reaching her home, a small, neat semi-detached house on the outskirts of Huddersfield, Helen Holden emptied the small carrier bag of items she had bought in town and set them in their intended places: fridge, larder, cupboard, drawer. The toothpaste, lip-balm and shampoo she had purchased in Boots, she took upstairs to the bathroom. She put the kettle on to make some tea for she had not yet fully recovered her composure from that unfortunate meeting in Boots with an ex-pupil —whose name she could scarcely remember—from Valley High: Natalie something, she vaguely recalled. It was not that she actively disliked her or that the girl had not been polite in the way she had approached her. The fact was that any encounter with that period of her life had the effect of setting her nerves on edge, leaving her vulnerable to impulses of anxiety of uncertain duration which floated like smoke through her mind, without precise cause or meaning.

She took off her coat and began the usual processes of re-establishing the habits and patterns of normality that would, hopefully soon, restore her equanimity. It was a year since she had last taken a tablet. She would have stayed on them longer if it had been left up to her, but the doctor had recommended the reduction over three weeks to nil. She had experienced some unpleasant side effects—some nausea and light-headedness—but she had stuck to it. There had been numerous occasions on which she had been sitting at this same table with her phone beside her, ready to phone the doctor, almost counting down the minutes to that inevitable outcome, but in the end something had pulled her back. *Maybe tomorrow. If it doesn't get any better, tomorrow definitely.*

She poured the cup of tea, added a single spoon of sugar and took a bite of a digestive biscuit. Something sweet usually helped.

'I'm OK,' she said to herself as she came to the end of the tea. 'I'll be OK now, I think.'

The summer holiday always posed a problem. It was all very well to have a little time away from it—to breathe, to read—but it was too long to go without a daily routine that filled most of the hours of the day. Most of the teachers at the little private prep school where she had been employed since leaving the Valley High School and after her convalescence, talked of going away on holiday—flying off to Majorca, motoring through France, walking in the Highlands of Scotland—but she could not trust herself to anything like that. She was accustomed to the narrowness of her own life. An occasional trip into town, to break up the day, was the most she attempted.

She drew a deep breath, cleared away and decided that a little housework, a little dusting and vacuuming, would fill in a half hour satisfactorily before some food—she had bought a cheese flan and some coleslaw—and then a shower before settling down for the evening to read some more of the *Master and Commander* series. It was not a subject matter that she especially enjoyed but the discipline of following all the nautical references and terminology somehow helped to keep her in a steady frame of mind until ten o'clock. Sometimes, at ten o'clock, she would watch the news or listen to some of it on the radio; at other times, she would go straight to bed.

But when ten o'clock came tonight, there was something else to deal with. It had been suggesting itself all through the evening, interfering with her concentration, rearing its ugly head. She rose quickly, putting *Master and Commander* to one side, and went to the sideboard cupboard from the back of which she drew a slender volume of poems: *The Angel's Share* by Adam Mitchell. She ran her finger down the spine and then touched the image of his fifteen-year-younger face with her fingertip. 'You!'

she said in a whisper. 'You again!' And then, as a sob broke from her throat, she cried to the picture. 'Did you not know? Did you not know that no woman ever loved a man more passionately, more completely, more devotedly than I loved you?'

CHAPTER 8

'Hello, you!' says Magda Bentley, opening the door of her studio.

'Hi.'

'I didn't know if you would come. I'm glad you did.'

Natalie smiles, a little shyly. 'Not come at an inconvenient time, have I?'

'No. Come in quickly. The guy across at the carpet place is watching.'

'Oh, who's he then?' asks Natalie.

'Guy sells carpets and stuff. Bit of a weirdo. I've just made some Earl Grey. Would you like some?'

'Oh OK. Yes, please.'

'Milk?'

'No. I prefer Earl Grey without.'

'Absolutely right too. Milk ruins Earl Grey. Sit on the chaise. We will use that in the pose.'

'Gosh. Have I got to pose?'

'Just an expression. All you have to do is sit there. Well, recline. Look relaxed and comfortable.'

'Have you been working?'

'Not really. Bit lethargic today. Some days are like that.'

They chat for ten minutes, drinking tea, and then Natalie positions herself according to Magda's instruction and the session begins.

'Oh, I have to be away by about six, by the way. Is that all right?'

'Absolutely. An hour is usually enough. More than enough. We'll both be tired by then. It'll probably take a few sessions overall. Are you OK with that?'

'Yes, I should think so.'

'I can do some work when you're not here, but mainly it'll be done directly, while I'm studying you.'

She pauses from the drawing for a moment and then says, 'Look, how would you feel about taking your clothes off?'

'Really?'

'Not shy, are you?'

Natalie shrugs her shoulders.

'You don't have to, if you don't want to. I just think it would be nice to do a proper life study.'

'I'm not sure. I've never been a model before.'

'I used to do it when I was a student. It pays reasonably well.'

'I'm not expecting to make any money.'

Magda laughs. 'Could be better than waiting on at the White Hart. But look, just sit there and try to be comfortable. I'll do you as you are.'

The room falls silent. Magda works on with concentration, her hand moving deftly, looking from the drawing to Natalie and back again every few seconds. Natalie, looking around at the detail of the studio, realises that being a model and staying still is actually quite hard.

'Would you like a rest?' asks Magda after twenty minutes.

Natalie sits up and stretches her arms.

'So, where are you off to tonight then?'

'Oh, just the pub.'

'Boyfriend?'

'No, just an old friend I bumped into. From school. Not seen him for ages.'

'Nice. Tell me when you're ready to start again.'

'Actually, I was thinking I will take my clothes off now, if you like.'

'Up to you.'

'So long as you don't exhibit it at the Gallery.'

'I promise I won't!'

'Not unless you paint a different head on it.'

'Now that would be defeating the object slightly.'

'So, should I…?'

'Go upstairs. There's a chair you can put your things on. And you'll find a dressing gown behind the door. Put that on to come down in. That's the etiquette. You're not expected to wander around in the buff. Oh, and better close the curtains up there first, just in case.'

Natalie made sure she didn't get to the pub too early for her meeting with Nathan. She recalled that he was not always the most punctual of people, and she had learned her lesson when once, in the first term at uni, she had gone into the bar waiting for someone and had been approached by at least three different guys who thought that because she was sitting alone she wanted male company. Such attention might have been flattering at first but it soon became a nuisance.

However, Nathan was on time and, meeting outside, they went in together. They got a couple of lagers and sat in the corner of a side room. Nathan had the usual bordering-on-scruffy look she remembered well. It couldn't possibly be the same grey Primark hoodie he'd had back in the day but it looked just like it. He was unshaven but it wasn't clear whether it was a beard in the making or whether he just couldn't be bothered.

'So how was Nottingham then?' he asked.

'Yeah, good. Good on the whole. Did you never…?'

'What? Go to uni? Finish my A-levels? No. Neither.'

'How was that then?'

'Difficult to explain really. Definitely not interesting anyway.' He took a sip of his drink. 'So what are you doing next then?'

'Teacher training. Yes, I know. Definitely not interesting either.'

'Definitely interesting, I'd say. Where?'

'Huddersfield, where else?'

'Secondary?'

'No. Primary. I thought I'd give primary a go.'

'Wise choice probably. You'll be good at it, I reckon.'

A silence followed but it was not uncomfortable.

'So,' she said at last, 'tell me what happened, Nathan. This is your old birthday-partner-girlfriend-who-is-not-a- girlfriend talking.'

Nathan shrugged his shoulder and twisted his mouth a little. 'Nothing happened. That's what sums it up best. Nothing. I went back to redo my A-level year but I couldn't hack it. I walked into college every morning, had a panic attack and walked straight out again. Basically, after that I just dropped out. It was as if my life had just stopped. As if everything was moving except me. I was stopped. Totally stagnated. My mum took me to see doctors. They put me on stuff, anti-depressants, that kind of stuff. I felt like a fish in a goldfish bowl. Then someone gave me some acid at a party and I went off my head. It was truly scary. They sectioned me and took me into a mad ward. People walking round watching you all the time in case you decide to top yourself. I guess I needed to be there at first, but in the end I felt I was more sane than the people keeping me there.'

'I wish I'd known,' she said, putting her hand over his.

He took in a breath. 'Probably nothing you could have done. You could have been nice and said nice things but I probably would have rejected it.'

Another silence, not uncomfortable, followed.

'Then, to cap it all, I got involved with an older woman.'

'Oh God! Not married, I hope!'

'No.'

'Thank goodness. Maybe it was something you needed.'

Nathan shrugged his shoulders.

'So who was it? What happened? Of course, if you'd rather not talk about it,' she added, sensing his reluctance.

'Not important. I just got drawn into it. It didn't last long.'

She tipped her head to one side. He smiled. It was clear he did not want to say anymore.

'All right, freak!'

Nathan gave a grin. 'It wasn't 'freak' it was 'creep'.'

'It was 'freak', I'm sure of it.'

'No. I remember it. Somebody—Valerie Thurgoland, I think—

called me a 'creep' and we took it up and called each other 'creep' at every opportunity.'

'Oh, yes, I remember now, creep.'

'It was hilarious, creep. We could keep it going for hours. Put it in every sentence.'

'Didn't we change it to 'freak' later though, creep?'

'No, creep. Well, we might have done but I can't remember.'

'Actually, I reckon Valerie Thurgoland was the biggest creep.'

'There was no shortage of them, come to think of it.'

They talked for a while of other people they'd known at school and in the sixth form, exchanging what bits of information they had of what they'd done, and their whereabouts now.

'So what have you been up to since you got back?' said Nathan at last.

'Oh, nothing much. Shopping in town, that sort of thing. Bumped into Miss Holden, do you remember her?'

'The one who disappeared suddenly?'

'Yes. Apart from that, working in here Saturday nights. I've been up to Magda Bentley's studio a couple of times.'

'Oh yes?'

'Is there something odd in that?' she asked, laughing.

'No.'

'Do you know her?'

'I went to one of her things at the Gallery. Didn't really get on with it.'

'Right,' said Natalie, deciding not to tell him that she had been sitting for Magda. 'So what are you doing now?' she asked.

'Well, I went over to Salford for a while. Just to get away. Stayed with a mate there a couple of months but he was getting seriously into smack so I came back. I'm on Jobseeker's. Do stints in a couple of charity shops. Try to make myself useful. Keep the demons at bay.'

Natalie nodded sympathetically, though she didn't really know what to say and, almost as if to save her, Martin's face peered round the door.

'Natalie, didn't know you'd be here tonight!'

His glance passed to Nathan as to a potential rival and then relaxed. 'Get you one? Nathan?'

'No. I'm OK thanks.'

'Natalie? White wine?'

He did not wait for an answer.

'You know him?' she questioned.

'Labour Party,' Nathan replied. 'I went to some meetings. Not my kind of Labour Party, really. But anyway, look, I'm going to get off. Don't want to be a…'

'You're not a… whatever it was you were going to say.'

Nathan produced one of his whimsical smiles, as of old.

'Give me your number,' she said. 'We should go for a walk. Or a picnic. A walk at least.'

Martin came back from the bar just as they were completing the exchange of numbers.

Nathan got up. 'Right, I'll see you then.'

'I'll text you.'

'Nathan Brook,' said Martin, sitting down.

'You obviously know him.'

'He came to meetings for a time. A bit of an idealist, quite angry underneath. The kind of supporter who will stop the Labour Party ever getting into power again. So how do you know him?'

'School and stuff.'

'Bit of a weirdo, some people say.'

'Well I wouldn't say that.'

Martin allowed this moment to pass. 'So what else have you been up to today?'

CHAPTER 9

Since bumping into Natalie on his Sunday walk, Adam Mitchell has had three days of complete sobriety. Not an agreeable lunchtime pint, not a leisurely couple early doors, not a bottle of chilled white, not a bottle of room-warm red, not even a nip of midnight whisky.

I'm cleaning my windows of perception, he said to himself. Could there be, he asked himself, some new access of creativity, some new direction, inspired by a girl at a gallery, a new girl behind the bar at the White Hart, a girl with a flushed face and dishevelled hair on a bike just below the reservoir at Old Lansley?

He sat patiently, with pen poised, each morning—always the best time for fresh ideas—and each slow afternoon. Some lines came, some images. Some sharp phrases, but when he looked at them afterwards, they were only phrases that would impress someone else. That was always the problem. Doing things because you knew they might impress, not because you actually felt them.

And what did he feel?

Three times he had recreated, almost in a spirit of pilgrimage, that Sunday walk. Here is where I stepped back to let a cyclist pass, here is where she stopped when she recognised me and when I recognised her. Here is where, for perhaps thirty seconds, we chatted pleasantly to each other. He summoned the image of exactly how she had looked astride her bicycle, and then pictured her riding onwards until she disappeared from sight.

Each time he repeated the walk, he had a preternatural sense of her presence: a feeling that at any moment she might appear, like a spirit summoned by his concentrated imagining of her.

This is patently ridiculous, he said to himself. I am becoming a figure of absurdity. A pathetic, helpless, middle-aged man in the grip of an adolescent's infatuation.

Was it the product of a disordered mind, a chemical imbalance, some subtle and perverse malfunction of the nervous system, affecting the all-unsuspecting mental processes, still imagining themselves capable of autonomous thought? Was it the case, as neuroscientists might argue, that all emotions, moods, states of mind, whatever you called them, were the by-product of micro-chemical chain reactions, cocktails of endorphins and pheromones and God knows what else swirling about in the psychological soup? Probably associated with some quasi-Darwinian rationale of self-preservation. Or possibly, self-destruction.

Possibly so, possibly so, but nevertheless, the feeling was there, however you reasoned it, inescapably and insistently present.

And as it flowed through your veins, your nerves, your thoughts, your brain, it was as if you were breathing in a rarified air containing something exquisitely fine, even if tinged also with exquisite pain.

Something about a girl he had seen three times, a girl quite easily young enough to be his daughter. Something that nevertheless had washed through him like a dye. Could a man make something of that, out of that invasion of anguish and energy? As late in the day as this? Was there some way that a man could take an unrealisable passion, a ridiculous, even pitiable devotion, and turn it into a work of art?

His pen hovered over the page. There was nothing written. He glanced up to the whisky bottle. He squeezed his eyes at the temptation.

He resisted.

CHAPTER 10

Martin Haslam is twenty-five. Originally from Oldham, he studied Politics at Hull, did an MA in journalism at Manchester, and was applying for jobs in radio and TV journalism before deciding to buy a flat in Milthwaite and pursue a career in local politics.

He is, as Natalie has discovered in the two or three times she has been out with him, very forthright and articulate, very confident in his own opinions.

Meeting Natalie at the White Hart on Thursday, he has arrived in his car, a new two-tone Mini Cooper of which he is inordinately proud, and drives them the half-mile to Marmaduke's.

'You should have let me pick you up at home.' he says. 'Could have saved you the journey.'

'It's not far. Besides, I enjoy the walk.'

Bars and modish eating houses come and go with some frequency in Milthwaite. What is now Marmaduke's began life as an Oddfellows Club—the working man's alternative to a Masonic lodge—in the late nineteenth century. Since then, it has been a pub (predictably The Oddfellows Arms), a Wimpy's, a night club and a wine bar. Now, and under new management for the last two years, it has become Marmaduke's, with an open kitchen where you can watch the chefs at work, and the most popular place in town for trendy diners.

'Have what you like,' says Martin as they look at the menu. 'It's on me, I insist. I'd recommend the Lamb Tagine.'

Natalie, who is always confused by menus, is even more thrown by this. If Martin is insisting on paying, she feels she should choose one of the less expensive options, but the fact that he has recommended a particular dish which is actually quite dear makes her feel she should look for something equally priced, and she is not especially keen on lamb.

Meanwhile, the bottle of Sauvignon Blanc which he has already ordered arrives. Martin samples it, swishing it round the glass and sniffing, and approves.

The wine waiter is followed swiftly by the are-you-ready-to-order waiter. Both Martin and the waiter are looking benignly but directly at her. 'I think I'll go for the er… Lamb Tagine,' she says, seeing—too late—the Sea Bass option which actually she would much prefer.

'Sir?'

'Ribeye steak,' says Martin without hesitation, and before the waiter can ask the question, 'medium rare.'

'Thank you, sir.'

'So, here we are,' says Martin, raising his glass. 'Cheers!'

'Yes,' says Natalie, picking up her glass.

'So what have you been up to today?' asks Martin.

'Oh, nothing much. Just visited someone for an hour or two,' she says, thinking that posing nude for a local artist is probably not the best material for small talk. Thankfully, Martin does not seem inclined to follow up on his question.

'How about you?' she says, handing it over.

'Been looking through the electoral register as a matter of fact, crunching the data.'

'Sound fascinating,' she says.

'Yes,' Martin replies, not sensing her irony in the least. 'Winning elections these days is quite a precise science. The days of riding through town with a megaphone are ancient history. It's all a question of targeting and messaging.'

He talks a little more about targeting and messaging, until their meal arrives.

The sauce is nice and the meat is tender but the taste of lamb is just something she has to endure.

'Of course,' Martin carries on, topping up their glasses,

'standing as councillor is just a start. Step one of the plan. I mean to go further. Westminster hopefully. I mean, if I can make my mark and then get adopted next time, I'll stand at the general election.'

'Do you think you have a chance?'

'Good chance, I'd say. Labour is always popular round here. That's partly why I chose them. Well, the politics too, of course. I mean, actually, my dad was an ardent Thatcher supporter, and I guess a lot of people start by inheriting their parents' politics but I soon hopped off that bandwagon. Not that she didn't get some things right, mind you, and I mean I'm no socialist in the big sense of the word but I think Labour have a better sense of the future. I mean, we really need a dynamic government, if you ask me. Blair was fairly dynamic for a time but then got involved in stupid foreign policy stuff: Iraq and all that. Of course, people blame Labour for the big crash but it wasn't really Labour policy that brought that on, it was the sub-prime market collapsing in America. I mean, I suppose you could say capitalism was the fault but that's too broad. You can't really get anywhere with that sort of argument. As soon as you start on broad things like that the voters start to distrust you. Think you're a Marxist. It's like saying you don't believe in the Queen. It's just a vote loser, especially when the tabloids get their teeth into it. What did you vote last time?'

'Green.'

'Green. Interesting,' he says, nodding his head slowly and considerately. 'I mean, I can totally understand why, from all sorts of points of view, but to me, and this is just my own opinion, it's like throwing your vote away.'

'Well, I just felt like using my vote to make a point.'

'Yes, of course, and I'm pretty big on the environment myself but the trouble is, again just in my opinion, there's too much identity politics about: LGBT, BAEM, Green, you name it. I mean, I have absolutely no problem with any of these groups per se, I support a lot of their aims, but they have the effect of dividing the opposition and its supporters, and if you don't get into power you can't do a thing. I mean the Tories are still massively divided over Europe, even post-Brexit, so I think it's time for Labour to fight under a broad platform of reform. You could say I'm a bit of a LibDem and fair play, I have some sympathies, but the Coalition was a bit of a disaster and I can't see them getting back any time soon. No, I feel that Labour is my home really. So what are your plans then?'

'Well,' says Natalie, suddenly surprised that he has come to an end, and at the disadvantage of having no really developed or extended plans, 'I'm going to do a PGCE next year and I suppose I'll just take it from there.'

'Right. I mean that's great. Education is so important. That's another big thing for me. I mean, my ideal job if I were ever to make it into the government, you know, the cabinet, would be Secretary of State for Education. That is something I would really relish!'

'I expect you'd be really good at it,' she says, and at that point the waiter comes to take away their dishes.

'Sweet menu?'

'Natalie?'

'No thanks. Not for me.'

'Coffee?'

'OK. Americano, no milk.'

'Same for me.'

They leave Marmaduke's and he drives her home.

'So,' he says, fancy going out again?'

'Yes, OK. Thanks for the meal.'

He looks at her. She doesn't feel that she can get out of the car without some token. She leans ever so slightly towards him, making possible a brief side-of-the-lips kiss.'

'I'll text you then, shall I?

She gets out of car, hurries down the path to the front door and hears his car travelling away.

'How did it go?' asks her mum.

'Yeah, fine.'

'Where did you go?'

'Marmaduke's.'

'Nice. And are you seeing him again?'

'Maybe. Yes, I think so. Probably.'

'Well, he seems a nice chap. Standing as a councillor, you said.'

'Yes.'

'And what does he do, I mean, when he's not doing his politics?'

'Oh, something to do with computer stuff. Crunching data.'

'Well, you could do worse than that.'

'Stop trying to marry me off, mum!'

'I'm not. I'm not trying to marry you off. Don't be daft. I'm just trying to show an interest.'

'Sorry.'

'How would you feel about going up to Manchester tomorrow? Shopping expedition. What do you think?'

'Yes. Sounds good. Do you think we could be back for four?' Natalie adds, remembering that she said she would call round at Magda's studio for another sitting.

'Yes. We'll get an early start. Do the shops, have lunch, then get the two o'clock back. How's that?'

'Perfect.'

CHAPTER 11

'Where's dad gone then?' asks Natalie as they stand on the platform, having walked to the station. Ralph has taken the car.

'Up to Leeds. He has something to do at the department.'

The train, when it comes, is crowded and uncomfortable and they have to stand by the door, but it is a short journey, and soon they are disembarking at Victoria and making their way towards Deansgate.

'It's years since I've been up in Manchester,' says Barbara. 'It always seems to change so much, you can hardly find your way around.'

'Maybe just Marks and Spencer first. I need to find some sensible clothes and shoes for when I go on teaching practice.'

'You need some nice summer clothes too. You only seem to have that tiny little mini-skirt and your student clobber.'

'It's not a tiny little mini-skirt at all, and I usually wear leggings under it anyway.'

'Just the same…'

She buys two navy knee-length skirts, two plain blouses, a pair of straight-legged charcoal grey slacks and some black shoes without a heel. She suspects female teachers these days are probably quite trendy but it's probably best to be relatively conservative at first, she thinks.

'What do you think of this?' says Barbara, who has been browsing in Per Una whilst Natalie has been making her purchases. The item she has over her arm is a light cotton print wrap-around frock. She holds it up against Natalie. 'It suits you. What do you think? Might as well while the hot weather lasts.'

'Don't say that, you'll put a jinx on it.'

'Try it on.'

A minute later, Natalie comes out of the cubicle.

'Yes!' says Barbara affirmatively. 'It's definitely you!'

'I do like it,' says Natalie, 'but I wasn't really budgeting for this sort of thing.'

'I'll buy it for you. Go and change back and we'll get it.'

An hour later, they are in the Riva Bar and Restaurant, perusing the menu.

'This is the second meal out I've had in two days,' says Natalie.

'Well, I'm paying for this too.'

'That's what Martin said.'

'And so he should!'

They place their order and look at each other across the table.

'You know, we really should talk more.'

Natalie scrunches up her face, and then shrugs her shoulders. 'What do you want to talk about?'

'Oh, you know, just mother and daughter stuff.'

'Oh dear, I'm not going to get a lecture, am I?'

'Not at all,' insists Barbara. 'I just feel that we've never really talked much. Over these last few years.'

'Well, I've been at uni and, well, quite often you've been involved in a play.'

'That's true,' says Barbara. They both know that this is not what's at the bottom of the matter, but it suffices to get them over the awkwardness of the moment.

Secretly, Barbara wishes she could tell Natalie the truth about Cyril. Natalie suspects that Barbara wants to talk about boyfriends and such matters, but it is not easy. There have always seemed to be secrets hidden away beneath family talks: things people didn't want to get too close to or bring out into the open.

As they eat their meal and later, on the return train where thankfully they find seats, the conversation finds lighter and safer avenues along which to travel.

When they arrive home, Natalie has a shower, changes, and sets out towards Magda's studio.

CHAPTER 12

The girl, Rob notices, has been there three times, three times that he has seen, three times this week. He has just looked up to see her arriving but tried to keep his head down because he knows the artist bird had clocked him the day before. Nice girl too. Very pretty. Nice figure. Nice tits as well. Nice enough. You always got a better sense of it in the warm weather, with the thin T-shirts and tops. He had managed to catch her briefly on the CCTV going in and coming out, and on the webcam too, but the images were fuzzy. But nevertheless! Wouldn't mind being in a threesome with those two, he ruminated. Christ! The very thought of it made him tighten in his pants. If you had to choose one as a hot fuck buddy, it would be the older one—the artist—but the young one, well, thinking about her, you could just let your imagination run wild!

At this moment in time, he is searching a website which deals in listening and spying bugs. Not extortionately expensive, he concludes; small, easy to install, wireless control. Now that would be the thing. Could he only find a pretext, a benign pretext for getting in there to do some kind of job: to fix something, like a good neighbour. Could he, for example, cause a malfunction in the plumbing and then be on hand to sort it out, meantime planting a little bug, one upstairs in the bedroom, one down in the studio. Worth considering. Definitely so. The opportunity didn't easily suggest itself but you never knew. Best be ready, even if just on the off chance.

Or a drone maybe. How would that work? Could you make it hover at a window, for instance, with camera obviously to catch a glimpse of what was going on inside. Could be dodgy. Was there any actual law against that kind of thing?

He clicked to purchase two radio-operated viewing devices; they even had, tiny as they were, the facility to move the angle of the lens. The wonders of technology! They were, perhaps appropriately, from Thailand.

He returned to the International Dating Agency, clicked on the Asian site, signed in and scrolled through numerous faces, some of which he had seen before. On this occasion, Quan-Lee from Ho-Chi-Min City attracted his attention. She was twenty-six. She liked his picture, she said, was very obedient, would be a very grateful, obedient wife and good mother to his children. *Would like come to England.*

It was pretty much as usual.

He clicks and says hello, says how often he has seen her profile but has been too shy to contact her.

No reason be shy, says Quan-Lee.

Quan-Lee very beautiful, he types.

Quan-Lee thanks you say so, Mr Rob.

He now proceeds to show Quan-Lee how to move from the site to private online chat.

It takes some time for Quan-Lee to comprehend all of this but eventually she agrees to connect.

Quan-Lee happy? he asks.

Quan-Lee very happy.

Show me screen shot of Quan-Lee happy face.

A few moments later, a screen shot comes through. Quan-Lee is smiling, and she is pretty but not as pretty as the photo on the site.

You like Quan-Lee picture?

Quan-Lee lovely picture. Quan-Lee make lovely wife.

Quan-Lee happy you say so. Rob want nice wife, come to England?

Rob want nice wife sure.

Rob younger than many men want wife.

Rob not just like old man want girl just sex, he says falling into the idiom.

Rob not want sex?

Rob not say that.
Quan-Lee glad.
Rob want children. Babies.
Quan-Lee, too, want babies.
Quan-Lee show titties? he asks.
Titties?
Quan-Lee breasts. Need see breasts for being mother.
There is a pause.
Then, *Quan-Lee be good mother, feed baby well.*

He thinks, and then types, '*Rob spend big money bring Quan-Lee England, nice house, very nice life. Just want screenshot, so can be sure.*

He waits. It is always a good interim, this anticipation.

After a moment, a screenshot comes through.

'Wow,' he says to himself. Quan-Lee very well-endowed. Quan-Lee loaded. He clicks to save the shot. One for the archive definitely.

Good? Yes? Good titties?

Very good, says Rob but then, the immediate satisfaction passing quickly, he goes on a new tack.

You like pleasure, Quan-Lee?

Pleasure, yes like pleasure, sure.

You like pleasure yourself, show me how you like pleasure.

How pleasure myself? How you mean?

How? Quan-Lee not know?

There is a pause of some length. Again he waits with mild excitement. Will-she-won't-she? Will-she-won't-she?

At last, Quan-Lee clicks out. It is not unusual at this stage. Only twice, with younger less experienced girls, has he managed to get that degree of compliance.

Of course, on the porn sites you could get pretty much whatever you wanted, explicit as you like, but the trouble was you never knew if it was real or fake. He often suspected the latter, though sometimes he went on just to see if there was anything new, just for the sake of it. And some of it was pretty disgusting too: the violent stuff, the stuff with animals; even he thought that stuff was disgusting. And it was expensive too. The deeper you went into it, the more expensive it was.

Why pay money when you could have these little interactions with real people—real girls—for free? The Quan-Lees of this world. Maybe he should have been a little more patient with Quan-Lee, teased her along a bit, gained her confidence more.

If he were ever to go to Vietnam, a Quan-Lee with knockers like that would be a sure port of call. Maybe he missed a trick there.

He clicked on her profile again but there was no response.

He clicked the key five or six times staccato fashion as if to convey his displeasure. Then at last, sitting back, 'Good riddance,' he muttered. 'Plenty more fish in the sea where you swim, my little Quan-Lee.'

CHAPTER 13

The White Hart was in its usual mid-Saturday evening scramble. For some of the younger clientele, it was a meeting place: a few shots before going up to Manchester or Leeds, even Huddersfield, to the night scene which would not truly begin until midnight. Then the place would clear by half nine or ten, leaving just the locals for the last hour or so.

Adam Mitchell was sitting in his usual corner, taking in —with a reverence that might well have been mistaken for surreptitious gaping—images of the creature who had so much been the object of his rapt thoughts and the cause of his abstinence during the whole of the last week. That he was here, drinking beer, now, was simply down to his wanting a pretext for seeing her again, knowing that this would be her second Saturday stint behind the bar. He was sitting thus, to all intents and purposes lost in his own thoughts, when he saw Magda Bentley entering the front door. His spirits plummeted. A meeting with Magda at this moment was almost as bad as being accosted by Moggy Morton, but though he studiously avoided acknowledging her, he knew from the corner of his eye that she was seeking him out amongst the crowd.

'There you are,' she said at last, sitting down beside him.
'Magda.'
'Aren't you going to offer to get me a drink?'
'Not sure the situation merits it.'
'That's not very gentlemanly.'
'Then it's in character.'
She laughed. 'How true.'
'What do you want?'

'Vodka and lime will do.'

He got up and went to the bar.

'Vodka and lime, please, Natalie, and the usual for me.'

He cringed slightly that he had used her name, but her smile was, he judged, the mildly private smile of one who remembered meeting him the previous Sunday. It was enough. More than enough.

'And yours,' he says, noticing that Natalie has glanced to see that the vodka and lime is for Magda.

'Thanks.'

'What is it, then?' he said, back at the table with Magda. 'For what particular reason, Magda, have you flown down here on your broomstick tonight?'

Magda paused, letting the insult drift away.

'I had a visit from our old friend, the teacher.'

'Oh Christ, what did she want?'

'She's mad. Delusional. She seems to think she can destroy your reputation and mine by somehow exposing us.'

'The answer is simple,' said Adam. I have no reputation to destroy. Neither have you. End of. Anyway, we've been through this before.'

'It's the midsummer madness. It always gets her. Poor cow.'

'We treated her badly.'

'You did. I had nothing to do with it,' insisted Magda.

'She was your friend. You introduced us. That's how it started.'

'She was desperate to meet you. What could I do? I didn't know you were going to shag her, did I?'

'And I didn't know how you were going to try to bugger it up for all of us, did I? Anyway, what's the point of all this, now?'

'Just to put you in the picture, give you the head's up. In case she comes to see you. You should be grateful.'

'Thanks.'

'And just wondering if you might just happen to want a naughty girl for the night but I see you've got your eyes on someone special.'

'What?'

'The barmaid. She's nice, isn't she?'

'I haven't noticed.'

'Of course you have, you old goat. Do you think I haven't seen your telltale beady little eyes straying in that direction? Ralph thingy's daughter. She's modelling for me, you know. Aren't you jealous?'

'Should I be?'

'In the nude too. That didn't take much persuasion. You'd like her even more if you saw that youthful form in a recumbent pose, Adam: comely bosom, slender waist, feather, and all.'

'Are you trying to provoke me?'

'Of course I am. Nice expression that, her 'feather'. Wonder where I got that from. One of your novels probably.'

'Have you read any of them?'

'Mmm, good point. Must have picked it up somewhere else.'

Despite knowing that she was trying to wind him up, Adam was as thoroughly piqued by Magda Bentley's words as she could have wished him to be. Without realising the full extent of it, she had pinpointed the very thing that had been exercising his thought, to the exclusion of almost everything else, since that day a week ago when she had spoken to him in the gallery, but now his tranquil meditations of the week lay in tatters.

'So is she threatening to come back again?'

'The schoolteacher?'

'Mmm.'

'God knows.'

'Well just ignore her, that's what I say. Do you want another?'

'No.'

'It's your round.'

'Well sod that! I can't stand his place anyway. Never did. Just wanted to let you know.'

Magda left, but not before going up to the bar to say hello to and exchange words with Natalie.

When Adam went to the bar, Natalie, it seemed, was on her break. He ordered a pint with a double whisky chaser and waited, finishing slowly, until she reappeared.

'You've got to admit she's a corker,' says Moggy, now joining him to take Magda's place.

'You've hit the nail right on the head there, Moggy.'

'Poetry in motion.'

'Poetry in fucking motion, Moggy. Couldn't agree more.'

Moggy laughs in his throat, as if he has caught Adam revealing his true colours.

The whisky chaser was followed later, at home, by more of the same. It was no good pretending he could achieve anything with words. No good at all. Like trying to play the guitar with only the remaining stubs of charred fingers. All he could do was summon forth her image to his mind.

Fuck Magda for having her to paint. No doubt Magda could capture all that. The slim form, the mildness of her features, the warmth of her eyes, the captivating smile – even more, the captivating half-smile.

And the 'feather'. What a cow Magda was to throw that into the mix. To hold a mirror up to all it is that is making my wayward, raddled soul stop in its tracks.

What was it Yeats said?: *Oh that I were young again and she was in my arms.* And Wilde: *Each man doth kill the thing he loves.* They understood the desperation. Could a man become a murderer to rid himself of that anguish? Like Othello: *Put out the light then put out the light.* Could the desire to kill be as strong as the desire to love? Could destruction be another form of the possession one craved?

Obliterate the desperation.

Destroy the anguish.

Make one's quietus.

He woke up at 4 a.m. The narcotic haze of the alcohol had departed, but not the post-alcoholic depression. It was the nothing time. But no, not the nothing time. Rather the time when every physical discomfort conspired with the withered spirit to flash up on the screen of consciousness, every negative judgement you have ever made on yourself. A waking nightmare.

A more real sleeping nightmare followed. A nightmare in which nets and grappling irons were dragging up meaningless debris, and then dead bodies—white and drowned—from the canal, in the net. And somehow, within the terms of the nightmare, the cause of all the trouble was his own grubby egotism.

He awoke again in a cold sweat but, realising that he was awake and that everything else was unreal, he felt a pervasive sense of relief. And in the light, pleasant slumber which followed, a peaceful, almost surreal, dream state came over him.

He was in the church,—St Wilfred's—with its white plaster walls, its pleasant soothing light and its equally soothing organ. And there she was, two rows in front: her brown hair combed and sleek, her face—which he could see in profile—pale and luminous. Occasionally, she moistened her lips with her tongue. Occasionally, too, he saw the blink of her eyelid, curved lashes which he had possibly noticed before but had not fully realised. What was she thinking? What was the colour of her thoughts? And then, as if sensing that she was being observed, she turned. Fearing any quick attempt to avert his eyes would appear furtive or evasive, their eyes met and her lips formed a pleasant smile which she held for a moment before turning back to the front.

And there the dream ended.

And it was then that he realised that something wasn't right.

He wasn't in bed.

He was at the bottom of the stairs.

He was cold. He was in pain.

And he had no ability to move.

CHAPTER 14

When Martin takes Natalie out, as planned on Tuesday, he drives her over to a tapas bar in Holmfirth and this time she insists on paying her share of the bill.

'I like Holmfirth,' he says. 'For some things it's as good as Manchester or Leeds.'

'Smaller. A lot prettier. Actually,' she adds, 'I was in Manchester the other day.'

'Oh yes? Anything special?'

'Just shopping. With my mum.'

'What did you buy?'

'Mainly some clobber for when I start at teacher training. Oh, and this,' she says, indicating the dress she has on.

'Nice.'

'I wanted to look for a new laptop for when I start too, but mum's not really into technical stuff, so it can wait. My old one's still OK. Just a bit clunky and slow.'

The route back takes them past the apartment block where Martin lives.

'Would you like to come up and have a look?' he asks.

'Mmm, OK,' she replies, for he is already slowing down. 'Just for a minute.'

'Just a quick look round,' he agrees.

His apartment is on the third floor of a woollen mill conversion. From the entrance vestibule, through double security doors and refurbished with polished marble flooring, a stone staircase with thick iron work railings—pitted but heavily painted in black acrylic—leads upwards. The alternative is a caged lift.

'Don't worry,' says Martin, leading her in. 'it's not the original lift, just a replica. They tried to keep some of the original features.'

He clangs the doors shut and presses a button. There is a buzz and then the cage lifts slowly with a tightening of metal, and they ascend, with each floor and landing visible as they move past. The entrance to his apartment is a heavy sliding door on metal runners, though opening with a key code.

'I had the option of changing it for a modern door,' Martin explains, 'but I chose to keep this. I think it's quite chic. Don't you?'

'Very unusual.'

'Well, come in. Here we are! Welcome to my world.'

'Wow!' says Natalie. 'I'm impressed.'

It is a spacious room with high casement windows opening to the outside in an old-fashioned style, though with internal double-glazed windows which open inwards. The internal walls are stonework, painted white, with some tinted Perspex panels between the buttresses and some exposed iron girders—rivets and all—beneath the ceiling and a steel conduit which looks as if it might be for heating but could possibly be just decorative.

The furniture is simple, a well-worn leather Chesterfield and armchair, a coffee table made of distressed blue wood, a workstation in the corner and a large thick-pile rug on the stone flags. There is some concealed lighting and a standard lamp, which Martin now switches on, between the settee and the armchair.

'Coffee then?' says Martin. 'Might as well while you're here.'

'OK, then.'

'I'll put some music on. Anything you like in particular?'

'No. Whatever.'

'I'll just put some background on. Something relaxing.'

Martin goes to the corner where the workstation is and a song begins, coming quietly from concealed speakers. He then goes through into what is evidently a kitchen area.

Natalie is reflecting that there is something unequal and to her disadvantage in all her conversations with Martin. She feels she has to parry questions and give bland answers because she doesn't really know what to say. He is nice enough but always seems to be a step ahead. She walks around looking at the paintings, half a dozen in number, all of which could be originals; one of them, she notes, is by Magda Bentley. It is of a woman dancing, in what seems to be a swirling dress, though when you look closer, the dress is made up entirely of swarming wasps, or bees, or maybe even barbed wire.

'I see you've got one by Magda Bentley,' she says when Martin comes through with the tray.

'Yes. Do you know her?'

'A little,' she replies, deciding not to give away any further information.

'I think she's quite good,' he says. 'Not that I'm any sort of real judge, but I like to support local artists,' he adds, putting the tray down and lowering the light slightly. 'I've met her at a couple of local meetings: community stuff, that sort of thing. Shall I pour? Come and sit down then. What do you think of the music?'

'Nice, yeah.'

'It's a playlist I put together for quieter occasions.'

'Yeah, it's good. Relaxing.'

'My taste is quite eclectic really: 80s, 90s, a little bit of classical now and then.'

They sit for a time sipping coffee, with a little more small talk about the apartment and her course.

'Can I ask you something?' he says at last. 'I wondered… I was wondering how you would feel about putting this thing on a firmer footing.'

'How do you mean?'

'Well – us,' he explains. 'You and me. Make it a proper relationship. I know we haven't been going out for long but I feel pretty good about it.'

'Oh,' says Natalie. 'I don't know. It seems so sudden. It's not as if… ' she shrugs her shoulders slightly, not quite sure of what it is she means.

'Not as if what?'
'I don't know. Well, I mean, we haven't even kissed.'
'You kissed me in the car last week. Well, a peck.'
'Just a peck. Not properly though.'

She means this to be both light-hearted and defining, but she sees immediately that she has offered a hostage to fortune.

'That can soon be remedied,' he says, and he moves his face closer to hers so that she must dodge awkwardly or meet his lips. It is tentative at first but, once started, he prolongs the kiss with increasing pressure and purpose.

'Try to relax,' he says, smilingly, breaking off for a moment and trailing a lock of her hair through his fingers. But before she can interject, he has renewed the kiss, now holding her shoulder and gradually moving his hand until it comes to rest lightly over her breast. Then, loosening the top fold of her dress, he slips his hand inside, over the cup of her bra and kisses her again, urging the strength of his feelings onto her as his hand now presses more firmly.

Her heart is thumping, though whether in panic or excitement she is not sure.

He kisses her neck and her ear and then, in a tense whisper, says, 'Let's go to the bedroom,' and standing, draws her up by her hand and leads the way.

Inside, he closes the door and kisses her again as they stand there. After a moment, he finds the knot of her sash and gently pulls it loose so that the dress drifts open. He presses the back of his fingers against the flat of her stomach and then lets his fingers play just inside the elastic of her knickers. Then, breathlessly, he urges her towards the bed, easing the dress away from her shoulders and drawing aside the straps of her bra.

'God, you're beautiful,' he says, looking at her uncovered breasts. He leans forward to kiss the pale flesh beside her nipple. Standing quickly, he then drops his trousers and then his underpants so that she sees him, swollen but not yet quite fully erect, and watches as, leaning over her, he begins to ease down her knickers.

'No!' she says, suddenly, recoiling. 'I'm sorry.'
'What?'
'I'm sorry. I can't do this.'
'What's the matter?'
'I don't know. It's just… '
'I've got some condoms if that's the worry.'
'No, it's not that,' she says, reaching to pull her knickers back into place.

He sits back, disappointed, resentful.

'Why?' he says. 'Why did you let me do all that and then just fuck me off?'

'I'm sorry.'

'I thought you felt the same as me.'

'I didn't know what I felt. It was so unexpected.'

He stands up and pulls on his underpants and trousers.

'I feel such a bloody fool,' he says.

'I'm sorry,' she repeats, fastening her bra and pulling her dress back into place.

He takes a deep breath and exhales. 'I should have taken things more gradually, shouldn't I? Shouldn't have tried to rush things like that.'

'It's not your fault,' she says. 'I should have said something. I thought it should be what I wanted, but I'm sorry, I just…'

It plays out at the level of awkward apologies.

'I'll drive you home,' he says at last.

'It's all right. I can just as easily get a taxi.'

'I'll take you home,' he says firmly, almost an order, as if claiming some moral high ground.

They go down to the car. The silence is awkward. He drives slightly faster than is necessary but she resolves not to say anything.

'Just drop me off here, please,' she says at the top of the close. 'Thanks.'

She is glad to be outside feeling the cool night air on her face as she walks the last fifty yards home, almost unaware that her face is streaming with tears.

The next morning, she receives a text from him: *Hey Natalie. How's it going? About last night. I know maybe I was a bit hasty, a bit too pushy. Sorry if it put you off. But, hey, not the end of the world. Let's start again, give it another go, just take things easy? Text me. Let me know if you fancy another date.*

Later, another text: *Hi Natalie! Did you get my text? I know these things sometimes go astray. Let me know.*

She feels that she is being moved into a position where if she does reply, it will be to say something she doesn't want to say, or something that could be misconstrued as that.

She does not answer.

CHAPTER 15

Adam Mitchell is on a ward in Celverdale General, having been admitted on Monday afternoon, as an emergency, to A and E.

He has, since then, been coming round gradually, in and out, from some realm of opaque consciousness and is aware that he is probably under the influence of sedatives because his brain is loaded with an unusual heaviness. He is afraid to move his body in case it sets off a chain reaction that will cause pain but gradually realises that within the confines of his bed, he can move his limbs without unpleasant consequences. However, the movement of his hand makes him aware that he is on a drip, and he makes the deduction that the discomfort around his midriff is caused by a catheter. In addition, some wires and electrodes connected to a device by the bedside are attached to his chest, evidently measuring the signals which indicate the continuance of life.

The questions he asks the nurses who stop by his bed, to monitor his observations and adjust the bits of equipment to which he is attached, are met with replies that are blandly pleasant and uninformative. The best he can get is that the doctor will be round to see him soon.

He has no alternative but to accept this and tries to induce in himself some kind of mental suspended animation. Later, he realises that he has since slept again and that the density which he felt earlier in his brain has lessened. He has no sense of time but knows from the light that it is daytime, and that when consciousness first came back to him it was night.

Finally, a doctor—or at least someone in dark blue scrubs, different from those of the nurses—draws up a chair by his bed.

The last time Adam Mitchel went to a doctor, the doctor was considerably older than him, which was somehow how it should be. This one seems inordinately young. A baby.

'Good morning, Adam. I'm Doctor Young.'

Adam wants to chortle and make a wisecrack but senses that it would be misjudging the nature of the discourse.

'How are you, Adam?'

'Well, I'm waiting for you to tell me.'

'You were admitted yesterday morning. You'd had a fall. We don't know how long you were there. You were very dehydrated. You were lucky. You were found in time. Any longer and you could have been food for worms.'

'I was found, was I? Who found me?' he asks, hoping that it might be Natalie so that he could officially claim her as his angel.

The doctor consults his notes. 'It was a lady called Miss Holden. Helen Holden? Does that name mean anything to you?'

'She's not here, is she?' asks Adam, warding off a wave of panic.

'No,' says Doctor Young. 'No, she called at your house and found you in a collapsed state. At the foot of the stairs. She thought you'd had a fall.'

'I was drunk. I must have passed out.'

'Well, yes, we know you were drunk, Adam. Quite drunk, in fact.'

'Yes, I was trying to drink myself to death.'

'Do you want me to write that down?'

'No,' says Adam, realising that this may put him in the way of mental health assessment and all that might entail in terms of unwelcome interference. 'Been teetotal for a while. I'd had a bit of a relapse. Over it now. Won't happen again.'

Doctor Young looks at him carefully and thoughtfully, and then continues, 'Well, the good news is there's no physical damage. A few bruises. Nothing broken. Bit of a bang on the head. Concussion, probably.'

'Right.'

'At triage they thought you might have had a stroke.'

'A stroke?'

'No need to worry. All the signs are that you haven't had a stroke.'

'Well, thank Christ for that! So, when can I go home?'

'Well, we've a few tests we still need to run. Give you a full MOT now we've got you here. Get some proper nutrition into you. Probably tomorrow morning. How does that sound?'

Adam wants to protest, wants to fling his arms up in the air, wants to discharge himself, but realises that such gestures, however true to his nature, are not appropriate.

He submits, passively, to another twenty-four hours of the hospital regime. Twice he is wheeled off by a porter into a lift and taken to some room in another part of the hospital for tests with different bits of apparatus. The drip is finally taken off and he is given a proper meal.

The next morning, he awakes to find the catheter has been removed. That augurs well, he surmises, but it seems an age before anyone comes along with his discharge papers.

He watches the door of the ward, monitoring every coming and every going. It runs along its own clockwork, he realises, and if that clockwork—at this particular moment—does not include you, there is nothing you can do about it.

By ten o'clock still nothing has happened, though he has had a proper so-called breakfast, has got out of bed to go to the toilet and has been allowed to dress in his own clothes. His patience is now running thin. He feels ready to hold someone to account and is waiting for the next nurse to come through when, looking towards the entrance, he sees—emerging and looking round as visitors do to identify a particular bed—the figure of Natalie Anderson.

For a moment, he thinks he has relapsed into some delusional state of fantasy but then, identifying his bed, she approaches, takes his hand in hers and with a furrowed brow, asks how he is.

'Well, I'm hoping they're going to let me out at any minute, but just help me out here, Natalie—here?'

'I met Miss Holden, you know, my old teacher, in the town; she said she was there to look at some property she was thinking of buying and she told me how she found you and called the emergency services. She went with you in the ambulance apparently.'

'Right...' says Adam, as if still awaiting an answer.

'Well, I didn't know if there was anyone else who would come to see how you are, so... so I borrowed my mum's car and drove over.'

Adam is about to formulate some reply of unfathomable gratitude when the doctor arrives at his bedside. Not Doctor Young this time but a lesser mortal. Natalie realises that the protocol is for her not to be present and moves away, out of the ward. He watches her go, thinking, *If I could have her visiting company for an hour, I wouldn't mind staying another day*, and then thinking, *Christ, she will never know, if it wasn't for her, I wouldn't be in here in the first place.*

The person now by his side is a healthcare professional from social services.

'My name is Louise. Hi!' she says, raising a salutary hand in a slightly comic fashion.

'Hi,' says Adam, raising—in a mockery which is just for his own benefit—a reciprocal hand.

'So,' she says, with long, rising and fruity emphasis, 'we are all clear from the medical point of view...' She says 'we', Adam reflects, as if she too were suffering from the same ailment as him.

'That's good,' he says, playing the game.

'So...' she says, again elongating the vowel into a provisional interrogative. 'we just need to address, Adam, we just need to address the alcohol issue.'

'Yes,' says Adam, again trying to play ball with acknowledgment and reasonability. 'As I said to Doctor Young, I've been teetotal for a while and, well, something came up and I was bothered and upset, and I slipped off the wagon. It won't happen again.'

She looked at him with the sympathetic look of one who

might say, *I've heard that declaration many times*. He looked at her with the look of one who might say, *Look, you've just deprived me of ten minutes conversation with the one person, the only person, who might actually make me feel better, so why don't you just fuck off and let me go home.*

'I can put you in touch with some agencies that might be able to help you, Adam.'

'Thank you,' he says, judging that abject compliance is now the best way forward.

And I've got some leaflets here for you, with information about alcohol and related issues, and some websites, and telephone numbers and links you can access if you feel you're not coping.'

'Thank you,' says Adam humbly, because he knows no other way of ending this conversation.

Louise stands.

'So can I go home now.'

'I think so. Nurse will be along in a moment. I'm sure she will set you free.'

'Thanks.'

'Can I just ask you before I go, Mr Mitchell, are you Adam Mitchell, the poet.'

'Yes, guilty as charged.'

'I studied you for exams.'

'Let me guess. GCSE, an anthology.'

'No. A-level actually.'

'Oh, things are looking up. Did you like it?'

'Yes, I did. But then our teacher did it to death. Took all the life out of it.'

'That's the way it goes.'

'I've got a copy somewhere. Dig it out now I've met you.'

'We can't take you home in an ambulance,' explains the nurse, 'but we can call you a taxi, if you like.'

'No. Never mind. I'll sort myself out.' He is anxious now, just to get the taste of freedom.

But Natalie is still there, waiting in the corridor just outside the ward. 'I had a feeling you wouldn't be long,' she says. 'I'll give you a lift home, shall I?'

CHAPTER 16

'So he's all right, is he?' asks Nathan as they walk out along Old Hall Lane towards the Westwood Brook.

'I think so,' replies Natalie. 'He seemed all right in the car coming home. Just said he had a fall. Miss Holden said it was drink.'

'And she's the one who found him?'

'Yes, she must have called to see him for some reason. Rekindle an old passion, maybe,' she adds, mischievously.

They cut down onto a narrow pathway that leads quite steeply between two large houses built, with their gardens, into the terrace of the hillside, and emerge below where the path evens out and runs alongside a small reservoir. It is a route they know well.

The reservoir is crossed—at its head—by a path, like a narrow causeway, which separates it from another smaller body of water, fringed by thick vegetation and surrounding trees whose lower boughs and exposed roots dip into it.

'Do you remember when we came swimming here that time?' says Natalie, standing in the middle of the causeway, looking to the main reservoir.

'Yes,' says Nathan. 'It was a really hot day and we didn't have any costumes, so we waded out in our underwear.'

Natalie lets out an explosive giggle. 'I think that might have been my first bra. There was hardly anything to go in it, but I was so proud of it!'

'And then there was a guy shouting at us from the other side and we made a dash for it.'

'How did we get dry?'

'Can't remember. Just evaporated, I guess.'

They cross a stile into a field at the corner of which deep cattle hoof prints have solidified to dry ridges in the sun, and then make their way across the meadow to where the wood begins. Steep steps lead down to the brook and then the path continues on the other side.

'Where shall we have our picnic then?' Natalie has bought two sausage rolls and two vanilla slices from Greggs, and bottle of Prosecco. That is the picnic. 'At the mill?'

'No, let's go further on. The mill's a bit gloomy.'

The 'mill' is an abandoned site by the stream—abandoned, probably, even before the start of the proper industrial revolution—but with remnants of walls and evidence of a sluice that was a mill race, and it has a kind of atmosphere.

'Do you remember,' says Nathan as they pass through it, 'we used to sit here and make up stories about what went on here in the past?'

'I do.'

'Murders and ghost stories.'

'I know! Sometimes, when I went home, I couldn't sleep and then had nightmares.'

They pass on as the path leads into the fullness of the wood with thickness of growth and heavy scents of late summer, honey-like, almost cloying.

At last, where the path turns again making a bridge over the beck, above a spot where the beck itself has made a deep pool below, they stop.

'Here?'

'Why not?'

'Here then.'

They find a place to sit.

'Here,' says Natalie, handing Nathan a sausage roll.

'Cheers.'

'Can you get the cork out of this?' she says, handing him the bottle of Prosecco.

'Hold my sausage roll then.'

'OK.'

Nathan struggles for a moment with the cork, and then it pops, suddenly, with an expulsion of foam.

'Have you got a glass?' he asks.

'No, I didn't' think of that!'

The foam subsides.

'We'll just have to swig it from the bottle then. It's maybe a little warm.'

'Well, I don't mind if you don't.'

Nathan takes a swig from the bottle, wipes the top and then hands it to Natalie. In exchange, she hands him his sausage roll. The picnic proceeds to its conclusion pretty much in this ad hoc pattern.

'So,' says Nathan eventually, 'how did your date with Martin go?'

Natalie gathers a stone from the bank beside her and throws it into the pool below. 'A disaster,' she said at last.

'As bad as that!'

'As bad as that, yes.'

'Oh.'

'We went to Holmfirth, which was all right, but on the way back, he took me to his flat.'

'OK, what, for coffee?'

'Yes, for coffee to begin with but then just to get me into the bedroom.'

'Well...' said Nathan with rising intonation.

'Well, what, creep?' she asked giving him a little knuckle punch on the arm.

'Well, creep, what I mean is, don't tell me you were absolutely totally one hundred per cent surprised. I mean, it's not as if you'd be expecting him to challenge you to a game of snakes and ladders, is it?'

Natalie lets out a snort of laughter.

'So... I mean you can tell me to mind my own business if you like, but did you actually...?'

'No, creep, actually not. I bolted.'

'Good for you, creep.'

'He was in such a dreadful rush.'

'Men usually are. Maybe if he'd taken things more slowly?'

'No, it wasn't that. Well, not just that. Come on, let's walk on a bit.'

They stroll on. The path winds upwards, coming up through the trees and then levelling out, bordered by a line of rowan bushes just beginning to show their berries, beside the emerald green sward of a golf fairway.

'Can I tell you something, Nathan?'

'Go on.'

'Can I trust you?'

'That's for you to judge.'

'OK, then. Here goes. What would you say if I told you that I thought I might be gay?'

'Might be?'

'Sometimes things are confusing. Are you shocked?'

'No, not at all. I mean, I sometimes wondered, you know, when we were at college…'

'If I was gay?'

'Well, possibly. I don't know. I mean we were thick as thieves, weren't we,? But there was never anything like that, never anything, was there?

'No. Did you want there to be?'

'I suppose I did. I used to have a fantasy that we were alone together on a desert island, and you know, well, you can imagine the rest.'

'Oh, creepy one, how sweet!'

'But in the real world there was always an invisible barrier, and I knew that nothing would ever, ever happen. I thought maybe it was just that you didn't fancy me?'

'And I always felt safe with you,' she said reaching out to squeeze his hand.

'Tell me though, why were you dating Martin if, you know, I mean if you, you know, like girls, why go out with Martin?'

'Because that's what people do. That's what is expected of me.

It's what my parents expect. What everyone expects. That I will go out with someone like Martin, and probably end up sleeping with him and marrying him.'

'So when did you first realise?'

'That I was gay. Or might be gay. I don't know. A long time ago. Thing is, you do know, underneath, but your mind does funny tricks with it…'

'Right.'

'I mean, at school, remember Mandy Aitken, I had a real crush on her.'

They both laugh, then Nathan says, 'So did I.' And they laugh again.

'I mean, I used to cuddle my pillow and pretend it was her.'

'So did I.'

'But then I had to put it away in a box because I knew it was odd and people would think me odd. Then when I first went to uni, it was party after party, and boys were all over me but usually they just ended up getting drunk and once, I was talking to a girl and we ended up in a bedroom snogging and I was really turned on.'

'Right!'

'Then someone crashed in on us and switched on the lights and it was all a big laugh.'

'Oh shit!'

'But I was thinking about her for days. And I really thought she must feel the same. But afterwards, when I talked to her, she just shunned me, just said we'd both been drunk, and I backed off completely. Well, it had been my first encounter with vodka. She was probably right. After that, I never really trusted myself.'

They walk back in the late afternoon.

'It's so easy to talk to you, Nathan. I'd forgotten how easy it is to talk to you. I've missed it.'

'Me too.'

They walk on for a time, hand in hand, and it feels natural and nice.

'So, what will you do?' he asks.

'Nothing. Just wait now until my course starts. How about you?'

'God knows,' he says. She squeezes his hand tightly for a moment and then they let go of hands as if they both realise, even after such a lovely day, that the future is probably going to be a mess.

CHAPTER 17

Adam Mitchell was developing an almost morbid preoccupation with Helen Holden. A neutral person might have supposed that he would be glad to see her, to offer a handshake, even a hug, to say thank you, thank you and thank you again; do you realise you quite possibly saved my life and I will be eternally grateful. But if such feelings might seem natural, they were far from the feelings he was actually experiencing. She had come to his house at a fortuitous moment, that was true, but the question was: why had she come at all? And—even more to the point—if she had come once, she might well come again. If she telephoned the hospital to ask how he was, they would no doubt tell her that he had been discharged.

He recalled that on Saturday night, Magda had made a point of coming to see him at the pub to tell him that the 'teacher' had been to see her, threatening some sort of revenge. Was it possible that she had hatched some sort of scheme and that her visit to see him formed part of that. Perhaps she was just mad.

Was she intending to put some emotional pressure on him? Even at the best of times, he was very bad at handling scenes, especially scenes with histrionic women. And what was it she had said to Natalie about looking for property in the town? He could think of nothing worse than having her live somewhere nearby, with the chance every day of seeing her on the streets, at the shops, in the pub. Christ, it didn't bear thinking about.

He made sure all the doors were locked, something he usually didn't bother much about even at night, even when he was out. In the back bedroom upstairs, the one which looked out over the road as it approached from the village, he set a chair so that he could use it as a watch-post. In truth, after his return from hospital, he was soon exhausted so to sit there, hour after hour, was pretty much what he would be doing anyway.

All I need now, he mused, is a shotgun across my knee.

CHAPTER 18

Natalie is now at her third sitting with Magda. It is eight o'clock in the evening and she has been there for an hour and a half. The atmosphere is, as usual, tranquil and concentrated: silence punctuated now and then with snippets of conversation.

She has told Magda about Adam, and Magda tut-tutted as if not at all surprised.

'One more sitting after this,' says Magda, 'and that will probably do.'

'Really?'

'Yes.'

'I think I'll miss it. I've never been so still. It gives me time to think.'

Magda smiles and gives a little laugh.

'How did your date go?' she asks a little later. 'With Martin, I mean,' she adds when Natalie does not reply.

Natalie shrugs her shoulders in a certain way and twists her mouth.

'Not good I take it?'

'There's just nothing there really.'

'For you or for him?'

Natalie thinks about the moment in his bedroom when they had been on the point of having sex. 'Both of us really,' she prevaricates.

Magda gives her a long, ironic look, then continues to paint.

'There,' she says at last, 'Enough for today. Lights fading.'

'Sorry. Maybe I should have come earlier.'

'No. We've done enough.'

She comes forward and lifts the gown from the chair. 'Here,' she says, draping the gown around Natalie's shoulders. Natalie smiles, slightly embarrassed at her closeness.

'Do you know what I've been thinking about for the last twenty minutes?' Magda asks, holding Natalie in eye contact. 'Mmm?' Natalie colours slightly, and Magda suspects she knows what is coming next. 'I've been thinking that I'd like to have sex with you.'

'Yes,' says Natalie, in a non-committal way, as if merely confirming a known fact.

Magda tips her head to one side. 'Meaning?'

'I mean, yes. That would be nice. I'd like to have sex with you too.'

Magda leans forward, lifts Natalie's chin gently on the crook of her finger and kisses her lightly on the lips.

'Let's go upstairs,' she whispers.

Definitely something funny going on there, Rob concludes. It is now half past ten and the girl is still there. The light went out in the studio downstairs at around half past eight and a light went on briefly in the room above. On then off. And off ever since. All is still. The stillness of the night. The stillness of sleep perhaps. It confirms his suspicions.

It is twenty to eleven when Natalie finally lets herself into the house.

'Are you all right, darling?' asks her mother, coming into the hall from the lounge.

'Of course. Why wouldn't I be?'

'It's late. I was worried.'

'I'm twenty-two, mum, not fourteen.'

'Yes. I know. But mums don't ever stop worrying.'

She says this lightly, simply relieved.

'Your dad's in his study as usual,' she says with a dry inflection, as if establishing the normality of the household. 'Been anywhere special?'

'Not really. I called in at Magda's studio. We had a glass of wine.'

'Oh good. How's the painting coming on?'

Natalie has mentioned that Magda is doing a portrait, but not anything else.

'Yes. It's OK.'

'Good. Do you want anything before you go up? Tea or anything?'

'No, I think I'll just go up.'

'OK,' says her mum with slightly overdone insouciance.

In her room, Natalie closes the door and then closes her eyes. Despite getting through the return home so easily, it has still been an ordeal. She is glad her dad is holed up in his study. He has put on a sour face every time she has mentioned visiting the studio.

She goes to the bathroom, then undresses and puts on her nightie, though she does not get into bed but sits in darkness looking out of the window, out to the summer night.

She waits until the sound of the television goes off, then until she hears her mum coming upstairs to bed, and then, at last, only when all the noises of the house have stopped, does she allow herself to open the Pandora's box which, like a swarm of butterflies, releases all her thoughts.

A tumult of images. Images which until now had been just that: shadowy imaginings, sometimes tinged with guilt and confusion, with denial, lightly dismissed. Now realised.

'I've known this all along,' she says to herself. 'I've wanted this all along.'

Had she ever truly imagined herself doing such things with another woman? She pictures Magda in the semi-darkness. Leaning over to kiss her, her breasts pressing against her own, and Magda's hand feeling its way between her thighs, and then her own hand doing the same, touching and being touched, loving and being loved.

It was a revelation.

'I can hardly believe this', she says, joyously.

She hears the door of her dad's study closing and then his feet on the stairs. It brings home a different reality.

'My God', she says to herself, 'I'm going to have to tell them. If I want to live my life, I'm going to have to tell them. And he's going to go through the rafters!'

CHAPTER 19

The final meeting of the organising committee for the Milthwaite Food and Drink Festival is taking place. No-one who has not, at some time, served on this committee can truly appreciate the gargantuan effort that goes into the making of the festival. Initial meetings that begin even before Christmas, delegation of roles and responsibilities, analysis of last year's festival, monthly meetings to give updates with regard to suppliers, equipment, marquees, PA systems and so on.

This final meeting, with the festival just a week away, is to liaise with the police and other emergency and first aid services and to brief those locals who have volunteered their services as stewards. At the front of the room is a large-scale map of the site, which is a field next to the local cricket club and adjacent to the canal, with the various stalls and attractions marked so that everyone can familiarise themselves with the layout.

There is a quick round-the-room for any last-minute updates. *The Frame,* a popular local band due to play between 6 and 7 p.m., have had to withdraw due to illness, announces Sue Bryans whose brief this is, but she has managed to secure *The Real Deal* to replace them. The good news is that Tom Sykes, a local solo performer, but one who has gained some national fame, has confirmed his availability.

Everything else seems tickety-boo, running like clockwork.

'Oh, but lest I forget,' says Emily Linton, the Chair of the Committee, 'it is, of course, the debut of the gin bar this year — and what a good idea of mine that was—so we welcome Barbara Anderson and Cyril North from the Players; the Players, of course, having nobly volunteered to head up this venture.'

'And at the same time,' says Cyril, 'to use it as a platform to boost our recruitment.'

This, which is deemed well-judged, causes a ripple of mirth.

'Indeed,' says Emily, 'and with my taste for gin, you may well have me signed up by the end of the day. Walk-on role only.'

Another roll of mirth.

Barbara, joining in with the laughter, had not, in fact, been expecting to be at the meeting at all. She had received a call from Eleanor Vance, i/c gin, at four o'clock. 'Look Barbara, something's come up. I won't bore you with the detail but you would be doing me a massive favour if there's any way you could possibly make itto the meeting in my place.'

Barbara, with a sinking feeling at the thought of an unscheduled meeting of any sort, is rapidly casting about for a plausible excuse when Eleanor adds, 'Cyril will be there, of course, and he's pretty well genned up, but you know, a bit of moral support wouldn't go amiss…'

'Yes, of course, Eleanor,' says Barbara, acknowledging guiltily that the sinking feeling has immediately reversed direction. 'What time does it start?'

The room listens attentively as Cyril runs through the arrangements and lists the extensive range of gins that will be available.

'Do we need to know all of them?' asks someone, not unpleasantly but evidently with a mind to the clock.

'Yes, we absolutely DO!' says Emily, again to appreciative mirth.

'Only a couple more,' says Cyril. 'and that's it.'

He sits down.

'Maybe I shouldn't have gone through the whole list,' he whispers, leaning his head towards Barbara so that for a moment his hair touches hers.

'Of course you should,' she replies, squeezing his wrist and then drawing his hand onto her lap.

It is now the turn of the police. It is a pretty low-profile event police-wise, their representative explains. There has occasionally been some rowdiness later on but no history of significant disturbance. There will be a car stationed near the entrance and a couple of Community Support Officers will be on patrol throughout the afternoon.

A question is asked about car parking, and this is picked up by Emily. All is in order.

There will be three first aid posts, it is revealed, staffed by the St John's Ambulance, equipped with defibrillation gear, and an actual ambulance to be descrambled to be on call, providing there is no major RTA situation to be addressed.

The meeting continues with its dry detail. Meanwhile, Cyril has globed his hand around Barbara's and is stroking her fingers.

'Shall we walk across, take a look,' he says to her as they come out of the meeting.

'Yes, let's. Best know what we're on about.'

It is only a few minutes' walk and perhaps recklessly, as if reliving Whitby, they walk there hand in hand.

'It's just been mowed,' says Cyril as they enter the field.

'I know, I can smell it. Isn't it lovely?'

'So, according to the plan, our dear old gin station will be about here.'

'Yes.'

'Can't say I'm looking forward to it much, are you? I suppose it's all for the cause.'

They cross to where steps lead to the canal towpath and there, with the camouflage of the surrounding trees, in the gathering twilight, they embrace.

In the bedroom of Cyril's house later, she says, 'That's the first time I've made love since we were together in Whitby.'

'The first time you've had sex?'

'I didn't say that. Sometimes, not very often, but sometimes, I've been used for sex. Do you understand what I'm saying?'

'Yes.'

'How about you?'

'Not at all,' he says, 'except alone, and thinking of you.'

'Yes,' she says, snuggling up to him, 'I know. Me too.'

The minutes pass by. She knows that soon she must leave.

'We made the wrong decision after Whitby,' she says at last. 'I know that now. Maybe I've known all along.'

'There didn't seem to be any other choice at the time.'

'My mind was all over the place. Things were already bad at home. I thought if I deprived myself, punished myself, it might make things better. But it didn't. His indifference remained utterly intact.'

'So…' he says, and then after a long pause, 'what are we going to do about it?'

'God, I don't know. I'll have to tell him. This time, I want to tell him.'

'If he really is indifferent, maybe he'll accept it.'

She shrugs her shoulders. 'He's very controlling. He belittles me whenever I say anything. I've always been frightened of him. But I feel that if I don't do something now, my life will just slip away. The thing is, I thought myself the lynchpin holding the family together, but I'm not. My daughter, who for some reason lately seems inordinately happy, never talks to me about anything essential, my son is in London and can't prise himself away, and my husband simply wants a settled base so he can go off on his philandering.'

'Maybe we should tell him together,' suggests Cyril.

'God no!' Barbara responds.

'It's just that after Whitby, I felt it was a lack of moral courage on my part. I let go too easily.'

'It was my decision,' says Barbara. 'If I'd asked you to, I know you would have stood by me.' She takes a long breath, squeezing his hand. 'No, I have to face up to him. I'll wait until Natalie goes to college, and I'll do it then. Alone. To begin with, at least. There will no doubt be lots of sparks flying, and it's then you'll have to be there for me.'

'It's a deal,' he says quietly.

CHAPTER 20

Rob Jenkins is trying to organise the files on his computer. There are one or two sequences from his security CCTV camera which he wants to download, but it's tedious work wading through hours of the footage to find what's worth keeping, and if you don't keep on top of it, every few days or so, it gets out of hand. Sometimes, it's tempting just to wipe the SD cards and start afresh. The webcam makes the problem even worse. It gives better quality images than the CCTV camera but leaving it on as he has for the last few nights, trained on the upstairs window of Magda Bentley's studio, has left him—when he returns — with hour upon hour of darkness to trawl through and he is beginning to reach the conclusion that it is a pointless task.

The telephone rings. It is a customer to whom he sold some stair carpet a week ago and who, politely but not without betraying some impatience, is asking when the fitter is going to turn up to lay it. Rob explains that he doesn't keep the fitter's diary for him but says that he will chase him up. He tries the fitter's mobile. It goes to voicemail. He makes a note to try again later or maybe tomorrow.

'What I really need,' he says to himself, giving himself a rest from the webcam footage, 'is to get those bugs in place.' He has already tried them out within the premises and they work a treat, but that's only half the battle. He knows from what he has seen of the inside of the studio that the general level of disorder is such that concealment will not be a problem, but it's the matter of getting in there that presents the challenge.

'I need a key,' he says to himself, 'it's as simple as that. I need a key.'

He returns to the task, trawling through the acres of blank darkness, and feels his eyes growing heavy. He decides to fast-forward at the fastest speed possible. Again, his eyes start to grow heavy but then, and gone as quickly as it appeared, a smattering of light flickers across the screen.

What was that?

He begins to run it back slowly. There is nothing. How far on had he run? Or perhaps it was just a trick played on him by his eyes; maybe he had fallen asleep for a second and imagined it.

He quickens up the reverse speed and is about to give up when the patch of lights flickers across the screen again, now in reverse.

He is about to run forward at normal speed when, to his great annoyance, the phone rings again.

It is the carpet fitter. 'Did you ring me, mate?'

Rob explains the situation.

'Yeah, I'm on my way there now. No problem.'

'Cheers, Phil.'

'So how's it going, pal? Must meet up for a pint some time, when you're free. How's the old girl, your mum, I mean?'

Phil keeps him on the phone until he reaches the premises where the work is to be done.

'Right, cheers, pal,' says Phil. 'Love you and leave you.'

It is a good ten minutes before Rob can return to the slow forward of his video cam footage but then, there it is.

'Fuck me!' says Rob, aloud.

He plays it through again, and then again, freeze framing. It is only twenty seconds long. A light goes on and twenty seconds later, a curtain closes, restoring darkness. But the twenty seconds between show the artist and the girl getting off with each other.

'Fuck me,' he says again, almost reverentially. 'That's definitely one for the archive. Pure gold, that is,' he mutters, 'Pure TV Gold.'

CHAPTER 21

The heat, some people say, has reached a point where it has become uncomfortable, unbearable at times. It is in the news that in some parts of the country hosepipe bans are in operation, and there have been fires on the moors further to the east: started, it is rumoured, by careless barbecues. In Milthwaite there has been no incidence yet of such drastic matters, but the lawns are all beginning to turn a tawny shade, like straw. What seemed, three weeks ago, like the freshest and most welcome visitation of summer, has become tired, heavy and oppressive.

Nathan and Natalie are walking along another of the routes which had been one of their haunts in their early teenage years. It begins where—unbeknown to Natalie—Barbara and Cyril had walked the previous evening, crossing the field where the festival is to take place, towards the canal.

'They're starting to put up the tents,' observes Natalie. 'You going?'

'Might do. Given it a miss for a couple of years but I'll probably have a walk round. How about you?'

'Yeah, probably,' says Natalie, recalling that at her most recent visits to the studio, also last night, Magda had said that she would be doing a face painting booth at the festival. 'Mum's lot are doing a gin bar.'

They turn onto the canal towpath, walk along for a hundred yards and then cross a bridge where the towpath crosses to the other side.

'Do you remember when we used to dare each other to walk across the lock gate?' asks Nathan, peering down into the dark water several feet below where rubbish has been swirled round into a pocket by the sluice.

'We did it too. We must have been crazy.'

'Yes, I think we probably were.'

They turn away from the canal and follow a path leading up the hillside between ever denser woodland and undergrowth.

'Too many pesky flies,' says Natalie.

'Midges,' says Nathan. 'They're midges.'

'Too many pesky creepy midges. Shall we turn back in a bit and find somewhere to have a pint?'

'Yes, if you like,' replies Nathan.

'I could just do with a pint.'

'I don't know what it is, creep,' says Nathan, 'but you seem very happy today.'

'How do you mean, creep?'

'Oh, I don't know, just something about you. You're bubbly.'

'Bubbly?'

'Ebullient.'

'Never heard of it. Have you been at the thesaurus again.'

'Ebullient. Yes, as if something really good's happened.'

'Oh yeah, forgot to tell you, I won the Euro Lottery, 80 million, so the first round is on me.'

Nathan laughs and they walk on.

'Actually,' says Natalie, 'let's sit down for a minute, and I'll tell you my big ebullient secret.'

'Ooh, that sounds tasty.'

They find a fallen tree trunk to sit on and Natalie begins. 'Well, you know I told you I'd been going to Magda Bentley's studio, sitting for her, you know, for a painting. Well, I was there the other night and then, completely out of the blue, something happened.'

'How do you mean, something happened? What sort of thing?'

'Oh, Nathan, use your imagination! Everything happened! Between us.'

She looks at him expecting some kind Nathan-like grin or matey response, but he has a sudden strained look in his eyes.

'Why are you telling me this?' he asks.
'Nathan?'
'Why?'
'Because you asked me what it was making me happy.'
'Look,' he says suddenly, 'I'd better be going.'
'But why? We've only just… what about that pint?'
'I need to get back. There are things I need to do.'
'Nathan?'

But Nathan is already standing and is now pacing away down the hill.

'Nathan!' she calls after him, beginning to follow. 'Nathan, stop! What the hell is up with you?'

They have reached the bridge by the time she finally catches up with him. She grabs hold of his sleeve and pulls him round to face her.

'Tell me what's up.'
'Nothing. I told you, I remembered stuff I've got to do.'
'No, you haven't. You've got something in your head.'

He shrugs his shoulders and looks away. 'I just don't understand why you wanted to tell me that stuff.'

'I told you because I'd already told you a secret I've never told anyone else. And because I trust you.'

She can tell from the look in his eyes that the steeliness of his resolve is melting.

'Come on,' she says, linking his arm, 'I'm taking you for a pint. Don't forget I've just won 80 million on the lottery.'

'You probably don't want to hear this,' says Nathan.
'Well, shoot away.'

They are sitting in the side room of The Feathers, a side-street pub, just outside the main town, each with a pint on the table.

'Come on then,' she says.

It takes him quite a while to get started.

'Well, you remember I told you, you know, when we first met up, that I'd got involved with an older woman?'
'Yes.'

He draws in a deep breath. 'What I didn't tell you was that the woman in question was Magda Bentley.'

'You're kidding me!'

Nathan's silence tells her that he is not kidding her.

'You had an affair with Magda?'

'Hardly an affair. It was nothing, really.'

'Well, obviously, it wasn't nothing. It must have been something.'

'It just happened. I went to one of her things at the Gallery. You know, trying to sort myself out. And she said I should come over to her studio, and I did. She said would I like to try drawing her, you know, naked. I said OK, trying to be cool about it and then afterwards, she was really coming on to me.'

'And you went up to her bedroom?'

'No. Not that time. But afterwards, I wished I had done and I couldn't get her out of my mind. So, in the end, I went back and she knew exactly why, and she teased me about it and it was then, yes, she took me upstairs.'

'Oh Nathan, you creep. Both of us. Oh shit.'

'I'm sorry. But look, I think you should finish it, whatever it is. I really think you should just get yourself out of it.'

Natalie sits back, taking herself out of the conversation for a few moments. She is trying to process all this.

'So,' she says eventually, 'obviously she is bi-sexual. But that in itself is not… is it?'

'Not what?'

'You know, not necessarily… ' she stops again, not knowing what her 'not necessarily' means.

People going into new relationships have often had relationships before. She is struggling to believe that any relationship Magda might have previously had, even with Nathan, should negate the passion and tenderness she and Magda have shared not once, but three times since that fateful evening.

She decides that it is not Magda's but Nathan's problem.

'Is that the reason you've been in a mess?'

Nathan chortles. 'No. Was in a mess before and after.'

'OK. Well thanks for telling me.'

'I'm sorry if it's upset you.'

Natalie shrugs. 'It's not the end of the world,' she says, though she says it as if it is.

'There is something else I ought to tell you.'

'What?'

'This is even worse.'

Natalie looks up, blank-faced. What could be worse?

'I did go back. A few times. It was like a drug. I'd call her and she'd say, "Let's do a video call," and we did. Don't ask me to go into detail, I would go back, and she would tease me and mock me and then let me have sex, well sometimes.'

'And?'

'And then, one time, I went there, and there was someone else.'

'Someone else?'

'I went into the studio. She wasn't there, in the studio, but it didn't take me long to realise that she was upstairs, having it off with someone else.'

Natalie gave a kind of silent, troubled consent to continue.

'I went outside. I had a compulsion to see who came out.'

'And?'

'It was your dad. I'm really sorry, Natalie, but I think your dad has had something going on with Magda. I'm sorry,' he repeats as he sees the tears welling in her eyes and then spilling heavily onto her cheeks.

CHAPTER 22

It seems that the worst fears of the organising committee of the Food and Drink Festival are about to be realised. Two days before the big day, the weather has turned and for the first time in over a month, the heavens have opened. Rain now cascades from the partially erected tents and awnings and workers scurry for shelter in the intensifying downpour. This, it is anticipated, is likely to cause considerable anxiety amongst the traders, by now stocked up and ready to go; it is one of the biggest days in the calendar. When, four years ago, it was cancelled because the field was under water, it spelled disaster. That couldn't happen again, people say the circumstances were unique with a July of incessant rain and the river breaking its banks just above the town causing localised flooding, but there is, nevertheless, some nervousness.

'Good for the garden anyway,' says Emily Linton stoically, visiting the site.

'The ground's dry,' says Ted Hull who is accompanying her and who happens also to be the groundsman of the cricket club, 'It can absorb a lot before it turns into a quagmire.'

'It's just a question of what it's like on Sunday,' says Emily . 'If it rains, people will stay away. Simple as that.'

Two miles away, along the canal and up the lane, Adam Mitchell is preparing to go out for the first time since he returned home from hospital. He is actually now feeling much better for several days of rest and abstinence, and the change of weather has had the effect of invigorating his mood. Besides this, he is simply sick of being stuck in the house. He is now ready to don his full-length raincoat and tweed hat and set off down to the village for a lunchtime pint.

He pulls the door shut and, not forgetting his new resolution to keep the door locked at all times, he splashes through the puddles already forming on the path and steps onto the lane.

He has gone no more than thirty yards when he sees a figure moving towards him, perhaps fifty yards distant. Despite the rainwear she has on, he immediately recognises the form of Helen Holden. In the same instant, he realises that she has seen him too and he quickly turns to retrace his steps. This, he acknowledges as he fumbles in his pocket for the key, is probably a mistake. He should have walked boldly on and outfaced her; turning on his heels like that will obviously have revealed his vulnerability.

He closes the door behind him but does not lock it. He just waits. Maybe she will take the hint and turn back. He listens and less than a minutes later, sure enough, he hears the sound of footsteps on the path. Then comes a knock on the door.

He does not move.

Another knock.

'Adam, I know you are in there. Are you going to open the door?'

'I don't want to see you, Helen. You know that. You should stay away.'

'If I'd stayed away, who would have called the ambulance for you last week?' she asks.

'You should have left me where I was. You were trespassing.'

'Don't be ridiculous, Adam!'

'All right, I'm grateful for you calling the ambulance but I still don't want to see you.'

'So you're going to leave me standing out here in the rain, are you?'

Finally, he opens the door but stands there barring her way in.

'Why are you so afraid of me, Adam?' she asks, curious.

He tries a derisory huff but it sounds weak, and he realises that the encounter is not going well. Everything he has said and done has contributed to handing over the moral advantage to her.

She looks at him steadily, holding his gaze, and then simply pushes past him into the house. He does not attempt to stop her; any physical action to that effect, he realises, would only make things worse.

'Where can I hang these?' she says, taking off her raincoat and hood. He takes them from her and hangs them on the stair newel post.

'That's just where you were when I found you. And a right mess you were in too.' She smiles. 'I'll put the kettle on, shall I?' she says pertly. 'I think I can remember where everything is.'

Adam takes a deep breath, sighs it out with slow impatience and then takes off his own coat and hat. Where, he thinks, is he going to find the bottom line of his patience before he kicks her out? After all, it had been done once before.

In the kitchen, she is filling the kettle and going about the business of making a pot of tea as if she is in her own home.

'It's all so familiar,' she says. 'Feels as if it could have been yesterday.'

There is a cheeriness about her which is quite unsettling, an affected chatty manner that does not ring true.

'Why are you here?' he asks.

'One sugar is it, Adam, or are you reformed?'

'I don't want any tea,' he says pointedly, and again realises that he merely sounds petulant. 'What do you want?'

'I don't really want anything, Adam. Just to renew acquaintance. I'm buying a property here. Just a little terrace but I've missed the place. I'd like to catch up with all my old friends.'

'The last time we met you hardly counted me as a friend, I seem to recall.'

'No, that's true. I was angry and distraught and I don't need to remind you why. I was very ill after that. You probably didn't know that and probably cared even less. But it's true. Between the two of you, you and Magda nearly ruined my life.'

'I have no idea where this is going, Helen, so if you wouldn't mind finishing your cup of tea and leaving, I'd be much obliged.'

'Are you sure I can't pour you one?'

'Yes.'

'All right. I'll explain. Some time ago, I met an old pupil of mine, from when I taught here. She mentioned you. I'm afraid I wasn't very pleasant to her because that time and what followed was so painful in my memory. But afterwards, I thought about it all very carefully and I thought to myself, why did I let myself become the victim in all this? Why am I the one who is on tablets? Why am I the one who is always on the verge of becoming a nervous wreck.'

'So where is this going?'

'Well, she inspired me. With her bright and breezy youthfulness and self-belief, though I can't even remember her name, she was just like I was then.'

'Natalie. She's called Natalie.'

'Yes, of course. I remember now, Natalie Anderson.'

Adam waits for what else she has in store for him.

'Anyway, thank you for the tea. Gosh, I've let you off lightly, haven't I? It might not be so light when I come to be your gossipy neighbour.'

'If you slander me, I'll take you to court.'

She laughs and they both realise this is a meaningless threat.

'Oh, it won't be as bad as that. Local gossip is so much more powerful than that. Besides, it will be nice to see you around in the village. In the pub, maybe. And I'll be sure to visit you, Adam. After all, we need to be careful of you having another nasty fall, mustn't we?'

She swills her cup, puts it upside down on the drainer and then retrieves her raincoat.

'I'll see you around then, Adam,' she says, letting herself out, 'Bye!'

'Damn you!' says Adam in a sharp hiss of breath.

Natalie has spent the greater part of the last two days in the confines of her room.

'I'm worried about her,' says Barbara.

'I'm sure there's no need for that,' says Ralph. 'Maybe she has work to do.'

'That's what she says but it doesn't feel right somehow.'

Ralph draws in breath silently. 'Have you tried having a word with her?' he suggests.

'Tried, yes. Maybe you could have a go.'

'I don't think she's going to say anything to me, is she?' he says with some impatience.

Barbara senses Ralph's characteristic reluctance to get involved in anything that relates to family intimacy and, as she has done for the last three days, she tries to imagine how it will be with him when she tells him about Cyril. Whatever her resolve, such a conversation seems impossible when she is actually in his presence.

'I'm not sure it's such a good idea for her to be seeing so much of Magda, really,' says Barbara. 'She's been there nearly every day over the last week. I mean, I know she's sitting for a portrait but I don't know, Magda is such a free spirit.'

Ralph does not reply to this. As a matter of fact, he too would prefer it if Natalie were to see less of Magda, if she were not to see her at all even, but he has his own reasons for this. That he has refrained from visiting Magda for the last two weeks is largely down to the fact that Natalie has made a chum out of her. He does not worry that Magda might spill the beans but it does rather stymie his own freedoms. He doesn't like it but for the time being there is nothing he can do about it. It will be much better when Natalie goes off to college again and finds a place to live at a safe distance.

'Do you want me to pop over to see Magda,' he says, the idea coming to him suddenly, 'have a word?'

'No, best not. Don't want Natalie to get the impression we're going behind her back.'

'No,' says Ralph, concealing his disappointment.

'There's Nathan too,' says Barbara after a few moments, 'she's been seeing quite a bit of him recently. I mean Nathan always used to be the nicest lad you could hope to meet, but according to his mum he's become quite cynical and apathetic since school.'

'What about this boyfriend she's been out with, the political chappie?'

'Seems to have died a death, more's the pity.'

'Maybe that's it,' suggests Ralph, now tired of the conversation and getting up from his chair, 'I'm sure she'll be right as rain when she gets up to college. Probably bored of being stuck around here.'

'I was thinking I might offer to take her on holiday for a few days. Just the two of us. Whitby or somewhere.'

'Now that sounds like an excellent idea,' says Ralph. 'I'm sure that'll be just the thing to lift her spirits.'

And then he is gone.

In her room, staring alternately at the wall and out of the window, Natalie simply does not know where to go with the knowledge she has gained. Today the rain has kicked in and so the prospect from the window has changed; that, at least, is something.

She wishes it would all just go away.

She knows her mum is fretting over her but she absolutely does not know what she can do about it. No mother and daughter heart-to-heart could ever have been invented that was more impossible. She tries to sound OK when she replies to her mum's questions, usually from the bottom of the stairs to the top or from outside the door to her room, but it is an act which is difficult to sustain.

There are books she has to read before the term starts and she tries to distract herself with them, but she can concentrate for no more than a few minutes before the painful conundrum returns. But nevertheless, she uses the books as an excuse.

'Are you ready for some tea, darling?'

'I'm just in the middle of it right now, I'll get something later.'

The dilemma has complicated itself like a wagon wheel in mud getting into deeper and deeper ruts with each attempt to move.

If not an open secret in the family, it is a shared supposition that Ralph has had clandestine encounters, probably with women at the university. It was her brother, two years older, who first told her this when she was fourteen. Deeply shocked, she had supposed that this was motivated by his antipathy towards his father, and she had simply gone into denial about it. By the time she realised that it was probably true, the shock had gone away. It just seemed to mirror the world that she was getting to know.

So, part of the conundrum was this: if her dad had relationships with other women, what was different about him having a relationship with Magda?

Probably nothing, was the answer.

Probably nothing apart from the fact that Magda had helped her to discover who she was and she had—foolishly, no doubt—trusted Magda and for a short time had been incredibly grateful to her, had even imagined herself in love with her.

She knew that at some point she was going to have to have some confrontations; she also knew that she was going to have to address the business of revealing her own sexuality to her parents and everyone. But at the moment, sitting in her room and watching the now lessening rain outside, she did not know where she was going to find the strength to do it.

After his attempt to get to the pub for a quiet lunchtime pint was aborted by the inopportune visit of Helen Holden, Adam Mitchell had kept himself more or less under house arrest until last night, Saturday. Then, despite the continuing intermittent downpours, he ventured out once again towards the White Hart, not disguising from himself that the prospect of seeing Natalie behind the bar once more was an additional incentive to the desire to quaff some beer.

Natalie, however, was not on her usual shift and, making a discreet enquiry, he found that she had phoned in sick. Moggy Morton approached with a Job's comforter-like commiseration on his stay in hospital which has somehow seeped into the flow of the local gossip.

'It catches up with you in the end, you see, doesn't it? That's how I see it anyway. Catches up with you in the end.'

'Well, thank you for that, Moggy, but as you can see, not quite the end yet.'

He raised his glass and Moggy gave him a special sorrowful look, patting him on the arm and nodding thoughtfully before going off to the corner of the bar where his regular drinking pals were standing.

There was much speculation to be overheard at the tables around him of the prospects of the festival being called off tomorrow, allowing people to give vent to acrimonious judgements about the deplorable unreliability of the weather forecasters and to bring forth well-rehearsed anecdotes about the floods that took place a few years back.

Adam began his second pint and, feeling the better for it, wondered why he has allowed Helen Holden to get so under his skin. Hell hath no fury like a woman scorned, as the saying goes. Except, of course, that she had not seemed to be particularly furious. Back then, when they—he and Magda—had contrived to shatter her little dream-world, she had been hysterical rather than furious. But now it's more a kind of sour vindictiveness coated with sarcasm.

Was she a threat?

Probably not. Without flattering himself, it might well have been a bit of a turn-on, as far as she was concerned, to be back in his cottage where it had all happened after so many years. As to whether she actually intended to move to Milthwaite, and buzz about like a fly round his ears, remained to be seen.

There is always the possibility, he concluded, that she is just a little bit mad.

He decided, virtuously, against a third pint but counterbalanced this as he walked home with the decision that so long as it is not cancelled, he would put in an appearance at the festival the next day. Who knew, if Natalie had recovered from whatever her indisposition was, he might catch a glimpse of her there.

When he awakes the next morning after what seems a good night's sleep, he is cheered by the sunshine at the window and sets about making himself a proper breakfast.

CHAPTER 23

'My prayers have been answered,' says Emily Linton. The ambiguous weather forecasts of the last two days have yielded, in the event, not an entirely cloudless sky but one sufficiently clear to cheer anyone who has an interest in the Milthwaite Food and Drink Festival.

She checks the weather on her phone again. It is now 7 a.m.: cloud with a corner of sunshine until 11 a.m., 30 per cent chance of rain; 11 a.m. until 5 p.m., clear sunshine. 'That'll do,' says Emily, jumping out of bed. Five minutes later she is back with coffee. 'Come on, Arthur,' she says, rousing her husband by the shoulder, 'time to get the show on the road.'

'What's it like?' he asks, sitting up and rubbing his eyes.

'Perfect!'

An hour later, they are at the site and Emily has the feeling of calm excitement that goes with knowing that everything is going to plan. Instead of a morning of making telephone calls to ensure contingency arrangements are good to go and flying by the seat of her pants, all is going as smoothly as clockwork.

The tents and booths are all in place, or in process, tables and chairs are being set out, the pen for the local livestock exhibition—always a feature—is being constructed. The merry-go-rounds and other attractions for children are pretty much ready. Dotted here and there, traders' vans are offloading their produce and the food stalls, the beer tent and the gin bar are all displaying reassuring signs of approaching readiness for the opening. The ever-reliable Mr Chippy looks to be set for business, the noodle bar—which, like the gin tent, is a new venture—is on site, and in addition the coffee and crepe stall, the smoked meats, the Greek souvlaki wraps and, last but not least, Barry's Burger Bar are all merrily setting up.

Some people, she knows, have been here since dawn; and walking around, visiting each in turn to convey the gratitude of the committee, she is met with affable banter. She senses that everyone is relieved.

Barbara Anderson is due to do two stints on the Players' gin bar, 12 until 1 p.m., and then 2 p.m. until 3.

'Why don't you pop down with me?' she calls to Natalie breezily' 'It'll make a nice change for you.'

'Yes, I might drop by later,' Natalie replies.

Earlier, when Ralph was out on an errand collecting some bottles of wine he'd ordered, Natalie actually came down for some breakfast, which was a hopeful sign.

'I wondered about going off for a couple days, just you and me. We could go to Staithes or Runswick Bay if you like.'

'I was thinking actually I might go over to Huddersfield,' says Natalie, without replying directly to Barbara's proposal. 'See if I can get into my flat early, maybe meet a few people from the course. Use the library, too.'

'Well, that sounds like a good idea,' Barbara replies, glad to hear anything that sounds positive.

Natalie goes back to her room. She has decided she simply does not have the courage to face any of the confrontations she has imagined taking place since Nathan's revelations. It's all just too unthinkable. The best thing to do, she has concluded, is to get away as soon as possible, to distance herself—much as her brother has done—from everything to do with home. Of course, Huddersfield is not as far as London, and she has toyed with the idea of getting in touch with the Education Faculty at Nottingham to see if there is any possibility of getting on the teacher training course there; she wishes now that she had done that in the first place as there are still people there she could go and stay with. It was just that, after three years she fancied a change, which as things stand now seems pretty meaningless.

'Right,' calls Barbara, 'I'm off. See you down there later?'

'OK. Is dad back?'

'No. He'll probably call in at the pub and go straight there. Why? Did you want a lift?'

'No. I'll get changed and then walk down.'

'OK.'

When Barbara has gone, she texts Nathan. There are numerous *Are you ok?* texts from him which she hasn't answered but now she quickly taps in a message. *Going to cut and run. Can't stand it any longer. See you at the fest?*

She waits a couple of minutes, looking at the phone and then it buzzes. *OK. Later.*

Rob is at his usual window, well placed to keep an eye on goings-on outside, when he sees Magda Bentley coming out of her studio. She has two folding chairs and other artist's paraphernalia which she is attempting with some awkwardness to carry. In an instant, Rob is outside.

'Going to the festival?' he calls.

'Yes,' she replies.

'Give you a lift if you like… '

'Well… '

'Unless you prefer to struggle.'

She smiles. 'Thanks. Very kind of you. Yes, please.'

'Just put your stuff in the back,' he says.

'I'm doing face painting,' she says.

'Nice.'

'Well, it gets a bit tedious but it's a nice little earner, as they say.'

'Not to be sniffed at.'

'Are you going?'

'To the festival? I don't know.'

'You should. It'll be fun.'

'Have my face painted?'

'If you like. I'll do it for free in return for the lift.'

Rob laughs but for a moment, surprised by her pleasantness, he wonders if this might be a little bit of a breakthrough moment.

'I'll have to see,' he says. 'I have my old mum to see to. Can't always tell how she's going to be. Sometimes, you know, I have to sit with her if she's had a bad turn or anything.'

'Right,' says Magda.

'If I can make it, though, I'll give you a lift back with your gear later.'

'Thanks a lot,' says Magda as she gets out of the car and retrieves her equipment. 'Maybe see you later, then, bye,' he calls, noting that she did not give a clear yes to the offer of a lift back. But then, he reassures himself, she wouldn't, would she? That would be too much of a giveaway.

He smiles to himself. Maybe this is my lucky day, he thinks.

CHAPTER 24

For Ralph Anderson, the annual festival is another of those annoying social occasions when he feels obliged to make an appearance, maintaining his profile as a figure in the community, however little he actually values it. He has, as Barbara suggested to Natalie, called in at the Vine on his way back from the wine merchants and has sent and received some messages to colleagues in the department ahead of the start of term, including one from Rosalind Helsby, who he once tutored and who is now an interesting new addition to the teaching staff.

At least, he reflects gratefully—returning to the theme of the festival—he has no official function to carry out, just walk around with a few well-placed hellos and a bit of conversation here and there. Of course, Magda will be there and if the situation lends itself, he might have a quiet word or two with her, maybe even persuade her to a rendezvous if it can be guaranteed that Natalie can be, as it were, disposed of for a while.

By one o'clock the festival is in full swing. It's a good turnout. A very good turnout indeed. There are healthy queues at all the food stalls and the beer tent is doing good business. Donkey rides are going on around the perimeter of the livestock area and the local 'Rock Choir' have, after initial problems with the microphones and PA, provided lovely vocal entertainment.

It is at this point that Nathan enters. He is not at ease in big crowds at the best of times—always likely to set him off on a panic attack—but he needs to see Natalie. He has been feeling guilty ever since their meeting at the Feathers. He thinks maybe he should have kept his mouth shut, should have let her find out some other way, but then again, is that what a friend does? He still has the image of her: first her tears and then just standing up, as if suddenly realising the full extent of it, as if she had seen a ghost, and walking out. Tears can be wiped away and forgotten; that look can't.

But how will he find her amongst these roving crowds? He tries calling but her phone is switched off. There is nothing for it but to walk around until he catches sight of her.

As he passes the gin bar, he sees Mrs Anderson—Natalie's mum—but he really doesn't want to speak to her. He turns, hoping to slip by unnoticed, and moves off in a different direction.

At this particular moment, Barbara is serving Martin Haslam who, as a candidate in the forthcoming council election, feels that it is no bad thing to put in an appearance, show his face around.

'I know nothing about gin.' he is saying, 'What would you recommend?'

'Well,' says Barbara, 'we've got Tanqueray, Sipsmith, Bombay Sapphire, Hendrick's.' She runs down the list, then adds, 'I'm afraid I can't really tell you much apart from the names.

'Bombay Sapphire,' says Martin, 'that sounds interesting.'

'Yes, it's quite popular, actually.'

'I'll try one of those then.'

Barbara is aware that her present customer is the one who took Natalie out three times but she doesn't say anything. I wonder what happened though, she thinks to herself. He seems a nice enough chap, a bit artificial perhaps, as if trying to give off an air of being 'someone', but pleasant enough.

'This is very good,' he says, sipping from his glass. 'I think I may be back for more.'

On the far side, near the livestock enclosure, Ralph is talking to Emily Linton. She is one of perhaps four people he needs to talk to, to make sure his presence has been noted.

'Yes, Ralph,' she says, 'Absolutely delighted!'

'So you should be,' he says, slightly ingratiatingly, making the observation that Emily Linton has a shapely bosom and a kind of middle-aged attractiveness that would make her quite interesting if she were in any way available, though obviously she is not. Still talking to her, he is actually watching Magda at her face painting station and waiting for a gap when he might talk to her.

'Will we make a profit, do you think?' he asks, as though one of the team.

'Oh yes. Probably our best ever if it keeps up like this.'

Their conversation is interrupted by the influx to the enclosure of a dozen sheep and the tannoy crackling up to introduce them. They are a particular breed—introduced from Norway by Albert Hartson, a local farmer, in the 1950s—and now thriving on several farms in the area.

Ralph uses the opportunity to saunter away from Emily Linton. Glancing over to Magda's face painting stall, he sees that she still has quite a sizeable queue. He is going to have to be patient, he realises, if he wants to have a private word with her this afternoon.

'I'm going to be popping out later, mum,' says Rob. 'Just for a bit.'

'Back up to the shop?'

'No mum. Going to the festival. Going to have a bit of fun.'

'Well, you deserve it, son. It's long overdue. You spend too much time working and looking after me. That's the truth.'

'I don't mind it, mum. You know that.'

'Course I do.'

'Only, tonight, there's a certain lady, ma, someone who I think might be the one.'

'That's such a pleasure for me to hear that, son.'

'I know. But don't build your expectations up too high, mum.'

'I won't,' she says. 'But then again,' she adds, 'maybe I will, it's high time.'

'High time all right. High time for me to get you your tea.'

'All right, son. Just let me sit outside a bit longer while the sun's on me.'

'All right, ma, no rush.'

Between three and four o'clock, Cyril and Barbara are to be found, as planned, on the gin bar together.

'Fancy going back for a coffee afterwards, when we're done?'

'Sounds wonderful, but…'

'But…?'

'Better not. Ralph is about. Oh, I know, I know what you're thinking, but I have to pick my own time.'

Natalie is on the lookout for Nathan. She has placed everyone — Magda, her mum, her dad, especially her dad—and is keeping them on her radar.

'Hi Natalie.'

The one person she hasn't pinpointed, she realises, is Martin.

'Hello.'

'How's it going?'

'OK.'

'Tried any gin yet?'

'Not yet.'

'I'm not usually a gin person,' he says, holding up his glass. 'But I think I could get a taste for this.'

'Yeah, maybe I'll try some.'

'You didn't reply to my texts,' he says before she can turn to go.

'No,' she said.

He cocks his head to one side as if he thinks she owes him an answer.

She shrugs her shoulders. 'Sorry. I just didn't have anything to say.'

He nods his head a few times, turning this over. 'I mean to say,' he carries on, 'I mean, I tried to apologise, in the text. You did read it, didn't you.'

'Of course I did.'

'And I mean, to be fair, Natalie, it wasn't all one-way traffic, was it? I mean, I genuinely thought you were giving me all the right signals.'

'I didn't really give you any signals at all, Martin.'

'Well, let's just think about it. You came out on a date with me, you came back for coffee, you brought up the matter of kissing, you let me undress you, without a peep, right up to the point where I genuinely thought you wanted to have sex with me.'

'Those weren't signals, Martin, they were just things you did to me.'

'So you're saying I was forcing myself on you?'

'No, but I'm saying you made a lot of assumptions. I should have said something earlier but I felt confused and that made me passive. It's pathetic, I know. But now that I've thought about it, I don't want to go on another date with you.'

'Well, so much is obvious,' he says, turning away with a sneer. 'So much is perfectly bloody obvious.'

Mentally, she raises one finger to his back. She has enough on her plate. She hasn't got time to worry about him.

Continuing her search for Nathan, she passes the beer tent where, much to her surprise, she sees Adam Mitchell sitting with her old English teacher, Miss Holden. She is on the point of going over to say hello when she notices that something of an altercation seems to be going on between them: nothing loud or dramatic, but the body language and facial expressions are of irritation and impatience. Best to move on, she thinks.

She finds Nathan at last, by the stage listening to a solo guitar singer playing up-tempo folk songs.

'There you are,' she says.

'I tried to call you but your phone was dead.'

'Yes, sorry. I switched it off in case my mum or dad called. Anyway, I knew I'd find you eventually if you were here.'

'He's quite good,' said Nathan, indicating the singer. 'Good guitarist, not bad voice too.'

'Why have you got your hoodie up, Nathan? Are you going incognito?'

'No, the opposite. I reckoned that if you were looking for me, this is the best way you'd recognise me.'

Natalie laughs. 'That's exactly true,' she says. 'That is how I knew it was you.'

'Shall we stay here or do you want to wander around for a bit?'

'Music's a bit loud.'

'OK, let's wander.'

'I know where my mum and Magda are. I've had one encounter with Martin and I don't think he'll be keen to see me again. Just keep an eye out for my dad. I really, really don't want to bump into him.'

'OK. I take it you've not said anything then?'

'No. I have absolutely no idea of how to break the news. I mean: 'Oh, dad, how lovely we're both having an affair with the same person.' and then, 'Did you get that, mum? We'd like to know how you feel about this unusual combination of circumstances.'

'Yeah, I see what you mean. So what did you mean about cutting and running?'

She explains her plan. 'I went on this app they gave me and identified a couple of flats. Officially it's not until the start of September but I might be able to get in early.'

'When?' he asks.

'As soon as possible. Tomorrow even.'

'Can you fix it that quickly?'

'Probably not. But I'll think of something. I just don't want to spend another day in that house.'

'What about your mum?'

'She'll be upset. But I know she's not happy. Hasn't been for a long time. I'll explain it all to her at some point, but I need to get away first.'

'You can come over to mine for a couple of days if you like. You know what my mum's like, it's all a bit chaotic but she wouldn't mind you dossing down for a bit while you get stuff sorted out.'

'Yes, thanks. I might just take you up on that.'

At this moment, they are passing by Magda's face painting station, and seeing that Magda has taken a break for a coffee, she suddenly feels emboldened.

'Just hang on a minute, Nathan. Or maybe just disappear for a minute so she doesn't see me with you; I'm going to grab hold of a nettle.'

'OK. Best of luck! I'll be back at the stage.'

Magda greets her with a beaming smile as she approaches. 'You!' she says, with emphatic gladness of mock surprise. 'Where have you been all this time? How am I meant to get my nude reclining portrait finished?'

'Maybe you'll have to do it just from memory.'

Magda tips her head to one side, quizzical.

'Or even better, just destroy it.'

'My oh my, what has brought all this on? Has it been too intense for you, baby girl?'

Natalie winces. *Baby girl* is one of the terms of intimacy Magda has used during their lovemaking.

'No,' she replies, a little feebly, feeling the same weakness and inarticulacy coming over her as with Martin.

Magda's smile comes back. She reaches forward and smooths a stray lock of Natalie's hair away from her brow. 'Baby girl,' she says, 'don't forget how good it was. Come back with me tonight, after this is finished.'

For a ghost of a moment, in spite of herself, Natalie is tempted. If she did not know what she does know, she would have accepted.

'You didn't tell me about my dad, did you?'

'Your dad? Tell you what?' says Magda in a kind of incomprehension, though already a mask has started to slip.

'You didn't tell me that you'd been fucking him.'

'Where on earth is this coming from?'

'Never mind where it's coming from. It's true, isn't it?'

The mask has now slipped completely and it is a different cynical and slightly hard-faced Magda who looks at her now.

'You've got a lot to learn about life, girlie,' she says.

'Yes, I'm sure I have,' says Natalie. 'But not from you, lady.'

She turns to go.

'How was it?' asks Nathan, when she rejoins him by the stage where now, a different act is performing.

She nods. 'Yes.' She says no more.

Nathan does not comment on how red-faced and uptight she looks.

'Come on,' he says, 'let's go and get a drink.'

'You get them. Bring them back here. Will you? There are some people at the beer tent I want to stay away from just at the minute. And I think my dad's still about.'

'OK,' says Nathan.

CHAPTER 25

It is four o'clock. The main festival finishes at five and some of the stallholders and food providers are packing up. Gradually the families will drift away, though the beer tent will remain open, and the rock bands will set up, taking the festival into its final session which will last into the night.

As the daytime crowds drift away, Magda's customers are becoming more sporadic. After a busy day, of which she is now heartily sick, she is ready to pack away as soon as possible, when another customer approaches. It is Martin who, she suspects, is slightly tipsy from the gin which is what he seems to be holding in his hand.

'How much?' he asks.

'Is that a face painting question or a proposition?' she asks.

He laughs. 'Take it however you want.'

'What do you want, Mickey Mouse or Spider Man?'

'Do me Spiderman.'

'Fiver,' she says.

'Cheap at half the price,' he says.

'Cheap at twice the price is what you mean I think, but a fiver it is.'

Martin giggles. 'A fiver then. Do it, do me Spiderman.'

'I may be wrong,' she says, applying the Spiderman paint for the fiftieth time of the day, 'but a young friend of mine, Natalie Anderson, actually told me she was dating you.'

'*Was* being the active word,' says Martin. 'She's, well, not to put too fine a point on it, frigid, I mean...' he shrugs his shoulders, 'she's just as cold as ice.'

'The thing is,' says Magda, 'I mean I don't want to put my oar in where it's not wanted, but she has been in my studio over the last week or so and, we've had conversations and, without putting too fine a point on it, I have absolutely no doubt that she is queer, gay, whatever you call it?'

'Are you winding me up?'

'Why would I do that?'

'Fuck me,' says Martin.

'Now, is that an expletive or a proposition?'

He thinks for a minute. 'I suppose it all makes sense.'

She holds the mirror up to his face.

'Spiderman.' she says.

'A dance later?' he says, 'I mean, when the band gets up.'

'Try to stop me,' she says.

'Who's on next?' asks Cyril.

'Er, Tom and Frances. Due to relieve us in five minutes.'

'Thank God for that!'

'Amen to that, say I.'

'I'll just go over and cash up this lot then. Then we should be done.'

Seeing the young politician chappie—as he calls him—leave Magda's stall, Ralph takes the opportunity he has been waiting for all through the afternoon to approach Magda.

'Lots of business then?'

'Not bad. Used to do this outside the football ground at Leeds. Made good money. Bit of a drag, though. Once a year is more than enough.'

'Look,' says Ralph. 'I need to see you. How about I come over tonight.'

'I've got to finish off here.'

'That shouldn't take long.'

She looks at him askance. 'Hope you are not trying to organise my life for me.'

'I need to talk to you about Natalie.'

'Oh, do you? Why?'

'Well, for one thing, because you seem to spend half your waking hours on this blasted portrait of her.'

'I'll treat that with the contempt it deserves.'

'I'm serious. I want you to stop seeing her. It's too dangerous. She's going to suspect something.'

Magda thinks carefully for a moment, arranging her paints and cleaning a brush, and then turns to him, face to face. 'She already does.'

'What?'

'You heard me, Ralph. She already does. I don't know how, but she knows. She confronted me over it.'

'When?'

'Just now, actually.'

'And?'

Magda shrugs her shoulders. 'And nothing. I haven't seen her since then.'

'You denied it, of course.'

'Actually, no, I didn't,' she says.

'Oh, for Christ's sake!' he says under his breath.

'Ralph, before you go any further, I think there's something you should know about your daughter.' She pauses for long enough to enjoy the perturbed expression on his face. 'Natalie is gay,' she says at last. 'She's gay, Ralph. I suspected it right at the beginning but then I found out for sure. You can probably guess how.'

She tips her head to one side, as if teasing him to make the connection. Then she shrugs her shoulders. 'Sorry if it's a bit of a shock and all that but there it is. Don't know what you're going to say to your wife.'

'You bitch,' he snarls. 'You absolute bitch!'

From a discreet distance, Rob is watching, waiting for the moment when Magda is ready to pack away.

Not seen you for a while, mister, he thinks, seeing Ralph. *Bit tetchy, that,* he thinks, reading the signs. *Definitely a bit of aggro there. Well, mister, maybe she's moved on. What is it they say, fresh fields and pastures new?*

'All right?' asks Cyril, returning from the cashing up.

'Hmm, not sure. Just saw Ralph talking to Magda Bentley. Well, I think he was intending to have a word with her, you know, about Natalie spending so much time over there, and then he strode off, almost at a gallop.'

'OK. And?'

'And… well, nothing. He seemed in a bit of a state.'

'No sign of Tom and Frances, then?'

'Not yet.'

'Well, I guess we just have to hang on a bit then.'

'Yes.'

'I'll just have one more Bombay Sapphire then,' says Martin, approaching.

'Are you sure, Martin? I mean, you have been our best customer.'

'I'm fine,' says Martin, 'but you can give me a large tonic this time actually. Make it last.'

'Very wise,' says Cyril.

'Cheers then. The night is yet young!'

Cyril and Barbara exchange glances and at that moment Tom and Frances appear.

'The relief of Mafeking,' says Cyril.

'Sorry, got caught up in the tombola.'

'What a relief.' says Barbara as they walk away.

'Coffee?'

'Very definitely coffee, I think.'

On the stage now, *The Real Deal* are setting up and starting their sound check for the next stage of the festivities, and some of the crowd are drifting over there to find good spots to watch and listen from. Grateful that her job for the day is now done and unrepentant for the two altercations she has had, Magda is packing away her equipment when Rob makes what he supposes to be a timely approach.

'Like I said,' he says affably, 'I'll take you back with your stuff, if you like.'

'Are you going back right now?'

'Yes,' he affirms.

'This very moment? Definitely?'

'Definitely,' he replies.

'Oh,' says Magda, as if issuing a suddenly discovered sigh, 'Thing is, I'm not going back quite yet myself, got one or two people to see. But if you're going you could take my stuff.'

'Right,' says Rob, feeling well and truly finessed.

'Here's the key. Just pop the stuff inside, then post it through the door.'

'How will you get in though?'

'I have one hidden,' she says archly, 'in a very secret place.'

'Bitch!' says Rob to himself as he lugs the folding chairs across to his Hilux. Walked into that one, didn't I? Bitch!'

Ten minutes later, he lets himself into Magda's studio. He deposits her equipment and then steps inside stealthily, just to familiarize himself again with the layout and to identify possible locations for a bug. If it weren't Sunday, he is thinking, I would get this key copied.

The first thing he sees, however, is the portrait—now nearly completed—of Natalie.

'Fuck me,' he mutters. 'She's gorgeous.'

He sits down and gazes, in a kind of crude reverence, and expletive follows expletive as he tries to express the sharp anguish that has hatched in his blood.

So maybe it was a bit of art for art's sake, he thinks, not a totally lesbian orgy after all. Or maybe a bit of both. Not a problem to me.

The girl will probably be there too, at the festival, he thinks. Art for art's sake is one thing, but half an hour with her on her own, or even in a threesome, would be one for the record, definitely.

He nods his head a few times slowly and then stands, backing away towards the door.

Magda has discovered Adam, sitting alone at the back of the beer tent.

'Billy-no-mates!' she says, sitting down with the pint of cider she has just bought.

He grunts with a kind of amused approval at this. He has been drinking steadily but very slowly through the afternoon, and he knows exactly where he is on the spectrum between sober and drunk. There is still some way to go.

'I'm incognito,' he says.

'Right,' says Magda. 'Well, I won't ask you to explain why, though I expect you're going to tell me.'

'I'm trying to avoid a run-in with a certain person.'

'Oh God, no!' says Magda, obviously getting the reference.

'I've had one encounter already this afternoon. One in the week too.'

'Really?'

'Like a stalker.'

'She always had it in for you more than me. Mind you, I haven't had a Christmas card from her for a while! Expect she'll be round at my place again next! Is she still here?'

'God knows.'

'Well, thanks for giving me the heads-up. I'll keep my eyes open. Can I get you a drink.'

'No thanks. Taking it steadily.'

'You were in Celverdale, I hear.'

'Yes. I've been thinking I might take out an advert in the paper just in case there's anyone who still doesn't know.'

Magda laughs. 'You know what it's like round here.'

'Two nights they kept me in. A timely warning. I've got to lay off the hard stuff.'

'Well, that's maybe no bad thing.'

'For a time, anyway.'

'You're an old rogue, Adam. I take it you won't be shaking a leg later on then?'

'You take it right.'

The band begin their first set at 6 o'clock. There is just the slightest hint of dusk in the light. The flashing, coloured lights above the stage and in the trees which surround the dancing area, create an atmosphere very different from the afternoon. A new crowd is now filtering in, comprising mainly the young, though some families have stayed on to listen and drink and dance whilst their kids play nearby.

'You staying on for a bit then?' Nathan asks Natalie.

'Might as well. Better than being at home.'

'Like I say, you can come back with me if you need somewhere to kip down.'

'Yeah, cheers. Thanks. Let's just hang out here for a bit, see how it goes.'

'OK. '

'Fancy a dance?'

'You know me and dancing, Nat. Why make more of an idiot of myself than I already am?'

'I remember you dancing like a dervish at the school disco.'

'The junior school disco, maybe. After that, zilch.'

'How come?'

'Dunno. Self-consciousness dropped on me like a thick fog.'

'Come on,' says Natalie, pulling him up semi-forcibly by the hand. She draws him into crowd of dancers. It looks for a minute as if he might just bolt and run, but then, as she sways opposite him, he slips into an awkward jagged shuffle which just passes as a dance.

'That was fun,' she says as they go back to their place which is one of the spaces between the roots of a sycamore tree. 'Let's have a shot.'

'OK. Double?'

'Let's do it.'

'I keep getting to the point where I'm about to tell him,' says Barbara, 'and then…'

'I know,' says Cyril. 'Well, I can't say I know because I don't, but

I can understand.'

They are sitting in the garden of Cyril's house, looking out over the canal.

'It's almost as if I've got it written like a speech, like lines I've learned, with all the possible cues and responses worked out, but when it comes to the moment, I just dry.'

Cyril grins at the theatrical references. 'Are you absolutely sure it's what you want?'

'Yes,' she says without hesitation. 'Are you sure it's what you want?'

'Yes,' he says. 'I can't tell you how often I've regretted that we didn't take the chance before. As I said yesterday, I think I lacked the courage. The stakes were so high, and then all the unpleasantness, the gossip, no doubt the moral judgements. I was afraid of all that. I didn't have that strength last time, but I do now. I am ready.'

She reaches across and takes his hand. Then she sighs heavily. 'I just wish he would somehow find out and challenge me with it. It's just making the first move.'

He squeezes her hand.

'Anyway,' she says at last. 'I'd better go.'

'I'll walk back with you.'

'Just as far as the canal path,' she says. 'Probably best if we aren't seen together in public just yet.'

'OK,' he says.

'Here,' says Nathan, handing a glass to Natalie and sitting down. They both throw the shot back. Natalie coughs. 'God, that's strong,' she says with a laugh. 'I wasn't quite expecting that.'

'Just seen you-know-who at the bar.'

'Magda?'

'No, Martin. Though he did have his face painted.'

'By Magda, obviously.'

'He collared me.'

'Collared you?'

'Yes. Obviously seen me with you.'

'Right. About me then?'
'Yes. He was mouthing off. Warning me about you.'
'Well that's a laugh.'
'*You do know she's queer, don't you, mate*,' he was saying. '*You do know she's gay*'
'Where's he got that from? You haven't said anything, have you?'
'Bloody hell, Nat. I wouldn't. You should know that.'
'Sorry. Course not. Who then?'
'Well, unless you've told someone else, the only other person who knows is the other you-know-who.'
'Magda?'
'Who else?'
Natalie nodded. 'I might have known. She is such a cow!'
'Let's have another one of these.'

Rob hears the thumping beat across the field from where his Hilux is parked next to the canal and sees the lights pulsing in time with the rhythm.

'Now,' he says to himself, 'I could just fancy a dance tonight. I feel just in the right mood for a dance.'

He goes to the bar and orders a vodka and coke which he downs quickly, then another.

He has already spotted both Magda and the girl. The girl is dancing with some geek, and Magda is just leaning up against a tree. He swigs back his drink and heads over.

'I brought your key back,' he says.
'Oh. Thanks. No need, as I said, but thanks.'
'It's all in order,' he says.
'How do you mean?'
'Just, well, just I dropped your stuff off and locked up.'
'Right. Thank you. You're a perfect gent.'
'Do you fancy a dance?' he asks.
'What?'
'A dance. Or can I get you a drink?'
'What's your name again? I'm sorry. I can't remember. Just

remind me.'

'It's Rob.'

'OK, Rob. Well look, I'm grateful you gave me a lift with my stuff and all that, but what I'd really like you to do right now is just fuck off.'

He looks at her with a blank look.

'Have you got that? Just two simple words: fuck…off.'

'Slag!' he says. 'I've seen you. Fucking slaggy. That's what you are.'

'Is there a problem here?'

It is Martin, suddenly appearing from the periphery. 'Is this chap troubling you?'

Rob stands his ground for a moment, as if intending to square up to Martin; then, pocketing the key and with a gesture of spitting, retreats.

'Piece of work,' says Martin.

'My knight in shining armour,' says Magda in a melodramatic damsel-in-distress voice.

'I'm Spiderman actually.'

'Oh, yes. But your face is a bit smudged. Come here, I've got a tissue.'

'I'm beginning to feel a bit pissed, actually,' says Natalie to Nathan. 'Think I might just go home and creep up to my room.'

'Really?'

'Maybe not, come to think of it.'

She closes her eyes and leans against Nathan. For a time, the rhythm and beat of the band grows distant; she feels dizzy and then drowsy, and then suddenly snaps awake.

'There's somebody watching me, Nathan,' she says, a moment later.

'How do you mean?'

'Just over there. That guy with the leather coat.'

Nathan peers across the crowd.

'He's seen us now,' says Natalie, 'he's moved away. No there, look, he's turned and he's looking directly across again. Can you see?'

'Yes. That's Rob. Rob Jenkins.'

'Do you know him?'

'Don't actually know him but he's the carpet man, the one whose warehouse is opposite Magda's place.'

'Oh, him! Magda said about him. That he's a bit weird.'

'He's moved off again now.'

'Creepy,' says Natalie.

'Dance with me, Martin,' says Magda, pulling him up by the hand.'

'OK.'

She draws him into the middle of the throng of dancers and there, to his surprise, she draws him into a smooch.

'Bloody hell, what's this all about?' he asks, between shock and delight.

'I've just seen someone I want to avoid. This is the best place.'

'Oh,' says Martin, a little disappointed. 'Not him again.'

'No. Someone else. I'm using you as a human shield. I'm watching her over your shoulder.'

'Natalie?'

'No. Someone else.'

At that moment he feels the soft pressure of her lips on his neck and simultaneously an electric thrill of arousal.

'Sorry,' she says. 'I was hiding my face.'

'That's all right,' he replies. 'Any time you want to hide your face in my neck, just go right ahead.'

She laughs. 'Like that?' she says, repeating the action.

'Yes, like that!'

'I think she's gone,' says Magda a few moments later.

'What a pity!' says Martin.

'Let's have another drink, shall we?'

'Have you seen the way she behaves! It's disgusting.'

Adam screws up his eyes and grimaces. Had he followed his own inclination to depart five minutes ago, he would have been spared this further encounter with Helen Holden.

'Look, Helen,' he retorts, 'I have absolutely nothing to do with Magda Bentley. I am not the guardian of her morals, nor do I wish to hear about her behaviour, however disgusting, from anyone else.'

After their earlier spat, he had thought she would leave him alone, even that she might have departed, but no such luck.

In between her two appearances he had had a remarkably pleasant time. He had had four pints—quaffed very slowly—and even had a civilised chat with Moggy Morton about cricket of all things and had felt, watching the world go by, generally at one with it. He now wishes he had downed this, his final pint, a little more quickly. By now he would be strolling home, enjoying the dusk; as it is, the remaining mouthfuls of beer have a flat brackish taste.

'Look,' says Helen who has seen Martin approaching the bar, 'he's the one. She was all over him. Disgusting.'

'I'm going to the loo for a piss, Helen, and then I'm going.'

He gets up and walks away without waiting for a response.

Martin, who at five o'clock was feeling that he might have to go home and lie down but has now regained at least some of his sobriety, is weighing up—as he makes his way to the bar—his chances of a fling with Magda before the night is out. She seems to have adopted him as her companion for the night and is in, if he is any judge, a flighty mood. A couple more drinks, he reckons, might just do the trick.

When he gets back to their place, however, she is not there. Possibly gone to the loo, he thinks, or maybe just playing fast and loose. He looks over to the entrance to the toilets and as his eye travels back, he sees her once more in the middle of the dancers, this time with Nathan.

He goes over to where Natalie is now sitting alone. 'What's going on?' he says.

'Don't ask me. She just came over and dragged him up.'

He leans in towards her with a vindictive face, as if determined to take this unexpected opportunity. 'I thought you were just a straightforward prick-tease, but you're not, are you?'

'Go away, Martin. You're drunk'

'It's not just that you're a little slag, is it? You're a rug muncher, aren't you? A bean flicker.'

He turns away with a laugh, pleased to see that his little attack has drawn tears. Serves her right, he thinks to himself.

'What's up?' asks Nathan, seeing the state she is in. 'I'm sorry,' he says, assuming it is Magda dragging him off that has upset her.

'It's not that,' she says, trying to control her voice through increasing sobs. 'I just, I just think I'm going to go.'

Coming away from the toilets, Adam sees that Helen has moved away from the seat she occupied next to him. He does not look around to see where she might have taken herself off to. As he makes his way across the field, however, he sees Moggy Morton and gestures a farewell before Moggy can ask him for another drink; and then he sees, on a trajectory that is shortly going to intersect with his own, the figure of Natalie Anderson.

It is clear from her demeanour that she is upset and, perhaps because she has not yet seen him, she makes no attempt to disguise it, nor to mitigate the pitiful sound of her sobbing.

His heart melts and his pulse leaps to life.

'What on earth is the matter?' he calls.

Startled, she gasps and veers away, as if to avoid him.

'It's all right,' he calls, trying to reassure her. She turns to look. 'It's all right,' he repeats calmly.

'I'm sorry,' she says. 'I didn't realise it was you. You startled me.'

'You're upset,' he says. 'What's the matter?'

'I'm a bit drunk I think.'

He nods. 'Well, you're in good company here! But it's not just that, is it?'

She shakes her head quickly.

'Is there anything I can do?'

She repeats the quick shaking of her head. 'I probably just

need to get home.'

'Yes,' he says. 'I think that's probably a good idea. Will you be all right?'

'I think so.'

'You sure.'

'I think so.'

'Would it help if I were to walk you home?'

'Would you? That's very kind. I feel a bit unsteady.'

'Here,' he says, 'Put your arm through mine. I'll make sure you're OK.'

'Thank you,' she says meekly.

'Which is the best way, Natalie?'

'We can go by the canal path and then cut through.'

PART 2 : AUGUST

CHAPTER 26

Monday

We trooped into the briefing room. Inspector Renwick, four of us from the team—me, Frank, DS Geoff Stone and DS Bob Keable—plus Home Office Pathologist, Dawn Wilson, who we'd seen down at the scene. DI June Lister and DS Ian Casey were out on a call.

Calling it an incident room is actually a bit of a joke. The space was not that great so we sat around as best we could on the corner of tables, leaning against the walls and cupboards. The whiteboard was empty apart from two photographs.

Renwick immediately handed over to Dawn.

The two photographs were of the victim's face. Pictures of murder victims are always pretty harrowing but it's something you just have to get used to.

'First thing to say is, yes, she did drown. But we are pretty certain that she was unconscious before she went into the water. There are two wounds, here on the forehead, which are consistent with a fall, possibly against the metal base of the lock which may have been enough to have caused a bit of shock, concussion—especially as she'd had quite a lot to drink—but not enough to knock her out. As we saw this morning, the path was quite muddy from last week's rain, so it would have been pretty easy for someone running to lose their balance and fall, especially, as I said, under the influence of alcohol. But the other wound, here on the side of the head just above the temple, was inflicted by a hard object, probably a stone, and this was administered with some force.'

'A stone, not a weapon?' asked Geoff.

'A stone can be a pretty potent weapon.'

'Not an implement, I mean.'

'No. There were traces of grit in the hair and in the wound consistent with stone – of which, as I am sure you are aware, there are plenty along the side of the towpath.'

'We can search for a stone tomorrow but chances are, I'd say, it's already at the bottom of the canal so unlikely we'd get any decent forensic from it.'

'Is the site secured?'

'Frank? Nula?'

We confirmed it was, both glad we'd taken the trouble at what we'd at first thought just an accidental drowning.

'Uniform'll stay with it overnight. Pity the poor buggers.'

'No further idea of who she is?'

Renwick shook his head.

The press statement's gone out and it'll be on local radio and television tonight, but no-one's called in a missing person. Give it until tomorrow morning, then it'll be a bit of foot-plodding for all of you, house to house, until we turn something up.'

'Hell of a lot of people at that festival yesterday. Not all of them locals either. Could be like a needle in a haystack.'

'Needles and haystacks. Our speciality.'

'Right, this is what I want.'

Renwick began to assign jobs. Until we got an ID on the body, it was all pretty basic stuff: fingertip search of the site, door-to-door inquiry, establishing any CCTV that might have been operational at the festival.

'Right, off you go,' he said at last, 'and try to keep the media at arm's length.'

Frank and I spent two hours doing house-to-house in the area surrounding the festival but it was thankless task. Without any further hard information to go by, the range of our questions was strictly limited. Evidence suggests that house-to-house inquiry will eventually, however long it takes, come up with something, some tiny nugget of information which will become a lead—and I believe it's true—but on this particular day, we got nothing.

'I'll drop you off, if you like,' said Frank as we began to drive home. Both our own cars were parked up at HQ and we were in a squad car.

'Pick you up at six?'

'Fine.'

Frank lives just a couple of miles further on from me and if we're on a job together, we often give each other lifts like this. We'd been going for about ten minutes when we heard the media release on the news.

A body, believed to be that of a female, was recovered from the canal near Milthwaite this morning. Police have been at the scene, which is cordoned off, through the day. No formal identification has yet been made.

We were nearly home when we got a radio message. *Just had a call from a Mrs Anderson, of 2 Crofters Mount, Milthwaite, reporting missing person. Daughter, name of Natalie Anderson, age twenty-two, did not return home after the festival yesterday.*

'Shit,' said Frank under his breath.

Can anyone pick that up? Mrs Anderson needs to be brought in to identify the body. It can't wait until morning.

Frank looked at me and I looked at Frank.

'Nula?' he asked.

'Do we have a choice?'

CHAPTER 27

Returning from the festival on Sunday night, Barbara had been, in all honesty, glad to find the house empty. She had thought at first that Ralph might be in his study, but seeing no light under the door, and then opening it, confirmed that the room was empty.

Funny, she thinks to herself, that could have been one of those moments. A blue-touch-paper moment. I open the door, he is there, I say, *Listen Ralph, we need to talk* .

Why, he says dismissively.

We need to talk because I have decided to leave you.

For days and days, she had been thinking of possible blue-touch-paper moments.

But Ralph is not there.

She draws breath in the silence of the house and then exhales back into the quietness.

It is not to be yet. Not quite.

Ralph, she conjectures, is probably at the pub. After his altercation with Magda—and to do him credit he was probably sticking up for Natalie—he probably fancied a few drinks at the White Hart.

About the fact that Natalie is not yet back she does not worry at all. Quite the opposite. If Natalie is having a bit of fun and staying out, so much the better.

She goes to the fridge, pours herself a glass of white wine and, free of other concerns, indulges the recollections of her own day. That she is in love with Cyril she has no doubt. They have been together now twice in the last week, and it has confirmed everything she felt those years ago in Whitby.

His attentiveness to her.

His care.

She never had that from Ralph. Never.

She goes to bed thinking of him.

'Cyril,' she murmurs as she slips into sleep. 'Cyril, my love. We will sort this out, we will make it work.'

When she wakes in the morning, it is already 8.30.

Ralph is not in the twin bed opposite and the bed is made. It is possible he came in after she went to sleep and got up and made the bed before she awoke, but she has no recollection of either. She checks her phone. There is no message from him and when she tries to call him, his phone is switched off. It is not entirely unusual. She texts: *Let me know what time you expect to be back.*

She has a shower and then goes downstairs—still in her dressing gown—switches on Radio 2 and makes coffee. She makes enough for two in case Natalie appears but she decides not to disturb her. It is quite likely, she thinks, that Natalie stayed out late.

Over her coffee and carrying on from her reverie of the previous evening, she begins to make plans. It is all very flimsy and fanciful, she knows, because as yet not even the first move has been made but nevertheless, it is pleasurable to let the imagination roam: where will they live in the meantime and then when it is all settled? Will she move into his house or will they get a different place of their own? What will their domestic routines be like? Where will they go on holiday when they can go wherever they like? Such things as these will form a completely new backdrop to her life.

It is not until ten o'clock, by which time she has finished breakfast and dressed, that she begins to wonder whether she should rouse Natalie. She makes more coffee, pours some into Natalie's usual mug, takes it upstairs and knocks lightly on the door.

'Nat?'

There is no sound of stirring.

'Nat? Coffee?'

Still no reply.

She waits a further minute, then pushes the door open just enough to see that the room is empty and the bed unslept in.

A series of possibilities comes quickly into her mind. The most likely explanation is that she stayed out with Nathan and went back to spend the night at his house. She may have met someone else from schooldays and gone up to town, clubbing until four o'clock in the morning—something like that—in which case she is probably just about now waking up on somebody's floor with a thick head. The other possibility is that later on, she might have run into Martin—hopefully a little more sober than earlier—and that a little bit of romance was rekindled. In which case—and she reminds herself that Natalie is twenty-two and not sixteen—they might well have gone back to his place and spent the night together. Each of the possibilities carries with it the chance that it will have snapped Natalie out of the gloomy mood which has been enshrouding her for the last week.

She returns to the deeper question of what is to be done in the situation with Ralph. Will it be best simply to come out with it, as in *I've decided to leave you*, or to make some sort of confession of her adultery and let the ensuing, no doubt rancorous conversation follow its own course. And in that conversation, will she be strong enough to hold her end up? It is possible that Ralph will fly into one of his rages, quite likely too that he will try to wound her with the barbs of his sarcasm; but these are not the main things she fears. Her main fear is that he will move her around the board, ridiculing her points, trivialising her perception of things, until she capitulates. It is unlikely to be the work of a single night, a single argument; she will have to regather her strength and resolve, and be prepared to come back, and come back again, until she finally gets it through to him that it is finished.

For all of these reasons, she calculates—once again—that it will be better to delay the start of it until after Natalie has gone up to college. It wouldn't be fair to subject her to a parental battle royal going on for days. And if Natalie has indeed decided to go up early, as she hinted, so much the better. 'I'll be able to sleep in her bed,' she thinks. It is a minor consideration but, nevertheless, something which may be necessary.

It is just after lunch that she gets a text from Cyril. He is coded as 'C.N. Players' in her contacts. *Everything OK? Give me a call when you can.*

She rings straight away.

'God, that was quick!' he says, sounding surprised.

'Well,' she replies, 'I'm alone in the house. Natalie stayed out last night and I don't know where Ralph is. I feel quite abandoned. So what is it? What's up?'

'Well, I don't know what's going on down at the field,' he says, 'well by the canal really, but there are police all over the place. I wondered if you'd heard anything.'

'No, not a dicky bird. Maybe there was a fight or something. There's been aggro before with people getting paralytic at the festival later on, anti-social behaviour and stuff, usually between locals and out-of-towners.'

'Yes, that's what I was thinking. Something and nothing probably. Still, thought I'd use it as an excuse to call you.'

There is a long pause, as if neither of them knows how to—or wants to—end the call.

'I've been thinking about it,' she says quietly, almost as if someone else might be listening. 'I've been thinking of nothing else.'

'Me too,' he replies. 'I feel so helpless. I just wish there was something I could do to help.'

'There isn't,' she says.

They talk again about the business of telling Ralph, going round the same circles. It is uncomfortable but also reassuring in that it affirms their commitment. He offers again the possibility of telling him together.

'No,' she says decisively.

'I wouldn't shy away from it, if you needed me there to support you.'

'I know,' she says. 'But no. It wouldn't work. Not in the first place. I have to do that on my own.'

'Right.'

'But don't think you're off the hook. I will certainly need you on my side in what will follow.'

'You got it,' he says with a supportive laugh.

'Anyway,' she says finally. 'I'd better go. Natalie might be trying to get hold of me.'

'OK.'

She clicks the call off quickly lest they should get into a ridiculous 'you-go-first-no-you-go-first' farewell routine.

She lets the phone call sink in, with all its affirmative elements, and then, coming back to the practicalities of the day, resumes the underlying question of where Natalie might be.

So far she has resisted the temptation to phone her, fearful that this might be seen as interference, but now she is beginning to feel sufficiently concerned as to need reassurance.

She clicks on her number. It rings for a moment and then shuts dead.

Is that reassuring or not? she asks herself.

She tries again. Dead straightaway.

Is that reassuring or not? she asks herself again.

She constructs a scenario. Natalie, either too hungover to reply or not wanting to reply because she is doing something else (never mind what) hears her phone ring and immediately switches it off.

She is twenty-two, not fifteen.

Reassuring, she reassures herself. Leave it for an hour.

She diverts herself by looking at the glossy playscripts which have just arrived. Next year's season. She quickly goes through the cast lists: male, female, age, type etc, wondering if there are any which she and Cyril can audition for to be in together. The Ayckbourn, certainly – that would be fun; maybe the J.B. Priestley. She looks at some of the scenes and imagines how she would audition.

Then she phones Natalie again. It is still dead.

What's going on? she wonders.

She phones Nathan's number.

'No,' says Nathan's mum. 'Not seen her. He was here this morning. Don't know when he came in.'

'Can I speak to him?'

'No, sorry, don't know where he is now. Out somewhere.'

Still not a cause for panic, she thinks, though on a reflex she wishes Ralph was here to pick up the problem.

She clicks on Messenger. He has not replied to her text from earlier.

She tries to call. His phone, too, is switched off.

What the hell is going on here, she asks herself, now feeling distinct bubbles of panic.

Her phone rings. She rushes to it, hoping it will be Natalie, even Ralph. It is Cyril.

She smiles, anticipating another minute or two of escape.

'Have you heard from Natalie?' he asks.

'Not yet, no. Why?'

'It's probably nothing,' he says. 'But look, I'm going to come over.'

'No!' she says.

'I'm coming over,' he insists.

By the time he arrives, she has watched the local news with its bulletin: *A body, believed to be that of a female, was recovered from the canal near Milthwaite this morning. Police have been at the scene, which is cordoned off, through the day. No formal identification has yet been made.*

She is sitting on the floor shivering when Cyril arrives.

He pulls her up and shakes her until she can make sense of what he is saying.

'We need to ring the police,' he says, 'report her missing. Are you listening to me, Barbara? We need to report her missing, they'll know what to do. They'll tell us what to do.'

'Will you ring them?' she says in a high-pitched, helpless whinny of a voice.

'Yes,' he says. 'I'll ring them now, I'll speak to them, but they will probably need to speak to you too.'

CHAPTER 28

We arrived at the address and went up the drive. A man opened the door as we approached.

'Mr Anderson?'

'No. Cyril North, I'm a friend of the family.'

We went in. Mrs Anderson was in bits, I tell you.

Frank sat her down and talked to her. To be honest, Frank is at his absolute best in situations like this. I mean, he might have antediluvian views on some things, but when it comes to talking to people, especially people in distress, he just has the touch.

'Right, Barbara,' he is saying. 'When you are ready, what we are going to do is this…'

Of course, it's hard because what we are actually going to do is identify a dead body which is probably her daughter, but Frank has a way of making distressed people feel as if they are being surrounded by some kind of protective coating.

The guy, Cyril, comes with us. We don't know exactly who he is but she obviously accepts him as her support, and that's as much as we need to know.

Of course, there is a dreadful tension in the car. Every so often Mrs Anderson stifles a sob and cannot prevent an occasional moan as if she is going through a moment of realising the full horror of it all.

We arrive at the mortuary, which is a part of the Royal Infirmary, and wait for a moment for the desk attendant but she knows who we are and is expecting us. She opens a security door to let us through and another attendant leads the way down a corridor. Outside a door, she stops and explains to Mrs Anderson what will happen. For a moment, Barbara's knees sag, as if she is going to faint, and Mr North supports her. It is all very harrowing.

'Would you like to sit down for a moment?' asks the attendant.

Mrs Anderson says 'No' in a barely audible whisper.

'A glass of water?'

She shakes her head quickly several times.

'Would you like anyone to come in with you, beside Mr North?'

For some reason, she looks at me with a plaintive expression, and nods her head.

We go into the room and the attendant draws forward a stainless steel trolley on which there is a white sheet obviously covering a human form. She brings Mrs Anderson to the necessary place.

'Are you ready?' she says quietly.

'Yes,' says Mrs Anderson in a surprisingly calm voice.

The attendant draws back the corner of the sheet and an involuntary moan of shock escapes from Mrs Anderson's mouth. It is some moments before she can control herself sufficiently to speak and when she does, the words become part of the moan.

'It's not her,' she says before breaking into a flood of tears. 'It's not Natalie.'

Outside the room, she sits down and I sit next to her, holding her hand. Mr North beckons to Frank. 'I can tell you who it is,' he says, white-faced. 'It's Magda Bentley. Would you like me to do a formal identification?'

It is some time before we are able to leave. After the identification, we take a statement from Mr North, which includes some details about the deceased to follow up on, and relay this back to HQ. Then we begin the journey back to Mrs Anderson's home.

'Where is she though?' she keeps saying. 'Where is she? Where's Natalie.'

'I'm sure she'll be back soon,' says Mr North. 'She may even be back there already.'

'But what if she's not? Is there anything you can do to find her?' she asks, now addressing us.

'Well,' says Frank. 'You've already reported her missing, and as she's twenty-two and not vulnerable, we wouldn't normally prioritise an investigation...'

'How do you decide if someone is vulnerable?' she asks.

'Look,' says Frank. 'We are going to be all over this area over the next few days. We'll do everything we can to find her if she doesn't come home, but as Mr North has said, it is highly likely that she will.'

'Can I phone you directly?'

'Not allowed to give out our personal numbers. I mean, strictly not. But I'll leave a message on the desk, and if you phone in and say you want to speak to Nula, they'll get me.'

'Thank you.'

When I got in, I was fit to drop. Wendy brought me a glass of freshly chilled white wine. 'You eaten?'

'Not hungry,' I said. 'Past it.'

'I'll run you a bath,' she said. 'So how did it go?'

I explained.

'Oh my God, no!' she exclaimed. 'You poor thing. And they don't know who it is?'

'Well, not until a Mrs Anderson phoned in to say her daughter hadn't returned home after the festival.'

'Oh God, sounds ominous.'

'Well, that's why I'm so late. We had to take her to the Rose Garden for identification.'

'God, it gets worse!'

'Well, as it turns out, it's not her daughter on the slab, but the chap with her says "Ey-up, I can tell you who it is," so, yes, we do now know.'

'I guess that's something.'

'Yes, anyway. Let me see Phoebe and then run me that bath!'

'Will do!'

Phoebe was pretty much asleep. I cuddled her into my neck for a while and then held her forward to look at her, trying not to think of what it had been like for Mrs Anderson. She opened her eyes, unseeingly, once and then went off again.

Wendy took her from me and put her in her cot.

I soaked, finishing my glass of wine, and then when I was dry, I slipped in between the sheets where she was already waiting and into the softness of her caresses; then, for twenty blissful minutes—and for six hours of deep sleep afterwards—I was able to forget the case.

How could I ever explain that to Frank?

CHAPTER 29

Tuesday

He picked me up, as arranged, at 6 a.m. and we were at our desks for twenty past, ready for a briefing. There was a buzz in the office that we had found out who the victim was. One or two from out that way knew Magda Bentley, or rather had heard of her as a local artist. I left a note with Jack on the desk, saying to put Mrs Anderson through to me if she called in.

We were in Renwick's office at 7.30.

'I'll be with you in a minute,' he said.

We were waiting for the others to arrive. Normally Renwick gets highly agitated when people aren't strictly on the minute, but he seemed quite calm. When it got to twenty-five to and still just the two of us, we began to sense that the operation had changed.

Finally he sat back in his chair. 'Thanks to you two,' he said, 'we've made a big step forward.'

'Thank you, guv,' we both muttered, overlapping. Speaking to him later, I realised that at that moment Frank was having the same thoughts as me. We both knew there was nothing really to thank us for, and we both knew that praise from Renwick seldom came without there being something to follow, some kind of rider.

'The fact that we now know who the victim is means we can now scale down the scope of the original investigation as we outlined it yesterday.'

Bob Keable and Geoff Stone had already been assigned elsewhere. Ian Casey was in court. June was doing some training.

Basically, it was going to be left to the two of us.

'Nula, I'm going to make you SIO. It'll be good experience for you and I know Frank won't mind. There are already six bobbies out there and they've retrieved some clothing and a purse from the undergrowth. You can hang on to the bobbies as long as they're any use. Keep them at it though, don't let them hang about kicking their heels. Now I'm sure you two are quite capable of cracking this one, so off you go. Keep me in the picture.'

'What about the team of divers?' asked Frank.

'What?' said Renwick with lacerating sharpness.

'To dive for the murder weapon. You remember, the piece of stone.'

'Fuck off, Frank!' said Renwick, seeing the funny side of it. 'Make sure you keep him on a short lead, Nula!'

'You all right with that?' I asked Frank as we made our way back to our desks.

'Absolutely,' he said. 'I've got eighteen months left. My career is going no further. Typical though, isn't it?'

'How do you mean?'

'Well, for flaming Nora's sake, it's a murder. There should be a full team on this. It's all right him saying he has faith in us, but well, we all know it comes down to cutbacks.'

He was probably right. It wasn't the first time something like this had happened, though personally I had to admit that I was chuffed to be SIO and I was feeling excited about the day ahead.

I'd just got back to the desk when my phone buzzed. It was Jack on the desk. 'It's Mrs Anderson asking for you. Will you take it?'

'Yes,' I said, 'put her through.'

'Hello? Is that...?' It was Mrs Anderson's voice, sounding tentative.

'Yes, it's Nula,' I said. 'Is she back?'

'Yes,' she replied. 'Last night. Not long after you dropped us off here.'

'Good news,' I said, mouthing *She's back* to Frank. 'Thanks for letting us know.'

'The thing is,' she went on. 'I think there is something else you need to know. Shall I come in?'

'No. We'll be with you in half an hour,' I said. 'Come on Frank. We're off. You can drive.'

'Yes, ma'am,' he said with an ironic grin. 'Cheers.'

'Feeling of Autumn in the air,' said Frank as we drove towards Milthwaite.

It was true. Along the valley, a thin skein of mist hung over the river and the canal, though by the time we turned off into the village and began towards Crofters Mount, the sun was already burning through, hinting at a pure blue sky beyond.

'We usually take our holidays about this time,' said Frank. 'Well, when the kids have gone back to school. Quieter. Cheaper too if you're going abroad.'

'Not this year, though?'

'No. Well Angela's waiting for a knee operation and if a cancellation comes up, she might get lucky.'

We pulled up on the drive and Mrs Anderson opened the door as we walked up the path.

'I've made some tea,' she said, ushering us through the hall into a sitting room. 'Is that all right?'

'Fine by me,' said Frank cheerily. 'Two sugars please.'

She came in almost immediately with a tray of tea and a plate of chocolate digestives. Frank's eyes lit up.

'So then …' I began. I was thinking all this is very nice, but I'm now the SIO and we need to get on.

Barbara took a deep breath as if picturing something in her mind before starting. 'As I told you, Natalie came in shortly after you left last night. After all I'd been through, I was intending to give her a hard time for staying out a night and a day without a call or even a message, but I was so grateful just to have her back, I just hugged her.

'Of course, I had to break it to her about Magda and she was extremely upset. Well, they'd seen quite a bit of each other over the last couple of weeks. She was doing a portrait of Natalie actually, and it was obviously a terrible shock.'

'Yes,' said Frank, reaching for a second chocolate biscuit. 'It must have been.'

'Well, she went absolutely white-faced and I was frightened she was going to pass out. 'Why don't you go and lie down?' I suggested,' continued Mrs Anderson. *'No mum,'* she said. And then she said, *'Listen mum, there's something I have to tell you. It's really important.'*

'And presumably she said something which made you call us this morning?' I said.

'Yes.'

'Is Natalie here now?'

'Yes, she's upstairs. But if you don't mind, it would be easier for me, and for her too, if I tell you on my own first.'

'OK,' I said.

It took her quite a bit of time to get to the bottom of it all, but what it came down to was this. 'My husband has been having an affair with Magda Bentley.'

Frank edged forward a little in his chair.

'And,' she continued, after drawing a deep breath, 'Natalie has also been having an affair with Magda Bentley.'

Frank swallowed a choke and looked at me. I gave him my sharpest look.

'What exactly did she say?'

'Well, in short, she told me that she was gay and wanted to come out as gay, and that as well as sitting for Magda as a model, they had become intimate.'

'And the other bit?'

'Yes. That she found out that Ralph, my husband, had also been in a sexual relationship with Magda Bentley.'

'Right,' I said. A little bit bowled over, I was struggling for a moment with where to go next. 'Your husband, then. I take it he's not also here now.'

'No. I haven't seen him since the day of the festival. He does sometimes go up to Leeds and stays over. He works at the university there.'

'But he's not contacted you?'

She shook her head.

'Maybe I ought to tell you that on the festival day, I did see Ralph—my husband—having a bit of an altercation with Magda. She was doing face painting, you see, at the festival, I mean, and I was on a different stall, but, yes, well, I thought I should mention it.'

We let this sink in.

'Possibly be a good idea if we spoke to Natalie now,' I suggested.

'OK, I'll call her.'

A minute later Natalie came into the room, and though her face had a haunted look, I have to admit that my first impression was of a strikingly pretty girl. She sat down and Barbara sat, almost protectively, beside her.

'I think, maybe,' I said, 'it would be best if we spoke to Natalie on her own.'

Barbara deferred and went through into the kitchen.

We went through the things Barbara had said and Natalie confirmed them all.

'She was doing a painting of me and we both realised we felt physically attracted to each other, and we had sex. About four times. Well, four occasions. And then someone told me they thought my dad had been seeing Magda, and I asked her, and well, it was obvious that she had had sex with him too.'

'And this was at the festival?'

Natalie hesitated for a moment and then, quite decisively, said 'Yes.'

'And what did you do then? You must have been upset.'

'Yes, I was. I got drunk.'

'And then you stayed away for the night and most of the next day?'

'Yes.'

I watched her for a time without asking anything else, trying to read her body language.

'Where did you stay, Natalie?' I asked.

'What?'

'Where did you stay? The night before last. The night of the festival.'

'Just with a mate.'

'A mate? Any names?'

'I got in with a crowd. We ended up at someone's, not even sure exactly who it was.'

'OK, Natalie. Thanks. Now, about Magda. I realise that it's difficult for you to talk about her in the circumstances, but did Magda ever say anything about anybody she might have had an argument with lately? Anything like that?'

'No. We didn't really talk about other people much, only in passing. The only other person she mentioned was the guy in the warehouse opposite. She said she thought he was spying on her.'

'Spying?'

'Well, you know, peeping, sort of thing.'

'Right. OK, thanks, Natalie.'

We called Barbara back in. 'OK, that's it for now. Thank you both for cooperating so willingly. It is appreciated.'

We drove away and then pulled in, out of sight.

'So, what do you think, Frank?'

'Fuck me,' he said, 'proper can of worms.'

'What next then?'

'If you ask me, we need to get hold of the father. He's an obvious suspect. I mean if she knew, not to put too fine a point on it, that he was screwing Magda, and he too knew that Magda was doing the deed of darkness with his daughter, there—unless I'm very much mistaken—is a motive.'

'*Doing the deed of darkness*, Frank? Where on earth did you get that one from?'

'But you get my point?'

'Yes, you're right,' I said. 'Let's call it in. Get in touch with Leeds. See if they can locate him and bring him in.'

'What did you think of Natalie?'

I didn't reply.

'Lovely girl, didn't you think though?'

'Fuck off, Frank!'

'All right. Sorry. Just saying.'

'I think we'll need to speak to Natalie again. She's not telling us everything. And, to be fair, what's a possible motive for him is also a possible motive for her.'

'Yes, I suppose so. And what about mum then? What did you make of her?'

'What are you getting at, Frank?'

'Well, Nula...'

'Ma'am,' I corrected, jokingly.

'Well, ma'am,' he said, 'what struck me was how easy she seemed to feel about sticking him up there in the frame.'

'Yeah, you're right, Frank. I got that too. Another can of worms going on there. Maybe Mr North is more than just a friendly neighbour.'

'What next then?'

'Get an alert out to Leeds about Mister. Take a look at what's going on down at the scene. Then take a look at Magda Bentley's studio. Check?'

'Check. No key found?'

'Not as far as I'm aware.'

'Better get a warrant then. Just in case it's a shoulder job.'

Down at the scene, the bobbies were getting bored, but sometimes that's just part of the job. They showed us where the clothes, presumably Magda's, had been found. A photograph of Magda had been acquired from her website and that was being processed so that the bobbies could do some door-to-door inquiries. Renwick had decided to delay a media release until later in the day, around teatime, just to give us chance to get our preliminary investigation done without being hassled, and I'd agreed with that.

We took a closer look at the spot where Magda's body had been found, trying to piece it together with what Dawn Wilson had said at the briefing earlier. The protruding metal at the base of the lock gear was fairly obvious now that Dawn had pointed it out.

'Do you reckon someone was chasing her?' asked Frank.

'Must have been.'

'Could have been a game.'

'Not with the injuries she ended up with, and whoever it was must also have pushed her into the water. If she was coming from this direction—and it's pretty obvious that she was—to fall and bang her head, she would have landed something like this.' I tried to show where I thought her hands and feet would be. 'She might have reacted, like turning over, feeling her head, drawing her knees up maybe. You know, like footballers when they've been fouled.'

'If she'd rolled over like them, she would have been straight into the cut!'

'She might even have been conscious enough to get up, maybe grab the rail. I wonder if Dawn did any testing for that.'

'Probably wouldn't help one way or the other. Someone clobbered her, then pushed her in, or let her fall in, and did nothing about it.'

'Let's try her place then. Her studio. Do you know it?'

'The old mill, yeah, went there to get some carpets a couple of years ago.'

As we made our way back to the road, we took a look at the festival site. The tents were now pretty much dismantled and there was just a lot of gear waiting to be ferried away. Oh, and the rubbish. Lots of that. It was difficult to imagine it the way it must have been on Sunday afternoon and into the evening.

'Did you ever come?' I asked Frank.

'Used to be a regular. Some good bands. You may not believe this but I once played in a band here.'

'Frank, is there no end to your talent!'

'No beginning, more like. I only knew three chords.'

At the gate, one of the bobbies came over. 'There's a chap over here says can he have a word.'

Across the road, there was a plumber's van with *F. Morton*

Plumbing and a cartoon of a cat with a spanner on the side. Leaning against it was a guy in overalls with a cap pushed back on his head. He straightened up as we approached and made a kind of casual salute.

'Felix Morton,' he said by way of introduction. 'Moggy to those who know me.'

The cartoon cat now made sense.

'And… you wanted a word?'

'Well, I was here all day on Sunday.'

'And you saw something that might help our investigation?'

'I saw lots of things,' said Moggy, tapping his nose, 'and that's because I keep my eyes open, and if I knew what kind of thing you were looking for, I mean if I knew what your line of inquiry was, I might be able to throw some light in your direction.'

'Our line of inquiry is not yet fully established,' I said, sensing that Moggy was just fishing for something to gossip about, or else one of those people who feel they gain some status by having some inside knowledge to impart.

'Do you know who it is yet then?' he asked.

'There'll be a statement later in the day,' said Frank. 'Keep your radio on.'

As we walked away, he called after us, 'There's one thing I can tell you.' he said. 'If it's to do with the girl from the pub, I can tell you I saw her walking off with the Mitchell fellow.'

'Who is he then?'

'Adam Mitchell. Mate of mine. Well, acquaintance really. Just see him in the pub. Calls himself a writer but more of a layabout if you ask me. Never known him do a proper day's work, let's say.'

'And who is the girl from the pub?'

'The new girl, works Saturday nights.'

'Has she got a name?'

'Nancy she's called, no, I tell a lie, it's Nattie.'

'Natalie?'

'Yes, that's the one. Is it her, then?'

'No, Moggy. I can tell you that it's not her.'

'Only he was crazy about her, he was. Adam Mitchell, I mean.

Couldn't keep his eyes off her.' He twisted his mouth downward slightly, almost as if he was disappointed that it wasn't Natalie lying in the mortuary. 'Anyway, here's my card, if there's anything else I can help you with. Or if not,' he concluded with a chuckle, 'if you need your boiler fixing.'

'Adam Mitchell,' said Frank as we set out. 'The name rings a bell. Think the wife read one of his books once when we were on holiday. Pretty mucky stuff it was by all accounts.'

We pulled up on the cobbled yard outside Magda's studio and tried the door which, as we expected, was locked.

'Shoulder?' asked Frank.

'Well, we've got to get in. Just have a walk round, see if there's another entrance. If not, shoulder; but your shoulder not mine.'

'Yes, boss. At your service.'

It only took us a minute to establish that there wasn't another door.

'OK,' I said. 'Let's do it. We'll send someone up later to secure the door.'

Frank was just going through his door-breaking warm-up, which involved some deep breathing and shoulder tensing preparation, when a voice called from the door of the building opposite.

'I've got a key if you need to get in.'

We turned to see a youngish chap, wiry and with a gaunt sort of face, approaching. He was holding up a key.

'Rob Jenkins,' he said. 'She leaves a key with me, just in case. Always losing hers. Well, used to, I suppose I should say now.'

'And why do you say that, Rob?'

For a moment he looked completely taken aback. 'Say what?'

'Say *used to* as of something that is no more.'

'Well it's her, isn't it. It's Magda. The one they found in the canal.'

'And how do you know that, Rob?'

'How do I know that it's her?'

'Yes.'

'Well, it's just been on the radio. Half an hour ago. *The woman found in the canal on Monday morning has been named as local artist, Magda...* I've been waiting for you to arrive.'

We both felt we had egg on our faces, and both silently cursed Renwick for jumping in before the agreed time. He rails against media interference but is all too prone to submit to pressure when the heat's on. An early press release probably just made his day a bit easier.

'Rob Jenkins,' said Frank as we went in.

'He'll be the one Natalie mentioned.'

'Seemed all right. Saved me doing my shoulder in anyway.'

It had all the chaotic appeal that you might imagine for an artist's studio, and everything about it suggested a pretty bohemian lifestyle.

'That's Natalie,' said Frank, referring to a nude reclining painting in the centre of the studio.

'Yes,' I said drily. I let him gaze at it. He was clearly unable not to gaze, at least for a few moments.

'I'm going to take a look upstairs,' I said.

After a while, he followed me up.

'What exactly do you think we're looking for?' he asked.

'Well, to begin with, we need to find out who her next of kin is, any relatives. So, birth certificate maybe, any medical paperwork, dental stuff.'

We looked in drawers and on shelves. There were signs of filing systems which had been started and then abandoned: bills, reminders, invoices, further reminders, subscriptions, reminders of subscriptions, postcards from a series of names from abroad. There was a funeral service programme for her mother, with a note saying 'Thought you might want to see this, sorry you couldn't attend.'

It struck me how complicated and disorganised people's lives could be, and how much they would not want other people to see the evidence they left behind. How many people leave a mess behind that they are no longer there to justify or explain? I sometimes wondered if my life might eventually end up like that.

'Snap out of it, Nula!' he said, bringing me back to the present. 'There's a diary on the desk downstairs.'

'We'll take that with us. Apart from that, I don't know. Bed unmade. Stained sheets. But we know already she was promiscuous. There's a pile of papers we could go through with a toothcomb, but to be quite honest, I don't think we'd find anything relevant. We know she was having some kind of affair with Natalie, and we know she was also screwing Natalie's dad. I think we have lines to follow up there. We'll keep this closed for the time being. I mean, if Renwick had given us more manpower, we could have people sifting through everything that's in here, but he didn't. End of.'

We went down into the studio.

'Of course,' I said, teasing Frank, 'we could impound the painting of Natalie.'

'Do you really think so?'

'Yeah, I do. But I think you'd have to keep it at your place.'

'More than my marriage is worth,' he said before realising I was taking the piss. 'Fuck off, Nula!' he said.

'Fuck off, ma'am, I think is what you meant!'

Frank laughed.

'Where to next?'

'Let's go back in. Check out what exactly Renwick's said to the media.'

'It's Tuesday afternoon. He could be on the golf course.'

'More than likely! But it might be useful to have another word with Dawn.'

We were ready to leave when, just to one side of the door, we found some gear which we hadn't noticed before. Two folding chairs and a bag with water paints, brushes, templates for tigers and Spiderman, and a cashbox, stuffed with fivers.

'This must be what she had at the festival,' I said.

'So how did it get back here?'

'Unless she brought it back herself.'

'Or someone else did.'

'There's a couple of CCTV cameras on the building opposite.

Worth a try.'

We walked across the cobbled yard to a door which led into a small warehouse with rolls of carpet, sample books and offcuts leaning up against the wall. A staircase led to an upper floor. There was no sign of Rob.

'Hello!' Frank called. 'Hello!'

'Anyone home?' I added.

'Pop my head upstairs, shall I?' said Frank.

He'd gone up three steps when Rob appeared at the top, coming down quickly as if to prevent Frank venturing any further.

'Yes. Can I help?'

'We noticed you've got a couple of CCTV cameras out there. We'd like to see your footage for the day of the festival.'

'I can tell you what you'll find on it,' said Rob.

'Oh yes.'

'I mean, if you're looking to see who went in and out, I think I can clear that one up for you. I mean, you'll find it's me going in. I brought her stuff up from the festival, put it in there. A favour. Like I said, she had me looking after the spare key.'

'Right. Well that would explain how her equipment got back without her. But maybe we can take the tape anyway.'

His initial reaction suggested reluctance.

'Problem with that, is there, Rob?'

'No, no. But I mean, strictly speaking, don't you need a warrant or something?'

'Strictly speaking, Rob, yes, you're perfectly right. But generally speaking, people tend to cooperate.'

He thought about this for a moment, and then said, 'OK, right, yes. Hang on, I'll just go up to the office then.'

He started up the stairs and when Frank began to follow, he turned. 'Won't be a sec,' he said. 'If you don't mind waiting.'

'What do you make of him then?' asked Frank as we drove away.

'I would have said friendly and helpful to start with, but he was definitely cagey about something.'

'Didn't want us upstairs, did he?'

'He's the one Natalie mentioned. Strange, you know, if she had a bit of a down on him, that she'd let him have the spare key.'

'Be interesting to see exactly what's on the tape.'

As expected, Renwick was not in the building.

We delivered the CCTV tape to Simon Pooley who was the team's specialist in digital media and the like, and then watched a playback of Renwick's media release. It showed him standing on the steps outside, cutting a smart figure in his uniform, naming Magda Bentley. It was quite circumspect, which was his style, nothing controversial apart from the early timing.

'He was in a bit of a rush,' said Jack with a knowing look, 'and the local meeja was blocking the switchboard. What more can I say?'

Dawn, however, was more than willing to see us and talk it through.

'Yes, I did,' she said in answer to our question about taking forensic from the lock gate rails. 'And no, she didn't leave any evidence there that I could isolate. To be honest, there was so much. I mean, hundreds of people must have held on, passing by the lock. If there had been blood or something, yes, I could have pinpointed it, but there wasn't. The only thing I've got to give you is on the clothes. They are all Magda's clothes. I mean, you could guess that from the fact that they are female garments: the blouse, the bra, the skirt. We can test for DNA but at this stage I can't really see any point, I think we can assume she was the one who was wearing them. The fact that she came out of the water with just her knickers and pumps on completes the picture. Of course, it may be the case that her clothing will contain traces of DNA from someone else, i.e. amongst others, the perpetrator; but whose it is will be impossible to say unless it is on the national database. Or unless you have a suspect.'

'Needle in a haystack again,' said Frank.

'Oh, finding a needle in a haystack is potentially much easier than this.'

'I've been thinking about our friend Moggy Morton,' I said to Frank on the way back. 'I mean, I know, a bit of a prat.'

'More than a bit of one.'

'Yes, but maybe we should keep him in mind.'

'As a nosy parker, you mean?'

'Yes. Nosy parkers are sometimes useful.'

'OK.'

'Have you still got his card?

'Sacredly stored away about my person.'

'Good.'

We drove on. The sun had been on the car while we were in the studio and I was feeling drowsy.

'So, what tomorrow, ma'am?'

'Let's see in the morning. And let's drop the 'ma'am', shall we? No longer funny.'

'OK, ma'am,' he said.

'I knew you were going to do that.'

'Sorry, ma'am!' he repeated with a chuckle.

'Enough!'

'Tell me though,' he said, 'I mean, just from a personal point of view, when we met Natalie this morning, if her mum hadn't already told us stuff, would you have known that Natalie was gay?'

I could tell he was still preoccupied with the painting of her we'd seen in Magda's studio and was pursuing his male fantasies.

'Have I got some kind of lesbian radar, you mean?'

'Something like that.'

'Like instant recognition at 50 paces? No, Frank, I haven't. Sorry to disappoint you.'

'Just asking.'

'See you in the morning, then. Six.'

'Yes, see you. Six.'

Wendy was waiting for me. She was making moussaka and while it was finishing, I had twenty minutes with Phoebe. I had texted Wendy earlier that Renwick had made me SIO. on the case and she wanted to celebrate, so there was wine; and after dinner, we sat for a couple of hours with coffee and another glass of wine.

By this time, Phoebe was awake and ready for a feed so Wendy told me to go and get straight into bed. As soon as my head was on the pillow I was out like a light, but when I awoke it was still the early hours and the drowsiness brought on by the wine had disappeared completely. Wendy was fast asleep beside me and I could just hear Phoebe's peaceful breathing in the cot at the foot of our bed.

For a short time, it was quite pleasant being awake and comfortable in the middle of all that peacefulness, but after a while my inability to get back to sleep became annoying and I knew it was a bad sign when I started to think about the investigation. Soon, I was processing the whole case, back and forth, back and forth. And my head was full of vague questions.

One of them was to do with Rob Jenkins. I know it's important not to jump to conclusions on appearances, but there was something about him that I didn't trust.

The other thing that kept on joining the merry-go-round of my thoughts was Moggy Morton. Probably an unreliable witness if ever there was one, but what reason could he have for saying he saw Natalie leave the festival with a particular person if it were not true – unless, of course, it was just to cause mischief.

I reminded myself that it was not Natalie who was dead – or missing. And as Mrs Anderson had told us, she was twenty-two and free to come and go as she liked. Whatever she got up to, she was not at this point, or at any point likely to be, part of the investigation.

I was vaguely aware of Wendy getting up to give Phoebe her three o'clock feed but by then my head was steeped in deep tiredness and I knew I had been asleep, and also knew that I was about to go back to sleep again.

CHAPTER 30

Wednesday

Renwick was keen to see us in the morning. He apologised for the early release of the media statement, saying that he had responded under pressure. He had been, in the afternoon, to a family funeral, so I was glad we had resisted any temptation to slip in a golfing innuendo. However, he wanted us to give him something he could use to reassure the 'jackals', as he called them, that the investigation was making progress. We told him how the day had gone and I could see his mind turning over to see how it could be crunched down into a suitable handout.

'About the CCTV from the neighbour,' said Simon, putting up a hand.

'Yes?'

'Pretty much confirms what he says. He lets himself in with the gear. Let's himself out again.'

'Right.'

'Only thing is, there's a gap of ten minutes between the two. Bit odd.'

I caught Frank's eye.

'Maybe admiring the artwork,' I said, deciding not to throw in anything about my misgivings about Rob Jenkins at this stage.

'OK. Good work,' said Renwick. 'What next?'

'Have we had anything back from Leeds, sir?'

It took him a moment to register this.

'Leeds. Mr Anderson, father of the girl who was missing,' I reminded him. 'Not seen since the day of the festival.'

'Right. OK. I'll get on to them now.'

He went into his office.

'How's it going?' asked Geoff Stone who had been hanging around with a coffee. 'I've got a couple of hours if you need help with anything.'

'Just waiting on this phone call,' Frank explained, nodding towards Renwick's office.

'Actually, Geoff,' I said, 'you could have a dig around, see if you can find anything on a guy called Rob Jenkins.'

'He sells carpets,' said Frank. 'Milthwaite.'

'Right, I'll see what I can do.'

'Oh, and Geoff,' I added, 'can you get someone in Records to see if they can find out anything about Magda Bentley's health information. See if that takes us anywhere.'

'No joy,' said Renwick, coming out of his office.

'No joy or no care?' asked Frank.

'Bit of both. They say they phoned through to his faculty and they said he's not due back until the start of term: sometime in September.'

'They didn't push it then.'

'Well look, they gave me the same answer I would probably have given them: workload pressure, manpower shortages etc. etc. I have the feeling they regard us down here as a bit of a backwater, to be honest.'

'Doesn't feel like it,' said Frank.

'Look,' said Renwick. 'If you think this guy is significant, why don't you go over there yourselves and try to flush him out. I'll get back on to Leeds and clear it.'

I looked at Frank and he nodded.

'Sir?'

'Nula?'

'I think it might be an idea to have Magda Bentley's studio secured. I've got the key she left with a neighbour but we don't know if it's the only one. We didn't have time to go through it fully yesterday and there may just be something that'll help.'

'I'll get it organised.'

'Thank you, sir.'

We joined the M62 at Ainley Top and it was clear as we descended the slip road that it was packed, bumper to bumper, with heavy goods traffic.

'I used to do traffic,' said Frank. 'Hated this stretch. Worst in the country for RTAs and long delays.'

It took us twenty-five minutes to get as far as Brighouse. The traffic had begun to ease off a bit by then. We came off at Morley and headed towards the city centre.

'Any idea where we're going when we get there?' asked Frank.

'Arts University. Blenheim Walk, just off Woodhouse Lane.'

'Don't really know Leeds. Apart from Elland Road and the cricket ground at Headingley.'

'Well, it's on the way to Headingley.'

'Know it then, do you, Nula?'

'Used to come here clubbing back in the day.'

'Did you now!'

'Also did a course here, on firearms.'

'Did you fancy being a shooter then?'

'No. Not at all. It was just a training module.'

We found our way through the ring roads and roundabouts onto Woodhouse Lane, past the University Tower and on to Blenheim Walk. It was a modern brick building in a pleasant setting with plenty of greenery. The foyer was very light and very quiet, with a distinct summer vacation feel to it.

We showed our warrant cards and the girl on reception was nervous and eager to help.

'Yes,' she said, 'someone called to ask for Professor Anderson yesterday but I explained that very few staff are here during August. If he'd been in, I'm sure I would have known.'

'Is there anyone else we might contact? A colleague perhaps? A friend?'

'I'm not sure if I should give out… I mean we have to treat confidentiality quite seriously.'

She was right to say this, of course, but she said it apologetically, as if she didn't quite believe it, and I thought it was worth pushing a little bit harder.

'This is a police investigation,' I said firmly. 'It's really quite important that we speak to Professor Anderson.'

She simpered a little, full of uncertainty. 'You could try this address,' she said uneasily, scribbling something down on a sticky note. 'It's in Kirkstall. Not far.'

'And who does this address belong to?'

'It's Gillian Selby. She's an associate lecturer from Ireland. She was working on a project with Professor Anderson last term.'

'Thank you, Sarah,' I said, reading it from the name badge on her lapel. 'You've been very helpful. Is there a phone number to go with this?'

In some pain, she consulted her screen and added a number to the sticky note. 'You will tell her that you insisted, won't you?'

'We will, Sarah. Don't worry.'

Back in the car, I tapped the postcode into the sat nav.

'Aren't we going to call her?'

The sat nav calculated: four miles, eleven minutes.

'Let's just go straight there,' I said. 'If he's there and we call, he might bolt for it.'

'Associate Lecturer. Working on a project together. Do you think we're talking nookie here?'

'Wouldn't surprise me. He's got a track record.'

'Of course, it may be that our little Sarah will call to warn her.'

'Chance we have to take.'

It was a small flat in a new build. The woman who answered the door was perhaps thirty with a shock of lovely black hair, and if Sarah had phoned to warn her of our imminent arrival, she would probably have taken a little more trouble to get fully dressed.

'Ms Selby?'

'Yes?'

We showed our warrant cards.

'May we come in?'

She took us into a nicely furnished room lined by full bookshelves with lithographs set between and a computer station and printer.

'We'd like to talk to Ralph Anderson,' I began. 'He's been away from his home in Milthwaite for several days, and we're anxious to locate him.'

I looked to Frank to pick up on this and, seeing his eye firmly fixed on the swell of Gillian Selby's bosom clearly displayed inside a V-neck sweater which was all she appeared to be wearing above her waist, gave him my sternest glare.

'We're given to understand he is a close working associate of yours and wonder if you can give us any information as to his whereabouts.'

'Well,' she said after an extremely awkward silence. 'He's here. I mean, as a matter of fact, he is just getting ready to go back to Huddersfield this afternoon.'

At this moment, the door opened and in stepped the man who was evidently Ralph Anderson.

'That's right,' he said. 'I heard about this terrible business yesterday. I'm just about to go back home. My wife and daughter, you see.'

'How were you intending to travel, Mr Anderson? By car?'

'No, by train. I came up here by train on Sunday night.'

'In that case, Mr Anderson. We can save you a lot of trouble. We can give you a lift.'

It was, to say the least, an uncomfortable journey back to Milthwaite.

'Do you mind explaining to me,' said Ralph Anderson, 'why you've come all this way to find me?'

'We just have some questions we'd like to put to you, Mr Anderson.'

'And are you going to tell me what these questions are?'

'In due course. A car journey is really not a suitable place for an interview.'

He sat back and said nothing for a few miles. Then he started again. 'Am I under suspicion? Is this what this is all about?'

'As I said, we can't carry out an interview except in a proper place.'

'Am I not entitled to some sort of explanation?'

'It's simply a matter of answering some questions about your absence from home and your whereabouts over the last few days.'

'Well, it's simple. I can tell you now. I've been in Leeds. You've met Miss Selby. You can probably guess the reason why.'

We did not respond to this, though I saw Frank's hand twitch on the steering wheel. Frank had obviously guessed.

Another few miles passed by.

'And where is this interview to take place?'

'Either at your home or you can come down to HQ in town.'

'And when? Today?'

'Tomorrow morning. We'll drop you off at home now. There are probably some conversations you need to have with your wife and your daughter.'

'I'll come in tomorrow morning. What time?'

'Nine o'clock?'

'Sooner the better. Will I need my solicitor?'

'You're not under caution so we are not obliged to provide you with a brief, but if you want your legal representative to be present, it's up to you.'

We dropped him off at Crofters Mount.

'Be some sparks flying there tonight, I don't doubt,' said Frank as we drove away. 'Definitely some feathers flying.'

'Which is it to be, Frank, sparks or feathers?' I joked.

'Probably both!'

'Well, you might be right. What did you make of him then, Frank?'

'Nula, I haven't got the vocabulary to describe what I made of him. Not in decent company, anyway.'

'Well, thank you, Frank,' I said, 'I'm flattered.'

'I'll tell you what though, Nula. I can see why his missus was so keen to put us onto him. I'm inclined to think less badly of her than I did before.'

'Result then,' said Renwick when we went back in. 'Nice work.'

'Bit of luck involved, guv, but we got him, yes.'

We went to the whiteboard in the incident room which now had, besides the pictures of Magda, photographs of the scene and of the clothes that had been found in the woods nearby.

'Right,' said Renwick, 'this is Day 3 of the investigation. We've made good progress but we're reaching the stage now when we need to focus in. So, right, persons of interest. Ralph Anderson, obviously.' He wrote the name down on the whiteboard. 'Nula?'

'Rob Jenkins, the neighbour. Maybe Adam Mitchell.'

'Who?'

'Local writer. Somebody thinks they saw him leaving the festival with Natalie.'

Renwick thought about this for a moment. 'OK, we'll add him. Maybe have a word. Now, I might be showing my ignorance completely here, but how do you spell Mitchell?'

Laughing, we helped him through it, though by the end none of us was sure we'd got it right.

'Good for team building,' Renwick suggested. It was difficult to tell if this was serious or a joke. With Renwick it is sometimes difficult to make that distinction.

'Natalie?' I suggested. All eyes turned to me. 'Well,' I said, 'I'm just saying she's a person of interest. She had just made a pretty devastating discovery about her father and her girlfriend – if that's what we call her - she disappeared for a day and a half and I don't know what Frank thinks but there is something about her account of things that somehow doesn't ring quite true.'

'OK,' said Renwick without consulting Frank and beginning to write. 'Fuck me!' he exploded. 'Is that with just a T or is it TH?'

At that moment, Geoff Stone came into the room. He looked at the board and immediately said, 'You've spelt Mitchell wrong.'

Nobody dared laugh.

'Right,' Renwick began to conclude. 'We've got one person here who is an obvious suspect and he's coming in for an interview tomorrow. Nula will you take it?'

'Yes, guv.'

'Frank?'

'Naw,' said Frank. 'Couldn't be detached. Probably end up thumping him. Let Geoff do it.'

'You up for it, Geoff?'

'Guv.'

'Right, that's settled.'

After Renwick had retired to his office, we all got coffees and gathered round Geoff's desk.

'OK,' he began. 'Magda is registered with a GP in Huddersfield. Receptionist tells me she's never requested an appointment for treatment though she was on birth control medication. Next of kin down as a Mrs M Bentley with an address in Wakefield. Follow up on that is that Margaret Bentley died six years ago, aged sixty-four. Presumably the mother. No other relatives that we can trace.'

'Nice work Geoff.'

'And your other little angel, Rob Jenkins, well no angel at all really. Minor drug offences as a teenager, nothing new there, complaints about domestic violence from his ex but she never preferred charges. Bit of a voyeur apparently, some complaints about his little peeping Tom activities but again no charges. Looks after an old disabled mother. That's his saving grace, but generally regarded as a bit of an unsavoury character.'

'I got my bloody carpets from him!' said Frank.

'Thanks Geoff. That's great. Corresponds with what Natalie told us.'

'How do you mean?'

'The peeping Tom bit. Apparently, Magda thought he was keeping a lookout on her.'

'In that case,' said Geoff, 'why not get all his CCTV stuff in, any computers, too. Have a good sift through. I'll organise that if you want.'

'Cheers.'

'I'll see Renwick first thing. Get a warrant sorted. Then get Simon out there with a team. Oh, and we secured the studio.'

'Thanks.'

'Anyone for the pub?'

'Just one,' I said. I texted Wendy to say I'd be a bit late. I didn't really want to go to the pub but there are times when you feel you owe something back to the team.

CHAPTER 31

Thursday

Ralph Anderson was on time for his interview the next morning. We were not. A major RTA up on the motorway near Hartshead meant it was all hands to the deck, with some of us out at the scene along with the rest of the emergency services and some of us covering at the station. It was nearly half past ten before he was escorted into Interview Room 2 and he was not well pleased.

I apologised for the delay and explained the context but he merely gave me a disdainful look, as if his time was a priority above all other considerations. He crossed his legs and half turned away.

Geoff explained the procedure. 'As my colleague has explained, you're not under caution, Mr Anderson. We are simply here to establish facts. For that reason, we will not be making a tape recording of the interview. If subsequently we find reasonable grounds to charge you, your rights will be read to you, interviews will be more formal and you will be entitled to legal representation. Is all that clear, Mr Anderson?'

'Do you think I'm an idiot. I'm a bloody university professor, for Christ's sake!' His flash of anger pinnacled and then subsided. 'Yes,' he said wearily, 'it is all clear, so can we now get on with it.'

'Nula,' said Geoff, inviting me to continue.

'Nula, nice name,' said Ralph Anderson and I could see his eyes doing a swift traverse of my upper body. 'Unusual, I mean.'

'You were at the festival on Sunday, Mr Anderson.'

'Yes.'

'And you stayed how long?'

'I don't know, about two hours, maybe three. I know some of the organisers, people in the community. I wanted to chat. About how wonderfully it was going.'

'You know that Magda Bentley's body was found in the canal the next morning.'

'Is that a question?... yes, obviously I do. It was on the local radio news on Tuesday.'

'We know from the post-mortem that Magda died sometime after seven o'clock and before midnight.'

'Long gone, my friends. Long gone by then.'

'Did you see Magda at the festival?'

'Yes, I did.'

'And did you speak to her?'

'Yes, I did.'

We waited.

'I spoke to her because I wanted to tell her that I considered her relationship with my daughter to be inappropriate – an opinion in which I now feel fully vindicated.'

'Was that the whole of the conversation?'

'No.' He took a long slow breath. 'As you are already aware, Magda informed me that her relationship with my daughter had become sexual. She also informed me that Natalie, my daughter, knew of the fact that I too had been, albeit very briefly, in a sexual relationship with her.'

'And how did you react to that?'

'I was shocked.'

'Shocked.'

'Yes.'

'Not angry? Your wife says she saw you talking to Magda and that you went off in quite a state.'

'If you're going to bring what my wife says into this, I'm going to terminate this interview with immediate effect.'

'There were plenty of other people around who might have witnessed what happened,' I said, thinking, a little mischievously, of Moggy Morton. 'We are getting a lot of information from our door-to-door inquiries.' This wasn't strictly true. In fact, it wasn't really true at all because we simply did not have the manpower to do extensive door-to-door, but it had the right effect.

'I might have shown momentary anger, but my anger is just that. Momentary. I am basically a reasonable being, and reason soon prevails.'

'So, tell me what happened next.'

'I went to the car park of the pub where my car was parked, decided I'd probably had too much to drink, called a taxi to the station in Huddersfield and caught a train to Leeds.'

'That seems to be a strange sequence of decisions.'

'Does it?'

'Wouldn't you say so?'

'Think about it.'

'Explain.'

'It's pretty obvious, I would have thought. But let me spell it out for you. If I go home as planned and as my nearest and dearest expect, I sip a relaxing glass of wine awaiting their return. All very cosy. They come in and the whole ugly business spills out like vomit. The alternative? Go to Leeds. I chose to go to Leeds.'

'You were obviously in a quandary, Mr Anderson.'

'Quandary, Nula, is not the word for it.'

'Do you have any proof to corroborate your journey to Leeds?' said Geoff Stone, coming in quickly to diminish the effect of his familiarity.

'Taxi driver from the White Hart. Small local company. Train ticket to Leeds which, happily, I just happen to have with me.'

He took out his wallet and produced a rail ticket dated Sunday, with a train specified: the 6.30 p.m. from Huddersfield.

'So you see,' he said. 'A good thirty minutes before the earliest time this death occurred, I was winging my way to Leeds.'

I felt non-plussed.

Geoff took the ticket and looked at it.

'This ticket isn't clipped,' he said.

'What?'

'This ticket hasn't been clipped so it isn't proof you actually travelled.'

'Oh for Christ's sake, is it my fault there was no attendant on the train between Huddersfield and Leeds?'

'We'll need some time to follow up on this,' I said.

'Follow up, how?'

'Taxis, CCTV.'

'And what am I to do in the meantime?'

'You're free to go back home, Mr Anderson.'

'Oh for God's sake, don't make me go back there,' he said. 'Can't you just put me in the cells for a while? Overnight if need be.'

'What's your view?' asked Geoff afterwards.

'Possibly guilty,' I said. 'How about you?'

'Possibly not guilty,' he replied. 'He may be a very unpleasant human being, but that doesn't make him a murderer. You have to ask yourself, Nula, is your view influenced by the fact that you want a result? It's your first SIO, obviously you want to make an impression. But one: if he was guilty, he would have called for a brief long before we got through that session and we would have had a sequence of *'No comment'*, and two: as far as I can see, unless he went into a total rage and was not answerable for what he did, he had absolutely nothing to gain from killing Magda.'

'Right,' I said, impressed with Geoff's cool reasoning but still thinking he might be wrong.

'What if,' I said, 'he is basically a narcissist. He controls the way the world is according to his own vision and then, when the vision is threatened, he sets out to destroy the person who he sees as his biggest antagonist.'

Geoff nodded. 'Well, that's one way of profiling him. Let's see what the CCTV comes up with,' he said. 'But bear in mind, even if there's no evidence on the CCTV to support his claim that he travelled up to Leeds, you still only have circumstantial evidence. You can't arrest someone for not going to Leeds.'

'But we could start digging deeper.'

'True.'

Renwick had come in on the end of this and was nodding his head in agreement. He had the troubled look on his face that he often had when he was being hassled by the media or hassled from above. It was Day 4 and we still had nothing definite.

'I think it's time to do another TV appeal,' he said. 'Put her photograph up, ask for any information, give a number to call. I've kept it to a minimum so far because I know the switchboard will be jammed with people who recognise her as the face painter, but if we sift through it, we might just get some crumb of a lead. Nula, you fancy taking that on?'

This came like a bombshell but I knew I had to do it. I stammered out a 'Yes' trying to conceal the sudden hot rush in my nerves.

'Good. I'll get the Press Room ready and have them in for two o'clock'.

Geoff tapped me on the elbow. 'You'll be fine,' he said.

Frank, who'd been standing in the background, gave me a look of commiseration.

'Frank, do you think you could sort out this CCTV stuff? We'll need the reels from Huddersfield and Leeds, between six and eight Sunday night. Oh, and try Alpha Taxis, see if he was picked up at the White Hart.'

'What about taxis at the Leeds end?'

'No. Too big. But if they've got any footage from the taxi rank at the side of the station, that might help.'

'OK, ma'am. I'll get on it straight away.'

It seemed funny the way 'ma'am' was beginning to sound natural from Frank. But my vanity did not take anything away from the ordeal that lay ahead.

Lots of coppers are nervous about speaking in public. Being in court can be an ordeal, especially if you're not totally on top of your notebook, but court has certain set patterns and routines and you get used to it, not least because it's something you have to do so often. Informal press statements aren't too bad because it's just a handful of guys in the room, but a TV appeal is a much bigger deal. For a start there's a camera in the room

—a TV camera that is—as well as the flashes from the press photographers, and you are doing it for the public. It might go out five or six times on local TV stations, might even make it into the National News. That, however sure you are of yourself, is scary.

I immediately started working on a script. It would only be a minute—maybe less—but I felt I had to know exactly what I was going to say, word for word. That meant a script and then learning it so thoroughly that I could deliver it as if it wasn't a script – if that makes sense. I had three coffees but couldn't eat a thing. Finally, I went to the restroom, did a little bit on my hair and face, did a last-minute rehearsal and then made my way to the Press Room.

There were more people there than I had imagined and, as well as the cameras, there was spotlighting on me so that I could hardly see through the glare.

'Just talk slowly and clearly straight to the camera,' said a young woman who sounded nice and helpful. She gave me more advice but by the time the appeal started I'd forgotten what it was. At the last minute, I noticed that a picture of Magda's face had been projected onto a screen to the side. Then I heard my voice talking. It seemed as if it was actually someone else's voice but there I was going through my script, staring at the camera, probably—I thought at the time—like a rabbit caught in the headlights. But I got through it: 'The body retrieved from the canal at Milthwaite on Monday morning has, as you already know, been named as Magda Bentley, a local artist. Many people attending the festival on Sunday will have seen her doing face painting sessions and we are asking for any specific information, anything unusual, perhaps anything untoward that might help with our inquiries.' I gave the contact number and said 'Thank you.'

And then someone said, 'Questions.' Questions! I hadn't realised there would be questions. My heart was in my mouth.

'You used the word *untoward*. Can you tell us exactly what you mean by that?'

'Well,' I said, 'if I knew the answer to that I'd probably have the case solved already.'

I hadn't meant to be funny, it was just what came out naturally, but it caused a roll of laughter and I have to admit that settled my nerves. The rest of the questions I was able to parry with standard police-speak about not being able to comment on an ongoing operation. Everybody said it had gone OK but I can tell you, I breathed a deep sigh of relief when it was over.

I got a sandwich and another coffee and went to my desk, giving myself a quiet breather just to think it all through and work through the next steps. Going back to Magda's studio was high on the list. Had we not had the drive up to Leeds, I would have done that yesterday. I also wanted to have another chat with Natalie. I still felt uneasy about the account she had given of things, and I wondered if there was anything to be ferreted out there. But I put those things on hold until Frank came back with information about CCTV and taxis. Despite what Geoff had said, I felt that if there was any reason to question what Ralph Anderson had said about travelling up to Leeds, our focus should be to get him back in and give him a grilling under caution. Brief or no brief, we could put him through it and watch his reactions.

Meanwhile, as Renwick came through to tell me, the presence at the site had been 'scaled down'. What he meant, when I pushed him on this, was that all the uniform officers had been pulled out and reassigned. He looked uncomfortable telling me this. 'We've got all we can from it,' he said, 'and the police presence just attracts prurient curiosity, but your TV Appeal was great. Well done, nice work. If that doesn't do the trick, nothing will.'

He patted me on the shoulder even as the word 'bullshit' emerged, fully formed but not expressed, on my lips.

I realised something in that moment that I hadn't before, and it has stayed with me ever since. Renwick wasn't concerned with the case on its own merits, i.e. the solving of a crime, he was concerned with how it would play out at a media level. As an unsolved crime, it would not greatly matter and the media would soon forget it. It was true, Renwick was dealing with inadequate resources and had to deploy manpower accordingly, but manpower deployed in the case of an obviously promiscuous and gay/bi-sexual woman did not rate highly in his priorities. I felt a stab in my vitals. Had he only made me SIO on this case because it was of such little importance to him?

The railway people were much more accommodating than the police in Leeds had been. By five o'clock we had digital copies of the CCTV reels we had asked for. Frank had already established that, yes, a taxi had picked up Mr Anderson from the White Hart going to the station in Huddersfield at 5.50 p.m. on Sunday. I clicked on the link and watched the footage from Huddersfield. There were a few people on the platform, none of them recognisable as Ralph Anderson. Then, at 6.28 p.m., just as the Leeds train was coming in, he appeared on the platform. In the movement into the train, it was unclear whether or not he had mounted.

I sat back and started to go through the Leeds footage. Leeds, a much bigger station, much more going on. Impossible to tell exactly who got off the 6.30 from Huddersfield. I went to the footage of the taxi rank. I had to rewind and play it through three times but in the end there was no doubt. There was Ralph Anderson, getting into a taxi at Leeds station.

I went home feeling utterly demoralised.

CHAPTER 32

At home, I had to submit to the embarrassment of seeing myself on the TV doing the appeal.

'You were fab,' said Wendy.

'No, I wasn't,' I said, remembering every bit of nervous self-consciousness and seeing it there so obviously on the screen.

'Very fanciable,' she said, and I think she realised straightaway that it was the least appropriate thing to say.

It somehow set the tone for one of those evenings. She'd had a bad day with Phoebe and wanted more from me, but I was drained. I had nothing to give.

'OK,' she said, just after eight, 'I'm going to bed. Phoebe will need feeding again at ten and I'm absolutely shot.'

She kissed me. It was a light, routine, meaningless kiss, though whether on her part or mine, I wasn't sure.

There had occasionally been times before when we had parted in a kind of silence, allowing each other the space to go away and think; but this was the first time it had happened since Phoebe had been born—the first time, probably, I reflected, since she had been conceived—that we had had one of our long overnight moody silences.

I don't know why I got into such a dark mood after she went to bed. I had only been back at work four days but already, it seemed, the strain was showing. What would it be like, I asked myself, when Wendy's maternity leave finished and she went back on her nursing shifts? We had talked about all that before, plenty of times, but always in that optimistic mood where you feel that there isn't anything in the world that is impossible, given the right mindset.

I suppose too, that at the back of my mind I was thinking about my career. I had always said that I was not particularly ambitious for a stellar career and that remained true, but I had to admit that being put in charge of the case had stimulated something new in me and I suspected that I would be hungry for a little more of that even after the case was over.

I went up to bed at ten, just when I heard Phoebe starting to cry. I changed her nappy as Wendy was sorting herself out and then got quickly into bed.

When Wendy got in twenty minutes later, I pretended to be asleep. She didn't say anything, just settled in with her back to me and was soon asleep, so far as I could tell. Perhaps she had been thinking the same thoughts as me.

As the previous night, tiredness was not a guarantee of sleep. Quite the opposite if anything, and tonight I didn't have the wine drowsiness to get me started. My mind was working overtime again but this time not on the case.

I seemed to go straight for my own jugular. What would happen if things ever got so bad that we reached the point of deciding to split up? It seemed unthinkable now, but then probably most—if not all—people who split up thought at one time that it could never happen. But if we did ever reach that point, what would happen to Phoebe?

Of course, my name was on the birth certificate too as a Responsible Parent—though we had had to jump through some legal hoops for that—but Wendy was the birth mother. Would that give her legal priority? If neither of us wanted to give her up, would we have to go through some process to determine custody? And how would either of us cope in that kind of scenario? It was too frightening to think about and yet here I was doing exactly that!

I met Wendy when I was twenty-four. I'd always known I was gay though I had a few boyfriends before I was absolutely certain. When you're going through all the changes of adolescence, with so much going on, your mind is sometimes like a kaleidoscope. There were a few girlfriends too, but nothing serious. I come from a Nigerian family, brought up in an Irish community. 'Coming out' in that context was not a realistic prospect so I couldn't officially bring a girlfriend home to meet mum and dad. There were other girls in the same boat though, as I discovered, so some one-night stands came my way, usually after parties and that kind of stuff. Then I joined the police and moved to England: to Liverpool first, where I started my training, and then to Yorkshire, and my career came first. Outside of work, I just wanted to party and have fun. I was the first to agree to go to the pub and often amongst the last to leave, and I think my main priority was just to fit in. I had sex with a few men. It didn't horrify me but I just thought it wasn't all it was cracked up to be. I think I was pretty shallow. Just rites of passage. Yes, now I've done this, yes, now I've tried that - in some ways it was all just a laugh.

And then I met Wendy and everything changed. I began to understand the meaning of being in a relationship. It was as if an important piece of my world jigsaw had suddenly fallen into place. Within a couple of months, I'd moved in with her and, quite importantly, I'd officially come out, not just to my family who were actually great about it, but to my work colleagues too. That took some building up to but when it was done, I felt a huge sense of relief. There were a few jokes and sideswipes, but nothing worse than the stuff all women get in the force.

I must have slept through Phoebe's two o'clock feed, but when I woke again it was half past five and, with all the detritus of my *what-ifs* of the night before, my head was full of disturbance and depression.

Then I felt the touch of Wendy's hand on my shoulder and immediately her hand slipped under my arm onto my breast. I felt the whole warmth of her body against mine and it was like heaven.

I turned towards her and we embraced. 'Let's make love,' I said. 'I want to. Please, I want to.'

'So do I,' she said practically, 'but it's six o'clock and you know what that means, don't you?'

As if perfectly on cue, we heard the little gurgles from her cot which meant that Phoebe was hungry.

CHAPTER 33

Friday

The first thing I did when I got into the station was to telephone Ralph Anderson to tell him that CCTV had confirmed his journey to Leeds the previous Sunday.

'So I'm off the hook, am I? You could have saved yourself a lot of trouble if you'd simply listened to what I told you. You've finished with me then, have you?'

'For the time being,' I said, a bit naughtily, hoping it would provoke a response. It did.

'What the... what exactly do you mean, *For the time being*?'

'We may need to speak to you again for more information,' I said. 'It's an ongoing inquiry. So, be a good idea to keep your phone switched on. Though, if not, we'll know where to find you in Leeds.'

He didn't like this, and I felt I had maybe overstepped the mark but Frank, standing next to me, was sniggering approvingly.

'Nice work, ma'am,' he said with a wink. 'Oh, by the way, we've got Rob's stuff in. I went out with Simon's lot.'

'Bet he didn't like that.'

'He did NOT like it one little bit!'

'Well, we'll see what it turns up.'

Renwick was right in predicting that the appeal would have the switchboard jammed – well, not the actual switchboard: it was a dedicated line where people could leave a message and contact number with the assurance we would get back to them if there was anything we thought could help the inquiry. Frank and I went through it for an hour, and if we were hoping for some precious little gem—something that would unlock the mystery, or at least set us on to our next step—it simply wasn't there. There were plenty of timewasters: some who said what a nice person she seemed painting their kids' faces, some who said she was fit and they wouldn't have minded giving her one, some who said she looked like a bit of a tart if you asked them. Quite a few didn't leave any contact details. Of course, we could have traced them and warned them about wasting police time, but to do that would have been wasting our time anyway, so it seemed pointless.

'This is getting us nowhere,' Frank said.

I had to agree with him.

'You all right, Nula?'

'Sorry, Frank, just a bit tired.'

'Who wouldn't be?' he suggested. That, I realised, was Frank's essential kindness, and I also realised at that moment that I valued it more, much more, than Geoff's clinical coldness.

'And in the meantime, I think we should go up and have a word with this guy Mitchell.'

'I thought the girl gave him an alibi.'

'She does, yes, and he gives her one, but only on the say-so of Moggy Morton. According to Moggy, they left the festival together. Let's assume that that bit's true. We don't know for sure that they stayed in each other's company, do we?'

His cottage was on the hillside above Milthwaite, near enough to walk into town, with a good view across the valley on one side.

'Good place for a writer to live, I would have thought,' said Frank as we approached the door.

It took a couple of minutes and a few separate knocks before he answered.

'Sorry about that,' he said on opening the door. 'I was lying down. Having a bit of a nap.'

'Sorry to disturb you, Mr Mitchell. Just wondering if you'd mind answering a few questions for us.'

He gestured for us to come in. 'Is it about Magda?'

'Yes, it is.'

'Thought so. Come through. Take a seat. Terrible business. Well, go on, fire away.'

'So tell us, Mr Mitchell, how long have you known her, Magda Bentley?'

'Eight years maybe. Something like that. Since she came here, more or less.'

'Long time then.'

'Long time, yes.'

'And how would you describe your relationship with her?'

He grinned. 'Close,' he said. 'I'd say close. We were lovers once, if you like, for a short time, back in the day, but that particular well ran dry a long while ago.'

'No ill feelings?'

'None. Best of pals. We're both artists, not always very steadfast in our affections. We understood each other, did Magda and me.'

'We have witnesses who can place you at the festival on Sunday.'

'I don't doubt it. I was there all afternoon.'

'We have a witness who claims to have seen you leaving the festival site with Natalie Anderson.'

'Let me guess. Moggy Morton.'

This, I have to admit, took us by surprise. It must have shown.

He chortled. 'Don't be dismayed by my supernatural powers of deduction,' he said. 'I saw old Moggy in the pub last night. He apologised to me for trying to get me clapped in irons.'

'Right, OK,' I said, regathering my composure. 'But the point is not who the witness is but whether or not it's true.'

'Moggy is always one for a good tale, especially if it's lurid rather than one that's accurate. He may have seen me talking to Natalie just before I set off for home but that is all he saw. But I presume you've spoken to Natalie herself.'

'We have, yes.'

He made a slight tilt of his head, as if allowing us to reveal what Natalie might have said, then smiled in a wry sort of way. 'Well, I won't ask you to betray witness confidentiality or anything like that, and I really, really don't mean to be rude, but the question remains: if I had left the festival in Natalie Anderson's company, what business would it be of Moggy Morton, or anyone else for that matter, present company included?'

'We're just trying to establish facts,' I said, knowing that it sounded weak.

'Unless, of course,' he continued, 'there is some other related matter, of a criminal nature. Then, of course, you'd only be doing your duty to give me a good grilling.'

'There isn't,' I conceded.

'Well, I'm glad to hear that,' he replied, smiling almost graciously.

'No flies on him,' said Frank as we drove away.

'No. Cool cookie. But I think we'll pay Natalie another visit tomorrow. Tie up any loose threads.'

'OK, boss,' said Frank. I think he'd decided that *boss* was something he could live with comfortably.

'Another thing, Frank. Just a hunch really, nothing more than that, but I think we should get someone onto Steeples.'

'The hardware place?'

'Yes. Just check if anybody's been in to get any keys cut this week.'

'OK, boss. Leave it with me.'

'You coming for a drink?' he asked when we got back in.

'No,' I said.

I just wanted to get back to Wendy and Phoebe.

That night I tried to do what I'd failed to do for the week so far: put the case out of my mind for a few hours in the evening. Wendy met me at the door with a hug.

'I've missed you!' she said. 'I've missed you all day. Every single minute of it.'

We stood by the door and embraced until we were both as

horny as hell.

'Look,' I said at last, 'much as I want to slip right in bed with you at this very minute, my darling, I haven't eaten all day and I am really, really, really hungry.'

'You and Phoebe both!' she said, laughing, though still not letting me go.

'Later?'

'Later,' she said. 'Meantime, you can call for a pizza.'

CHAPTER 34

Saturday

Next morning, just after ten, we pulled up again outside Crofters Mount. Mrs Anderson opened the door; Natalie was standing behind her in the hallway. Mrs Anderson gave us to understand that her husband was not there.

'I take it you know that we checked his alibi and it confirms he was in Leeds from early evening on Sunday.'

'At least he's not a murderer then,' said Natalie with some bitterness.

'He came back here on Wednesday after you interviewed him. It wasn't very pleasant but it gave us the chance to sort some things out. He's gone back to Leeds now. He won't be coming here again.'

We explained that we'd come to have another word with Natalie, to ask her a few more questions. Natalie said that she wanted to do it without her mum being present. Mrs Anderson obliged by going out into the kitchen.

'What is it, then?' asked Natalie, looking very uncomfortable.

'Well, since we saw you last, Natalie, we've been working through a lot of statements from potential witnesses and according to one of them, you were seen leaving the festival with a chap called Adam Mitchell at about seven o'clock.'

'Do you know Mr Mitchell?' asked Frank.

'Yes. He comes in the pub where I work.'

We waited. It was clear that Natalie did not have Adam Mitchell's composure when confronted with the question.

'Did you leave with him?'

She nodded her head.

'And is that where you were overnight? At his house?'

She nodded again.

'When we spoke to you on Tuesday, why didn't you tell us where you'd been?'

'I didn't think it mattered. I was confused. I didn't want to get him in trouble.'

'Trouble? Why should you think he'd be in trouble.'

'Because if people knew I'd gone back to his house, they might think badly of him. They might jump to conclusions.'

'Did he try anything on, Natalie?' asked Frank.

'No,' said Natalie, shaking her head emphatically. 'Nothing like that. It was all my fault.'

'You mean something happened between you and it was your fault?'

'No!' said Natalie again, now with something like exasperation.

'OK, Natalie,' I said, feeling that Frank was being a bit heavy-handed. 'Just tell us how it was, just so we can get a clear picture of everything. Why do you think you were in some way at fault?'

'Because it was me who put pressure on him to let me go home with him and stay. I didn't want to come home here. You know the reason for that. I had nowhere else to go. He was kind to me when I was upset and I took advantage of it.'

'So he didn't ask you to stay?'

'No. I knew he felt awkward about it but I just sort of coerced him into it. I just couldn't face the prospect of coming home if my dad was here.

'So you can vouch that he was at home between Sunday night and Monday afternoon?

'Yes. Well, apart from when I was asleep. Even then.'

'How do you mean?'

'Well, I was in a spare room. But I didn't actually sleep very well and every time I woke up, I could hear him snoring.'

'Right.'

For a moment, I smiled to myself at this moment of absurdity:

the potential for a murder case hanging on a witness testimony of having heard someone snoring.

'So, Natalie, you were saying just before that Adam Mitchell was kind to you?'

'Yes.'

'When you were upset?'

'Yes.'

'And were you upset because of something that happened at the festival?'

'Yes.'

I waited for a moment. She didn't elaborate.

'Was it at the festival that you found out about your father's affair with Magda?'

'No,' she conceded.

'You already knew?'

She nodded.

'But you would have seen her at the festival?'

'Yes.'

'That can't have been easy. Did you say anything to her?'

'Yes. I confronted her about it.'

'And...?'

'She was just very rude to me.'

'So was that why you were upset?'

'I suppose so, yes.'

'You suppose so?'

'I'd been up and down for a few days, because of her and because of my dad, and I had a bit to drink, and then I just got upset.'

'OK, thank you, Natalie. Just one last thing. If you already knew about your dad and Magda, who was it that told you?'

She looked stumped.

'Someone must have told you, Natalie. It must have come from somewhere.'

For a moment, there was a sense that she was resisting something, but an equally strong sense that she was going to give way.

'Nathan,' she said at last.
'Nathan? Who is Nathan?'
'Nathan Brook. He's a friend. An old friend from school.'
'And he knew your dad and Magda were having an affair?'
'Yes.'
We waited.
'He'd seen them together.'
'OK. So did he tell you where and how he saw them?'
'At her studio.'
'This is getting complicated, Natalie.'
'OK, for fuck's sake!' said Natalie, losing it for a moment. 'He'd been another one of Magda's 'things'. Like me. He went there to see her and my dad was there. End of story.'
'And can you give me an address for this Nathan?'
'What for? He's got nothing to do with it.'
'Just to rule him out of the inquiry.'
'This is just like a nightmare,' said Natalie. 'When is it going to stop?'
I felt sorry for her but I also knew we had to get some kind of formal grip on all this.
'I'd like you to come with us to make a statement, Natalie, just so we've got it all clear.'
'Oh God, am I a suspect?'
'I didn't say that but we'd like you to come with us anyway. Just voluntarily. That would be much better than under caution.'

Half an hour later then, we had her in the interview room, though in the circumstances we had agreed that I would take her statement alone.

'So, Natalie,' I explained, 'because there are different accounts of events on Sunday night, particularly with regard to yourself and your movements, I want you to go through what happened from you leaving the festival up to the point where you turned up back at home the following evening. Is that OK?'

'I think so,' says Natalie nervously.

'Just go through it step by step. I'll write down what you say, and you can check it as we go along and change it if you think what I've written isn't what you meant. Then at the end, you'll be able to read it all through and then sign it to confirm that it's accurate.'

'Right.'

'When you're ready then, Natalie.'

'I left the festival with Mr Mitchell. I was a bit upset about something and he said he would walk with me back to my house. We walked along the towpath by the canal. It was comforting.'

'How do you mean, comforting, Natalie?'

She narrowed her eyes, concentrating, as if to bring it back into focus. 'He let me link my arm through his. I felt safe. There was even a smell about him, like the musty smell of a man's coat maybe, a soothing smell maybe even like the smell of shaving soap.'

'Well, I don't think we need to include all of that.'

'No, perhaps not. But it was important to me because I thought it was like being a with a real father, one who cared about me, one I could trust with all the things had been bothering me.'

'OK, Natalie, go on.'

'I asked him if he was better. He'd been in hospital, you see, and I visited him, and I wondered if he would ask me why I was upset but he didn't. But I told him I was going to do teacher training and he asked me about it. Then, when we came to the path from the canal which was nearest to my house, I asked him if we could walk on a bit further.'

She took us through to the next morning.

'He told me I had to go home. He made me some toast and coffee and then said I had to go straight home, straightaway, and I would have done too but then, as he got up from the table, he fainted. Well, I mean he slouched back onto a couch but he obviously wasn't right.

'It only lasted a short time but afterwards, he didn't seem quite right. I asked should I call an ambulance, but he said no. So I stayed there until I was sure he was OK.'

'And then, eventually, you went home.'
'Yes.'
'OK, Natalie, so now tell me about Nathan.'
'Why? Nathan's got nothing to do with all this.'
'You know that isn't strictly true, Natalie, don't you? Mmm? So tell me about Nathan. Let's get this done properly, shall we?'

'OK, Natalie', I said to her finally. 'Just read this through and tell me if there is anything you want to change.'

Natalie pushed a strand of hair away from her face and began to read through what I had written.

I left the festival with Mr Mitchell. I was a bit upset about something and he said he would walk with me back to my house. We walked along the towpath by the canal. When we got to the place where the path goes off towards my house, I asked him if we could walk on a bit further. He said we could walk as far as the bridge and then turn back. I knew the bridge was near his house so I asked if we could go back there for some coffee. I ran on ahead. I didn't wait for him to agree. We had some coffee and I asked for a whisky but he said no. I then asked if he would let me stay there overnight. He said no and said he would walk me home. I was then upset again and in the end, he said I could sleep in the spare room as long as I phoned home to say I was safe. I went outside and then told him there was no reply but I'd left a message. In fact, I hadn't left a message. He made breakfast for me in the morning and told me quite a few times that it was time to go home. I kept on delaying, partly because he seemed to be unwell. In the end, I did go but I went for a long walk on my own before I actually went home. I told Mr Mitchell that I would tell people that I had stayed over with some friends.

Nathan Brook is an old school friend. It was Nathan who told me that he thought my father was having an affair with Magda Bentley. He told me he had seen them together. I had told Nathan I was having an affair with Magda Bentley. He was worried for me and wanted to protect me.

'Is there anything else you want to add, Natalie?'
'No.'

'Is there anything that you want to take out?'

'No.'

'Would you say that the words in the statement are yours, Natalie, and not words anyone else has suggested?'

'Yes.'

'OK then, Natalie. It just needs your signature at the bottom.'

After she had made her statement, I offered to drive Natalie home but she said she would prefer to go home on her own. I got myself a coffee and waited for Frank to return. Meantime, I tried using the phone number Natalie had given me to get hold of her friend Nathan. There was no reply. I asked Jack in reception to find me an address.

I told Frank that I'd called Nathan a few times with no reply. 'I've got the address so maybe we'll pay him a visit. First off, though, I think we'd better just see if we can wipe the slate clean with Mr Mitchell.'

A storm was blowing down the valley as we drove out there: the tail end of one of those cyclones that start over the Bahamas and wreak havoc in the southern United States. The rain was lashing against the windscreen.

'They should keep their cyclones to themselves,' suggested Frank, 'then we'd all be a lot happier.'

'You should have been a diplomat, Frank. I don't know what it is, but you've just got it.'

Torrents of water were swirling down the lane outside Adam Mitchell's cottage.

'Two visits in two days.' he said, opening the door to us, 'To what do I owe this honour?'

'May we come in?'

'By all means. Come in, take your wet coats off. The kettle is on if you would like some tea.'

'That won't be necessary,' I said, blotting out a response from Frank which sounded dangerously as if it was going to come out as *Yes, please, thank you, that would be very nice, have you got any biscuits?*

We sat down. He waited, fingers poised in a cage, for us to begin.

'When we spoke to you earlier, Mr Mitchell, you told us that Natalie Anderson did not accompany you from the festival and that she did not spend the night and some hours of the next day here with you.'

'I did,' said Adam Mitchell with the calm confidence of someone who is not at all perturbed.

'Natalie has, since our visit to you yesterday, made a detailed statement to the effect that the opposite is the case.'

'Good,' said Adam Mitchell.

'Excuse me?'

'She told me that she was going to say that she stayed with friends. So as not to cast any unpleasant speculation on me, I think. Of course, at that stage, neither of us knew that there had been… that Magda had been murdered. What you said to me yesterday obviously came not from her but from Moggy. I had to assume that she had maintained the story of staying out with friends.'

'You could have saved us time if you'd told us this yesterday.'

'I'm sorry if I've wasted your time. I was trying, in my own no doubt misguided way, to protect her from salacious conjecture.'

'From what?' asked Frank.

'Gossip.'

'Tell me something, Adam, did it strike you at all that Natalie might have a motive for wishing harm on Magda?'

'For heaven's sake, no.'

'You say you looked after her because she was upset?'

'Yes.'

'And did she tell you why she was upset?'

'No.'

'And did you ask her?'

'No.'

'Why not?'

He took a long breath. 'I'll tell you why not. The truth, sad and ridiculous as it is, is that I have been completely infatuated with that girl, infatuated to the point of distraction, ever since I first saw her. Infatuation is a cause of distress to the sufferer but it is not a crime. To have probed into her personal life, into her reasons for being upset, her reasons for unhappiness, would have been to sail my little boat into dangerous waters, waters where I might have offered more comfort than was warranted. I judged her to be vulnerable. I did, in spite of my own vile heart, what I thought was the right thing to do.'

The rain was just beginning to ease as we drove down the lane. Across the valley opposite a gash of blue and a corona of lemon sunlight had appeared in the sky.

'What do you reckon that was that all about then?' said Frank.

'I think we can eliminate them both, Frank, don't you?'

'I reckon so. But tell me one thing, Nula?'

'Go on.'

'Am I right in reaching the conclusion that he, Adam Mitchell, still doesn't actually know that she, Natalie, is gay?'

'I think that is the right conclusion, Frank.'

'Well, all I can say is, he's either a villain or a saint.'

'I'll ignore that, Frank. He's neither.'

'OK, boss, so where next?'

'Let's try the address of this mate of Natalie. This Nathan. Shall we?'

'You're the boss, boss.'

The address was for a small, terraced house in Slant Gate, about two miles from the middle of town.

The woman who answered the door looked frightened and apprehensive but it was the kind of apprehensiveness that seemed to be part of her natural expression. You could imagine that she would meet the supermarket delivery man, or the man to read the meter, with the same expression. The expression of someone who always expected something bad.

'Nathan?' she responded. 'He's not here.'

'Do you know where he is?'

'No. No, I don't.'
'Do you know when he'll be back?'
'No. Why? What is it?'
'We just want a quick word with him. A few questions.'
'Is he in trouble?'
'No. It's just that he might be able give us some information.'
'Is it to do with that murder in the news?'
'Why do you say that?'
'Because that's what everybody's talking about.'
'So when do you expect Nathan back? Later today maybe?'
'He just said he wanted to get away for a bit. He often does that. Just goes off, tries to get his head clear is what he says.'
'And when was that?'
'Two, three days. Wednesday, I think.'
'So where do you think he might go?'
'He doesn't tell me anything.'
'Any relatives or friends he might get in touch with?'

She shook her head slowly. She had the really vulnerable troubled look of someone who does not know any more than they are actually saying.

'Well, if he gets in contact with you, will you let us know? Or if he lets you know where he is? OK?'

She nodded her head.

'I'll leave this card with you. That's the number. Ask to speak to Nula. That's me. It's on the card.'

We got into the car and started the run back to HQ.

'What do you make of her then?' asked Frank.

'Don't think she's hiding anything. But it's odd that Nathan should go walkabout just after the murder.'

'Very odd. I mean, if, as Natalie says, he'd been messed about by Magda, same as her, I mean same as Natalie, his friend, then you can begin to see a motive taking shape.'

'Maybe. But his mum says he didn't take off until Wednesday.'

'She didn't seem very sure though, did she?'

We drove on in silence for a time. I think we were both tired. It'd been quite a week.

'Think I'll take tomorrow,' Frank said after a while. 'You be OK?'

'Yeah, you take it, Frank. Get a rest. Doubt if we'll get anything on Robbie-boy's computer stuff until Monday. Chase him up then and see if Nathan's turned up. I'll go in first thing, then sign off. Spend some time with Wendy and Phoebe.'

'Nice one.'

'Only been back a week. Feels like a lifetime!'

I was in bed by eight o'clock, just after Phoebe's feed, and I got up for the 12 o'clock, hoping to let Wendy sleep through. I was dog-tired, as if half my brain was still steeped in sleep, but there was something really secluded and peaceful about it: as if me and Phoebe were totally in our own world, insulated from reality. Everything I'd been thinking about for the last six days—of Magda Bentley and Rob Jenkins and Natalie—seemed to dissolve away into nothingness.

I awoke briefly at four, just as Wendy was getting up for the four o'clock. She kissed me lightly on the forehead. 'Thanks for last night,' she whispered. 'Now go back to sleep.'

I must have slept quite deeply for another two hours and when I awoke, I was trying to shake off a murky dream which at one point had me in a car chase after Ralph Anderson but had then slipped into a shapeless incoherent mess. I could see from the light under the curtain that it was a much brighter day. By now Wendy was back in bed and I slipped out, trying not to disturb her, to make some coffee.

CHAPTER 35

Sunday

At times, Sundays at the nick can be as manic as any other day but today happened to be one of those sleepy Sundays when there are very few people in the office. I switched on my laptop and ran through the notes I'd been keeping in rough form during the week to check that it still all made sense. Then I copied in Frank, just to make sure he was up to speed, and ran a check on Nathan Brook. There was a brief reference to him having been sectioned under the mental health act on something drug-related, but there was no follow-up and certainly no suggestion of violence or other criminality.

I was about to sign out when Simon Pooley came through the door.

'Ah, the very person I was hoping to see!' he announced. Simon is our computer whizz-kid. 'Frank not with you then?'

'Day off,' I said, shaking my head.

'I don't know, putting his feet up watching the cricket, no doubt, whilst we are here fighting crime.'

This was something of an in-joke as it was usually Frank who had a dig at Simon along the lines of sitting in front of a computer screen all day whilst others were out there fighting crime.

'Anyway, joking aside, I had a thoroughly entertaining evening going through your man's digital wonderland last night. Thought I'd come in and do my report while it's quiet.'

'And... don't keep me in suspense, Simon.'

'He's obviously made an effort to delete some stuff. But he's not as familiar with his own computer as he thinks he is. Not difficult to retrieve.'

'So you think he got wind of us coming for him?'

'Quite possibly.'

He sat down next to me, opened his laptop and performed a series of taps and clicks. The screen showed a sequence of images of Magda going into and coming out of her studio.

'You can have as many of those as you like, Nula. Gets a bit boring after a bit. Also, this chap...'

'Ralph Anderson,' I said.

'And, more recently...'

'Natalie Anderson.'

'Also, this, which, if I'm not mistaken, is the same girl. I make no other comment than that.'

The screen clicked to show a photograph of the nude painting of Natalie.

'He also has a second CCTV camera which is trained, at least part of the time, on the upstairs window of the building opposite. It makes for pretty boring viewing actually, unless you like curtains, but then there is this, from his webcam, from the week before last.'

He clicked again and, framed by the window, in the dim illumination of a yellow lightbulb—which nevertheless contrasted with the dusky evening light outside—Magda and Natalie are embracing. It continues for about twenty seconds and then Magda, in just a bra, comes quickly to the window and pulls the curtains shut.

'That's about it,' says Simon. 'I mean, he watches a lot of porn to judge from the sites he subscribes to, but nothing that strays too far into the dark side. And he chats to girls on dating sites and online: mainly Asian girls, Thai, Cambodia, Chinese. Oh and he has two bugging devices but they're still in their packaging, or at least in opened packages, but point is, I suppose, whatever he intended to do with them he hasn't done it yet.'

'Is there anything we can get him for?'

Simon shrugged his shoulders once and twisted his mouth

slightly.

'If I stick up a security camera and you walk through it, technically that's not my fault. And mucky footage, it's usually when people do it for harassment or extortion, revenge porn— you know making it public—that it gets to court. I mean some of this stuff wouldn't look good if you got him for something else, something serious I mean, but on its own, probably not. That's what I'll say in the report.'

'OK, thanks, Simon. I'll have a think about all that. Meantime, I'm going to knock off.'

'I know the feeling. See if you can remember where you live.'

CHAPTER 36

Monday

Frank picked me up at the usual time.

'Another Monday!' he said in that tone of dour resignation that he tended to use to greet the start of each new week. 'Let's hope there are no nasty surprises this week.'

We allowed ourselves a brief exchange on what we'd got up to with our families on Sunday, and then I gave him a run-down of what Simon had said.

'Doesn't surprise me, I have to say.'

'Anything on the keys?'

'Got uniform on it. Nothing so far. Not Steeples. They'll keep on it.'

'Simon's probably right then, not enough to nab him with.'

First thing, we were in the incident room for a meeting with Fenwick. As we summarised the work we'd done, it was clear that he wasn't happy.

'I asked for progress,' he said. 'What I'm hearing doesn't amount to any progress at all. Time to get our fingers out, ladies and gents.'

As Renwick went on, I could see Frank bristling. I knew what he was thinking and I had a feeling it wouldn't take much for Frank to call him out. I looked over and gave him a 'back off' look. Renwick was known for his Monday morning black moods. His storms were best left to blow themselves out.

'So, we've eliminated Ralph Anderson, we've eliminated Natalie Anderson, we've eliminated Mitchell. He crossed them off the board in brusque swipes. Now, who is this Brook whose name has magically appeared?'

'Nathan Brook. Friend of Natalie,' I said. 'The one who told her about her dad and Magda Bentley.'

'So he knew Magda then?'

'Yes.'

'Well, we need to get him in then, don't we?'

'On it, guv. Been to the house. Not there. Mother didn't know where he was.'

'So that leaves Jenkins. Where are we up to with him?'

I updated him, regarding Simon's report.'

'Right, so you're telling me this guy Rob Jenkins has form for various stuff, that he's got footage in his computer that looks dodgy. Why isn't he in here at this very moment, under caution?'

'We only got the stuff from his computer over the weekend, guv.'

'We don't know if it's really relevant.'

'It's a murder investigation. Everything's relevant.'

'Yes, guv.'

'Get him in. Let's hold his feet to the fire. And this Nathan Brook. Get over to his house again. Search his bedroom. Squeeze his mother. She probably knows more than she's saying. Right, get on with it.'

He made a rapid exit.

'Don't worry,' said Geoff. 'He'll mellow once the weekend whisky is fully out of his system. June, you come with me, we'll bring in Jenkins. I'll enjoy that. Nula, you and Frank pay Nathan Brook's mother another visit?'

'Excuse me, Geoff,' interjected Frank. 'But last I knew, Nula was SIO on this case.'

'Sorry,' said Geoff. 'Sorry Nula. Your call.'

'No, that's fine, Geoff,' I said. 'But I want to be in on the interview with Rob Jenkins.'

Everyone seemed to be nodding.

'Right,' I said. 'Let's crack on with it.'

We filtered back from the incident room to our desks and got ready to go out. Just as I was closing down my computer, a call came through from Jack on the desk. 'Call from a Natalie Anderson. Do you want to take it?'

'Yes, put her through.'

'Hello?'

'Hello, Natalie. This is Nula. How can I help?'

'Well, it's Nathan. I'm worried about him. I phoned his mum and she said the police had been round.'

'Yes, that was us. We had to follow up on what you told us.'

'He's not a suspect, is he? I mean, God, Nathan wouldn't hurt a fly.'

'We just need to speak to him, Natalie. But as you probably know if you spoke to his mum, he's gone missing.'

'Just because he's away doesn't mean he's missing.'

'No. No, you're right, Natalie, but we still need to speak to him. Do you have any idea where he might be?'

'Not really. We were friends at school. I've only just met up with him again recently. The only thing is, well, he did say that he had a friend in Salford that he'd stayed with at some point.'

'Hmm, Salford, big place, Natalie!'

'I know, I'm sorry. I'll leave a message on his phone. Tell him to come back. Maybe if he knows it's from me.'

'OK, thanks, Natalie. Let us know if you hear anything.'

If anything, Nathan's mum looked even more careworn than she had the day before. It wasn't a neglectful mother we were dealing with, but a mother who cared but didn't know how to cope.

'He was so glad to meet up with Natalie again,' she said. 'She was such a good influence him. You know what he used to say? He used to say, *'Mum, Natalie's the only person who makes me feel normal. She's the only one who doesn't make me feel like a freak.'* Of course, I tried to tell him he wasn't anything like a freak at all. But who believes their mum? He believed Natalie, he didn't believe me.'

I squeezed her arm and then said very quietly, 'Is it ok if we just take a quick look at his bedroom?'

Like a teenager's bedroom, Nathan's room was just one small step from complete chaos. His mum stood just outside the door. 'He gets annoyed if I try to tidy after him,' she said apologetically. 'Makes me feel ashamed.'

'Don't worry, Mrs Brook,' said Frank. 'I've seen worse, and that's from personal experience. Got three of my own.'

'But he's twenty-two. You'd think he could straighten his bed, at least, once in a while.'

We tried to make light of it but I think that by that time, we'd both noticed that amongst the detritus of the room—the CD covers, the scattered clothes, the discarded books—were several sketches of women, or rather of one woman: a woman who looked remarkably like Magda Bentley.

'I don't suppose you'd mind putting the kettle on, would you, Mrs Brook? A cuppa would go down a treat.'

She was all too willing to oblige.

'What do you make of that then?' said Frank in a hushed tone as we heard her feet descending the stairs.

'Well, maybe not supremely talented, but good enough to draw out a likeness.'

'From life, do you think?'

'Difficult to say. I'm no expert. Quite likely though, I'd say.'

'What do you think then?'

'Get some photos. Just on the off chance they go missing like him.'

'OK.'

'You all right with that?'

'Yeah, why not?'

'Don't want you getting over-stimulated, Frank!'

He muttered something under his breath that sounded vaguely like a familiar obscenity, and whilst he was getting his photos, I had a closer look around. There was no computer, though it was quite possible that he would have a laptop and that he would have taken it with him. There were notebooks though, and loose sheets, with poems—some crossed out—and other paragraphs of a colourful and emotional nature, evidently written with a 'she' in mind, though the 'she' was not named.

'The tea's ready,' Mrs Brook called up the stairs.

'Right! Just coming.'

I took a few photos of the writings, exchanged nods with Frank, and we went down.

By the time we got back to HQ, Rob Jenkins had been brought in and was waiting in Interview Room 3. There was no time to discuss with Renwick what we'd found in Nathan Brook's bedroom at this point, so after a quick word with Geoff, I went straight into the interview.

Geoff switched on the recording machine. 'Interview with Robert Jenkins, Monday 8th August, 1125 hours. Present DC Nula Ryan, DS Geoff Stone and Mr Jenkins's legal advisor, Mr Jefferson.'

Jefferson was the usual brief we called in when people didn't have their own on call. He was an old hand, always sat in a slouched way and gave the impression of being totally disinterested, though he was quick enough to resort to the *no comment* tactic, if he felt you were pushing too hard.

We confirmed Rob's identity and address and Geoff went on with the formalities.

'So, Mr Jenkins, you know that you haven't been arrested or charged but you are being interviewed under caution. That means that anything you say could be used as evidence if later a criminal case were to be brought. Is that clear?'

'My client has said that he is prepared to cooperate,' said Jefferson.

'So, Mr Jenkins...' Geoff began.

'Might as well call me Rob. I don't stand on ceremony.'

'Rob. OK. Thank you. Nula?'

'Tell us a bit about your relationship with Magda Jenkins, Rob.'

'Didn't have one really. Kept ourselves to ourselves.'

'But you held a key, took her gear to the festival and back.'

'Just chance thing. I saw her struggling. Offered her a lift. End of.'

'I've got here, Rob, a summary of what we found on your

computer. For the benefit of the recording, I am showing the witness the report prepared by DS Simon Pooley into equipment from Mr Jenkins's commercial premises, opposite the studio occupied by the deceased, Magda Bentley.
It says here, Rob, that there was a considerable amount of pornographic material on your computer, including recordings from dating sites where you ask young women to perform certain acts of a sexual nature. Would you like to comment on that?'

Rob shrugged. 'I like to get to know people. The girls, I mean. Wouldn't do it if they didn't want to, would they? Not minors. I mean, it's private. I don't show them anyone else. That's not illegal, is it?'

'My client is right,' said Jefferson. 'But more to the point is what is the relevance of this line of questioning.'

'It provides some context. There is also footage from your CCTV camera and from your webcam, some of which contains images of the deceased, Magda Bentley, seen through the upstairs window of her studio: the bedroom window. Are you aware of that?'

'Accidental,' said Rob. 'The camera must have slipped in the wind. Pure chance that it ended up there. I didn't even realise until I was checking through the tapes. I don't check them that often to be honest.'

'But this footage is on your hard drive, Rob. You would have had to download it for it to be there, wouldn't you?'

To this, Rob seemed to have no answer. Jefferson whispered something in his ear.

'Shall I repeat the question, Rob?'

'No comment,' he recited, predictably.

'You tried to delete some files from your computer, Rob, didn't you? Now, why would you do that?'

'Normal housekeeping. Doesn't everyone do that?'

'There are also numerous photographs, both of Magda Bentley and of Natalie Anderson, at the entrance to her studio, and a photograph of a portrait of Miss Anderson which Magda Bentley had painted.'

'No comment.'

'Also found at your premises were two surveillance devices.'

'Never used,' said Rob, coming in quickly.

'Never used, maybe, but presumably you bought them with some purpose in mind.'

'I bought them to keep an eye on my mother at home. She has mobility problems, you see. She sometimes has falls. But I bought the wrong ones. I was going to send them back.'

'I see.'

At this point there was a knock on the door and Frank popped his head round. 'A minute ma'am?

Geoff suspended the interview.

'What is it, Frank?' I asked, going outside.

'We've got something on the key, Nula. Day after the festival. Over at Tesco other side of town. Woman said she remembered. Fits Jenkins's I.D., but they'll have it on CCTV too.'

'Good work.'

'Not me. WPC. Hampson.'

'Tell her good work then.'

We restarted the interview.

'On Monday morning, Rob, the day after the festival, you had some keys cut at Tesco, didn't you?'

'No comment.'

'We have a witness who can identify you, formally if necessary. Were the keys you had cut keys to Miss Bentley's studio? Again, that is something which can easily be verified.'

Rob had a private word with his solicitor and then, turning back, said, 'Yes.'

'So how do you explain that?'

'Like I said, I helped with her gear down to the festival. I gave her a lift. Then later, I went back to help her bring the gear back. But she wanted to stay on. She gave me the key to let myself back in, I said I'd take it back, she said no need, she had another.'

'Where?'

'She didn't say.'

'So the key you gave us wasn't a key you were holding as a friendly neighbour, but the one she gave you at the festival. You hung onto the key. And then had it copied.'

Rob shrugged and nodded faintly.

'For the benefit of the recording.'

'Yes.'

'Why?'

'No comment.'

'Did you get the spare key cut so that you could let yourself into her studio to take more photographs, maybe to plant surveillance devices?'

'My client is not required to answer such speculative and tendentious questions,' said Jefferson in his flattest tone of voice.

'Just one thing,' said Rob, coming in over his solicitor, 'what would I be doing getting keys cut on Monday if I knew she was already dead.'

'What did you do after dropping off her stuff?'

'Went back to the festival.'

'And what time was that?'

'I don't know. About six o'clock. After the bands started.'

'And did you see Magda Bentley again when you went back?'

'Might have caught a glimpse of her. There were a lot of people dancing. She might have been there. Can't really remember.'

'And what did you do after that?'

'I stayed on for a while. Had a couple of beers. Then went home.'

'You went home?'

'Yes. The band was too loud. I don't like loud music. And I saw that they were going to let off some fireworks. Well, mum doesn't like fireworks. They frighten her. So I went back to make sure she was all right.'

'And you stayed there?'

'Oh yes, all night. We watched TV Gold together all night. It's her favourite station. She likes the old sitcoms. So do I for that matter.'

'She will be able to verify this, will she?'

'Oh yes. Go and ask her. She's getting a bit dodgy on her pins but all the marbles are still there. She'll remember it. She'll remember asking me to turn the sound up when the fireworks were starting, for one thing.'

'Is that a dead end then?'

'Not necessarily,' said Geoff. 'There's a lot of stuff that would look very suspect in court, and he wouldn't have the luxury of *no comment* under cross-examination, but it's as we thought: all circumstantial. He could have been caught planting one of his bugs in the rafters over her bed but, unless we can prove that he killed her, it's no use to us. I don't know what Renwick was expecting but that feller, scrote as he is, is not going to break down under questioning and give us the confession we so urgently desire.'

'Just one obvious thing though,' I said. 'His point about not getting keys cut after she was dead. I mean I thought that too, to be honest.'

'Could be a double bluff. Possible but unlikely. Don't think he's that bright.'

That just about summed it up. I agreed. 'If he's still a suspect, though—and I think we have to say he is—we need to go through all the statements we've got from people at the festival and get round to them again with pictures of Rob's ugly mug. See if we can get any more confirmed sightings.'

'In the meantime?'

'We have to let him go. Keep him on the back burner.'

'What about checking with his mother?' said Frank who was now up to speed with it. 'His alibi, I mean.'

'What do you think, boss?' asked Geoff, taking me by surprise.

'Chances are he's primed her,' I said. 'The references are too precise: the fireworks, the TV Gold. But maybe we should, just for the record.'

'OK, I'll go out there with June right away,' said Geoff. 'You keep him here another half hour, then let him go. You can tell me about your visit to Nathan Brook's place later.'

I must admit, I was pretty disheartened. I'd heard plenty of stories of investigating officers knowing, without a shadow of a doubt, who the perpetrator of a given crime was but not being able to get hold of the crucial evidence that would clinch it. On the grapevine, you also heard stories of officers who had planted evidence to get a result; but when you heard things like that, you didn't really know if people were just trying to impress you with the 'dark' side of policing. I suppose it's something that must have happened, but I don't really know.

We let Rob go, not without being subjected to a self-satisfied smirk from him as he left.

When June came back in, she confirmed that if it was a script, Rob's mother had 'learned her lines' impeccably.

Meantime, Geoff had been called out on another case.

We spent the afternoon, Frank and me, going through the statements that had been gathered by uniform in the three days after the festival, and drew up a list of people we could show a photo of Rob to, to see if it nudged anything that might be significant. It seemed like needle-in-haystack syndrome again, but it was all we could do.

When I got back home, Wendy's mother was there. She'd travelled over from Chester to see Phoebe and was going to stay over.

'I've booked a table,' said Wendy. 'Just you and me. Don't argue. Just get ready. Now!'

I was pleasantly shoehorned out of what otherwise would have been a tired continuation of my frustrating day and did as I was told. I was ready in half an hour and Wendy had already called a taxi.

It was amazing how the atmosphere of the restaurant changed my mood. We had a gin and tonic, then a starter between us, then a shared seafood platter, washed down with a bottle of Pinot Grigio.

Wendy put her hand over mine across the table.

'We haven't done this for ages,' she said.

'I know, and I haven't felt the need to talk about the case all night.'

'I know. That was the general idea!'

I squeezed her hand.

'I'm thinking Greece,' she said.

'Greece?'

'Next Spring. You, me and Phoebe. Skiathos maybe. Or Corfu. Sunshine.'

'Sounds heavenly.'

When we got back, Wendy's mother was about to go to bed, reporting a peaceful evening. Wendy did the midnight feed and then slipped into bed beside me, full of intent.

'Are you fast asleep?' she asked.

'No. it's just…'

'Just what?'

'What about your mum?'

'It's not a problem,' she said. 'You'll just have to be quieter than you usually are!'

'OK,' I agreed. 'I'll do my best.'

37

Tuesday

'Cheer up,' I said to Frank on the way in.

'Cheer up? What for?'

'Oh, I don't know. Something good is bound to turn up today.'

'Whooosh!' he hissed.

'What?'

'Oh nothing. Just an elephant flying by.'

'Do you mean a pig?'

'You what?'

'Well, an *elephant in a room,* and a *pig flying by*, as in *Oh aye, and pigs can fly.*'

'Smart arse,' he said.

But my words might have been prophetic. We signed in to find that Moggy Morton was waiting for us.

'Got a busy day,' he said, greeting us. 'Thought I'd call in before I get down to the graft.'

'Thank you, Moggy. So what've you got for us?'

'Well, when I spoke to you the other day, I didn't know it was her—the artist lady I mean—who had copped for it.'

'And?'

'Well, I had my eyes on her,' said Moggie, 'at the festival, I mean.'

'How do you mean, you had your eyes on her?'

'Because she was a looker. Straight up. Well, I mean, she had assets a man notices. I'm sure you know what I'm on about,' he added, addressing this last bit directly to Frank. 'Well, I noticed this guy who was all over her, a bit pissed I think he must have been. Anyway, I thought no more about it until yesterday and then I saw this picture and I recognised who he was.'

'What picture, Moggy. Have you got it, this picture?'

'No, I haven't got it personally but it's all over the billboards. In the public domain, you might say.'

'Cut to the chase, Moggy.'

'It's the whatsit guy, the guy running for the council, Martin something.'

'Martin Haslam?'

'That's the one. Martin Haslam. Your Labour candidate.'

'Right. And you're saying what, he was dancing with her?'

'Dancing with her, yes, looking as if he was after a bit more than dancing, if I'm any judge.'

'OK, thanks, Moggy.'

'My civic duty.'

'Oh, whilst you're here, what about this bloke?'

We showed him Rob's photo.

'The carpet guy.'

'You know him?'

'The carpet guy. Yes. The carpet feller. Well, we trade people get to know who each other are for when our paths cross. Yeah, he was around. I mean, I saw him hanging around later. You know, like sniffing around for any spare skirt but not necessarily with her. Not to my recollection. I mean, she was putting herself about, dancing with anyone, but more with this Haslam bloke, really.'

'Thanks, Moggy, you're a mine of information.'

'Eyes and ears of Milthwaite, me!'

'We'll be in touch.'

'Well,' said Frank uncertainly. 'Breakthrough?'

'Maybe, but someone in the public eye. You'd think he would have come forward. Too much to lose.'

'Unless he actually did it.'

'Well, yes, unless that.'

We were pondering this when I got called through to take another call from Natalie Anderson.

'Natalie?'

'It's Nathan. I had a call from him. He's back. He's been in a bit of a mess, but he wants to talk to you.'

'Thanks, Natalie. When did you speak to him?'

'Just this morning. Just now.'

'And he's at home, is he?'

'He was on the train. From Manchester. He said he's going to come here.'

'OK. Just tell him to stay with you. We'll come out to pick him up.'

We set out more or less straightaway, deciding Martin Haslam could wait until later. When we arrived at the Anderson household on Crofters Mount, Nathan had not yet arrived. Natalie was obviously distressed about Nathan, and Mrs Anderson was fussing over Natalie, though her friend Cyril was doing his best to keep both of them calm.

'Are you going to arrest him?' Natalie asked.

'No. We just need to talk to him.'

'Can you talk to him here rather than at the police station?'

'No, I'm sorry, Natalie, that wouldn't really be appropriate.'

'Can I come with him then? Only he'll be frightened, you see. I can probably reassure him.'

'Well, yes, no reason why not, if you think it will help. But when we question him, he'll be on his own.'

'OK.'

We sat in an awkward silence, the four of us. At last, I went to the window and a moment later, a young man in a grey hoodie and with a backpack came round the corner. He stopped for a moment, seeing the police car. It was obviously Nathan. Natalie went to the door and ran down to meet him.

We put them in the car straightaway. They didn't speak at all during the journey but I could see that Natalie was holding his hands across her lap and every so often she would say, 'It's all right, Nathan, don't worry, it's all right'. My guess was that his hands were trembling.

When we got him into the interview room, he was shivering and looked as pale as a ghost.

'Have you had anything to eat this morning, Nathan?'

He shook his head.

'Would you like a cup of tea or something.'

'No. I just want to get this over with.'

'OK, Nathan. We're not going to caution you at this stage. You've come in voluntarily and we want to ask you a few questions and see where we get to. Do you understand that?'

'Yes.'

'OK. So, Nathan, you know the background to this, and am I right in saying that you were acquainted with Magda Bentley?'

'Yes.'

'How would you describe your relationship with her?'

'I went to one of her art courses and then she asked me back to her studio.'

'To do more artwork?'

'Yes, to begin with, but then she wanted me to have sex with her.'

'And did you?'

'Not at first, but yes, later. I did. Yes.'

'Did you know that we called at your house yesterday, Nathan?'

He sat up sharply at this. 'Did you speak to my mother? She'll be upset.'

'She was already upset, Nathan, about you disappearing.'

'Yes.' He slumped back in the chair.

'We had a quick look in your bedroom, Nathan. There were a lot of sketches there. Were they sketches of Magda?'

'Couldn't you tell?'

'Well, yes, actually I could. We could. There were some poems, as well. Were the poems about Magda?'

'Some of them.'

'Were you in love with her?'

'Not in love, no. She wasn't always nice to me. But I was a bit obsessed with her. For a time.'

'You know that she upset Natalie, don't you?'

'Yes.'

'And how did that make you feel?'

'Angry. But for Natalie's sake not mine. Natalie was in love with her. She told me. And she was happy. But it was me who had to tell her the truth, and that was pretty horrible.'

'Did you see Magda at the festival?'

'Yes. She was doing face painting. During the day, anyway.'

'And later?'

'Yes. After Natalie left, I had a couple of drinks and watched the band. I saw her then, dancing with people.'

'With people?'

'Yes, she was the kind who would dance around, laughing and stuff, getting other people going. Having a good time.'

'And that was the last time you saw her, was it, Nathan? When she was dancing?'

'No.'

There was quite a long pause after this. We waited.

'When she left, she was walking over towards the canal and I followed her.'

It was at this point that I stopped the interview. It was clear that we had reached a point where informal voluntary interview was no longer appropriate. I took Frank outside and explained that we were going to have to caution him and get it on tape. Geoff, who'd been following from outside, agreed. I was glad that I'd made the call. If I'd left it a minute later, he would have intervened.

We went back in and explained the procedure to Nathan. He didn't seem surprised. He was still as pale as a ghost but he had stopped shivering. We asked him if he wanted a brief but he declined.

'I just want to tell you what happened and get it over with,' he said.

Frank read him his rights and we switched on the tape and began the formal interview. For the benefit of the recorder, we went over some of the questions we'd already asked. He looked a bit weary of it but he was compliant.

'So, Nathan, we've established that you watched Magda dancing for a time.'

'I didn't *watch* her dancing, I saw her dancing.'

'Is that not the same thing?' asked Frank.

'Not really. But yes, she was dancing and I saw her, so I suppose I must have been watching to some extent.'

'And when she left the festival, you followed her?'

'Yes.'

'In which direction did she leave?'

'Towards the canal.'

'And can you tell us why you followed her?'

'Prurient curiosity, I suppose.'

'Prurient curiosity,' Frank echoed, 'those are big words, Nathan. Can you explain to us what they mean?'

'An unhealthy interest in seeing something happen.'

'You've still not got me, Nathan.'

'She wasn't on her own. She left with someone. A man. I thought they were probably going to go off and have sex. I wanted to see if I was right.'

'And were you?' asked Frank.

'Just a minute,' I interjected. 'You said she left the festival with a man, Nathan. Can you identify who that man was?'

'Yes.'

There was another long pause here, as if he were reluctant to put a name to the person.

'Well?' I said at last.

'It was Martin Haslam.'

'Are you sure of that, Nathan?'

'Yes.'

'OK. So Magda left the festival with Martin Haslam and they went towards the canal.'

'Yes.'

'So, tell us what happened next.'

'They went across the bridge and stopped for a minute snogging. Then they went up into the woods. Not far. Just enough to be out of sight.'

'Except from someone who was following them?'

'Yes. I know that part of the woods quite well. I often go walking there. It was quite easy for me to find somewhere to hide, where I could watch.'

'And what did you see?'

'They started taking their clothes off.'

'And did they have sex?'

'No. They were just playing about.'

'Playing about? How playing about?'

'Playing about with each other and laughing. I think they were both quite drunk. And he tripped over trying to get out of his trousers, and she was laughing at him, and he got up eventually, just in his underpants, and sort of fell onto her, well, grabbed hold of her. And then, she started to run off.'

'Why did she run off. Was she upset?'

'No, it wasn't like that. It was more like a game. I mean, laughing.'

'And he was running after her?'

'Yes, like I say, a chase.'

'And they ran down to the towpath.'

'Yes.'

'And then what? '

'She fell over.'

'Into the canal?'

'No, against the post of the lock gate. She tripped and fell against the post and banged her head.'

'And what did he do?'

'He went up to her.'

'Was she unconscious?'

'No. She was moving a bit. I think.'

'And then?'

'I slipped away. I ran off. I'd had enough of it.'

'Ok. So, you ran off and what did you do then?'

'I went home. Didn't think any more about it until I heard about her on the news.'

'And at that point, you ran away again,' suggested Frank.

'Yes,' said Nathan in a hushed voice.

'Why was that, Nathan?'

'I panicked. I was frightened it would come back to me. That someone would try to pin it on me.'

'Where did you go, Nathan?'

'I've got a friend in Salford. I went there. And then Natalie texted me and I saw sense, and knew I had to come back.'

We terminated the interview and kept Nathan in custody. I went out to let Natalie know. I suggested that she should go home.

I saw the look of panic in her eyes. 'Have you charged him?'

'No,' I said. 'But we've got other angles to cover. It could be quite a while yet.'

'I'll wait then. Will you let me know?'

'Yes, of course.'

I showed her where she could get some coffee and a snack if she wanted to, and then went back to the room with Frank.

'What do you make of it then, Frank?'

'My money's on him. We know he had form with her before. What was it Natalie said? That she'd treated them both as playthings?'

'*Things* is what she said but I suppose it amounts to the same.'

'What's your take on it then, Nula?

'Well, he was obviously there. No doubt about that. And the key details of his account are borne out by the facts.'

'And what do you make of him implicating Haslam?'

'Maybe it's true. Remember what Moggy told us.'

'He only told us he saw Haslam dancing with her and fawning over her.'

'And that he was pissed.'

'Yes, but Nathan could have seen that too. What if it was him —Nathan, I mean—and not Haslam who went into the woods with Magda? Same story, just a different player.'

'We need to get Haslam in.'

'Yes, we do. But it's Nathan for me. And to me it's the absconding that clinches it.'

'Do you think so?'

'Yes. I mean, what was to stop him coming in on Wednesday morning and giving us the story he's just given us now, if it's true?'

'Maybe he thought it was stacked against him. He's got a possible motive, he'd put himself in a dodgy position by following her, he's a bit of a drifter, plus, his word—possibly—

against a man who has some standing in the community.'

Frank sat back in his chair. 'I'm sure coppering used to be a lot simpler than this.'

'Come on, Frank, let's pay this Martin Haslam a visit.'

His apartment was in one of those mill developments just along the valley. I'd seen it in passing quite a few times, and Wendy and I had once talked of going over to see if it might suit us, so —other things aside—I was quite looking forward to seeing the inside and if it lived up to its reputation. However, there was no reply when we pressed the doorbell.

Frank suggested that we should drive back into the village and check at the office that they used for party political stuff. There were two or three people working there, and Martin Haslam was clearly recognisable from the photo on his campaign material dotted around town.

'Do you think we could do this somewhere more private than here?' he asked.

'Certainly, sir,' said Frank. 'If you'd like to come with us, we can find a nice quiet room at the station.' Sometimes Frank has a brilliant way with words!

Quarter of an hour later, we had him in the same interview room where we'd questioned Nathan an hour before. We went through the formalities and prefaced the business. Martin Haslam's manner was polite, almost deferential, with a kind of calmness that would give you confidence in his rectitude.

'So, Martin, we've established that you were at the festival on the Sunday in question, and that you'd been drinking gin during the afternoon.'

'Yes, far too much actually,' he said with a bit of a smirk.

'Now, Martin, we have a witness who identifies you as the person who left the festival with Magda Bentley at some point during the evening. And that you went with her into the woodland on the other side of the canal.'

'Is that a question?' he asked, as if to maintain an air of detached control.

'Is it true? That's the question,' said Frank.

For a moment, it seemed he would find some form of words to parry the question but already we could see the mask beginning to slip. He closed his eyes and kept them closed for quite a time.

'Yes,' he said at last, in a husky voice.

'Would you like to take us through what happened then, step by step.'

'It was very stupid of me, I know, and very unprofessional, given my position, but there was an atmosphere of jocularity and as I say, I'd had a few glasses of gin—which I'm not at all used to, I have to add—and, well, she was dancing with me in a very familiar, not to say intimate, way and yes, I do admit that I found her very attractive, so that when she suggested that we should go off together somewhere privately, I'm afraid I succumbed.'

'You went off in the woods with her?' said Frank.

Martin Haslam cleared his throat and gave another husky 'Yes'.

'Go on then.'

I could see Frank was enjoying this.

The continuation of his account squared pretty much to the detail with the one Nathan had already given us, right up to the point where Magda slipped and banged her head against the post by the lock.

'And was she still conscious, Martin?'

'Yes.'

'Was she aware? Did she say anything?'

'She didn't say anything. I'd say she was groggy. Stunned.'

'And then you left the scene?'

'Yes.'

'You didn't think of getting help. Calling an ambulance. You just left the scene?'

'No. I mean, yes, but it wasn't like that. You see, I saw someone else coming up the path. I was all but naked, for fuck's sake! I'm standing for the council. In the heat of the moment, I thought this person would find her and see that she was looked after. And so, yes, I ran back to where my clothes were and left.'

'So that was Sunday night. On Monday a body was found. On Tuesday it was identified as Magda Bentley. On Wednesday that information was made public. It's now a week later, and in all that time it didn't occur to you to make a statement to the police?'

'I woke up with a terrible hangover. To begin with I couldn't remember a thing. Then it started to come back to me, bit by appalling bit. Next thing it's in the news that there's a body, then that it's her. I went into a flat panic.'

'So you decided to keep shtum.'

Another husky yes.

'Hoping it would all go away.'

'Yes.'

'Big mistake, that, Martin. Big mistake.'

'Can I go now? I've told you everything. I don't know who killed her. But I know I've probably lost my entire career over this. So can I please just go?'

'I'm afraid you'll need to stay here a little longer, Martin. There is a possible murder charge. But if not that, there may well be other charges.'

'Can I have a break then?'

'Yes. The only other question, for the moment: this other person. Did you recognise them?'

'No,' said Martin. 'No. Just that it was a woman.'

'Smooth talker,' said Frank when we'd finished the interview.

'Very eloquent.'

'Won't be so eloquent in the local rag. *Local politician in stark bollock naked sex romp with randy artist murder victim.*

'I hope you turned the tape off, Frank!'

'Think I might make a good headline writer, you know, Nula.'

'You missed your way, Frank. The question is: supposing the rest of his story is true, who is this mystery woman, and in the phrase they use in *A Question of Sport*, what happened next?'

'I didn't know you watched *A Question of Sport*, Nula. Wouldn't have had you down as the type!'

'Let's get Nathan back in.'

'So, Nathan, you've taken us up to the point when she'd slipped, was maybe stunned.'

'Yeah.'

'And he was standing over her.'

'Yes.'

'And then he ran off.'

'Yes.'

'You saw him run off.'

'Yes.'

'You didn't tell us that before. You said that you ran off because you'd had enough of it. Now you're saying that you saw him run away?'

Nathan didn't respond to this.

'Is that how it was? You saw him run off.'

He nodded his head.

'For the tape, please, Nathan.'

'Yes.'

'So there she was, in trouble, stunned, concussed, semi-conscious. Why didn't you do something?'

'Because I saw someone else who came to look over her. And I felt sure that this person would look after her.'

'A woman?'

'Yes.'

I exchanged a glance with Frank.

'And why didn't you tell us about this woman earlier?'

He looked at us squarely and said, 'Because she used to be my teacher.'

CHAPTER 37

After that, a long day turned into an even longer evening.

One of the last things I remember was going into the waiting room and finding Natalie curled up asleep on the bench, still waiting for Nathan. But before that we had to wait for Renwick to be called so that we could run everything by him and get clearance for the actions we were proposing. He was annoyed and prickly at first—we suspected that it was his golf afternoon that he had been called back from—but when he realised that we had a possible result that he could take some credit for, he definitely changed his tune. Martin and Nathan were finally released without charge but still under police caution, and Helen Holden's address and details were ascertained with a view to an arrest and questioning. I drove Natalie and Nathan home, first to Natalie's house, but then insisting that Nathan should go home and explain everything to his mother.

'Have you got a *Good Work* ringing loudly in your ear,' asked Frank on our own way home.

'Faintly, maybe. Not that loud though.'

'No. Just what I thought. Think I might be in need of a hearing aid, Nula.'

Helen Holden was arrested and taken into custody in Leeds the next day. She made an immediate confession to Magda Bentley's murder and was charged and remanded pending trial.

I later read the transcript of her interview. There had been some history with both Magda Bentley and Adam Mitchell which had left her with bitterness and resentment, and which had brought on a 'complete breakdown'—as she described it—

from which she had never properly recovered.

On the evening in question, she said she had left the festival to follow Adam Mitchell but had turned back when she saw him returning to his house with a young woman who she supposed to be just another foolish female being seduced as she had once been. She had wanted to shout out a warning, she said, but the words just stuck in her throat. After that, she said, she had just wandered for a time, feeling that it was like a second betrayal. Then, on her way back, she had witnessed a woman running along the canal path and falling, injuring herself. The man she was with had turned to run off. She had approached, intending to help the woman, but had then recognised her as Magda Bentley. In a fit of rage, she said, hardly knowing what she was doing, she had picked up a stone from the side of the path and had smashed the stone several times against Magda's head. *When I realised what I had done*, she said, *I was horrified, and when I pushed her into the canal, it was as if I was trying to hide it from myself.*

According to the arresting officers, she said, 'I've been waiting for you. I don't know why it's taken you so long.'

She was described by the officers who questioned her as calm, articulate and precise.

After that, however, it seems that she went into some kind of nervous crisis. She was referred for psychiatric assessment and eventually was declared unfit to stand trial. As far as I know, that is still the case.

Eventually, no charges were preferred against Nathan or Martin, though possible charges of *Perverting the Course of Justice* and *Withholding Evidence* were considered and dismissed by the CPS. Both were issued with a formal police warning. Martin withdrew as candidate for the council and moved away from the district. His press headline was not quite as bad as the one Frank had drawn up for him, but it was bad enough.

No action was taken against Rob Jenkins. However shady his activities, it was decided that they did not, at this stage at least, merit further investigation.

In the absence of a will, Magda Bentley's affairs were put in the hands of legal administrators with a view to discovering who, if anyone, was her next of kin. The owner of the studio was informed that the contents and Magda's possessions could be put into storage pending the completion of this process, and that the associated costs could be claimed via the administrator against Magda's estate. As the owner was Barbara Anderson, this chore fell to her. A distant cousin of Magda Bentley later authorised the sale of her completed work at an auction house in Wakefield. The portrait of Natalie was not, apparently, on the inventory.

At the inquest, Ralph Anderson, now relocated permanently to Leeds, along with others who had had dealings with Magda —including Natalie, Nathan and Martin Haslam—were called as witnesses. It could have been an ordeal but the coroner made a point of saying she was interested only in establishing facts and not in probing into people's private lives, so it was not as bad as some people feared. There had been no trial but the evidence of the pathologist was sufficient, she decided, for the coroner to record a verdict of unlawful killing.

A few months later, just after Christmas, Frank was offered the opportunity to become Home Security Officer for the local authority and he accepted. As a spin-off, he now appears regularly in training videos on the topic and, as we joke affectionately at the nick, the camera loves him.

I was made up to Detective Sergeant in April. The three of us—Wendy, Phoebe and I—took a fortnight's break in Croatia in May. After that, Wendy's maternity leave ended, and another totally new and unpredictable phase of our lives began.

AFTERWORD

CHAPTER 38

There is another gathering at the Gallery. It is almost exactly a year since the gathering to celebrate the life of the local watercolourist, Duncan Tomlinson. On this occasion the gathering is smaller, for the person whose life is being commemorated is not so well recognised a local personality as was Duncan Tomlinson, but he is acknowledged—in his own way—as a significant figure, nevertheless. It is the writer Adam Mitchell who died in May, and the gathering has been organised by Cyril North, a member of the local amateur theatre group.

Julie Brown, the gallery curator, is present, as is Paul Phillips the rector of St Wilfred's, Cyril's partner Barbara and her daughter Natalie, who has brought along a college friend, Melanie. Standing with them is Nathan Brook who now works as a part-time assistant at the gallery, and Felix Morton, a local plumber, who looks awkward in suit and tie but who is there, as he has told people, because he feels he should pay his respects to an old friend and drinking companion.

Cyril is giving a speech which he has promised will be short.

'I can't claim to have been a deep or long-standing friend of Adam,' he begins, 'but during the last months of his life, I had a number of conversations with him. He was a complex character, very aware of, how shall I put it, his own shortcomings as a human being, as I suppose—if we are honest—are we all.'

Looking up at this moment to where she is standing, he sees that Natalie is crying, silently but without control, but he has to continue.

'His illness was diagnosed as recently as last October. He was passing out, fainting, in the White Hart where he was a very familiar face, at home, even in the street. *Was it the drink?* people asked, *Is it the drink?* he asked himself. Tests proved otherwise.'

He looks up and sees that even Moggy Morton is now crying.

'It was a fourth-degree brain tumour, inoperable, and he was given three months to live. I went over to see him quite a few times after that. He was reconciled to dying and seemed to have no obvious dread. I reminded him of his achievements, the works he would leave behind. He told me his novels meant nothing and could be consigned to a dustbin. *'I put my talent to the service of a debased art form,'* he said, *'and I helped to debase it further.* 'But the poetry? *'Yes,'* he said, 'I'd like to think of kids in schools reading one or two of those, maybe, even if it's just for their exams.'

'The conversations with him were always ones I felt might be an ordeal, but in fact, they never were. And on one occasion, speaking of his illness, he said, "Actually, I'm grateful for it, it's given me one last chance to see things clearly, a last chance to say something maybe, and I just hope I'm spared the time to say it." Well, ladies and gentlemen, he did finish it, and here it is.'

He is now holding up a slim volume of poems with the title, *The Pale Dawn*.

'They are poems,' Cyril explains, 'which Adam wrote in the last six months of his life. In the very last conversation I had with him, he gave me a manuscript, and asked me to do what I could with it.'

'The first poem,' says Cyril 'is called *Standing There*, which may put some of us oldies in mind of a certain song by The Beatles, but it is in fact taken from a poem by W.B. Yeats, as is the epigraph *Oh, that I were young again and held her in my arms.*'

He reads the poem aloud and Natalie, knowing that the poem is about her but not wanting to draw attention to herself, has now dried her tears and has made herself calm.

'A simple love poem, I suppose you could say,' Cyril concludes, 'as are all the poems in the collection, simple lyrical poems with the wistful detachment of an old man looking back perhaps, but also with a vivid sense of the present, together with a stark sense of the ultimate mystery of the universe and the potential emptiness we all face. Ladies and gentlemen, Adam Mitchell.'

There is a round of applause and then Cyril says, 'I should add that copies of *The Pale Dawn* can be purchased here today at the very reasonable price of £9.99, and all profits will go to this, our much-loved gallery.'

This cheeky reference to the commercial side of things causes a ripple of mirth and it effectively breaks the sombre atmosphere.

Julie pops the cork of a bottle of Prosecco with her usual giggle and Nathan sets up at the counter to sell copies of *The Pale Dawn*.

Natalie is his first customer and when the purchase is complete, she leans towards his ear and says, 'See you down at the pub later, creep, I want you to meet Melanie.'

Thank you for reading this book. If you have any particular thoughts or reactions, why not leave a review on Amazon?

Further titles in the Detective Nula Ryan series are:
The Irini House
The Playroom

Both to be released on Amazon soon.
As a taster, here are the first two chapters of 'The Irini House'

THE IRINI HOUSE

CHAPTER 1

I know that the feeling of being alone at the end of a long relationship is not new. And that loneliness, and feelings of abandonment and self-pity are not unusual. Though when you feel them, they are intense, and you think yourself the only person in the world who has ever been in this desperate empty place.

And you think you will be quite incapable of going into work the next day. But still, you do go. You go in, and that, in the end, is what saves you. I was a Detective Inspector. I had had a partner and a child. Suddenly, being a DI was all I had.

We had been together for seven years.

When we took Phoebe into school together that very first day, Wendy and I, it seemed that all was well. Her first day at school. The beginning of another chapter in our journey of being single-sex parents. The school knew. We had made a point of telling them, proudly, who we were, and they had been abundantly welcoming.

We had agreed that the school runs should be shared as equally as possible. As a nurse, it was easier for Wendy to arrange her shifts than it was for me. I did my best, but there were times, often, when I had to call her and say, *look can you just do it today, I'm really in the middle of something.*

And she did. By and large she did. Though it was not without tensions.

And it was at the school gate, as it turned out - more fool me - that Wendy met the lady with whom she decided to have a fling, a fling which - by the time I found out about it - had become a full-blown affair.

Tanya, she was called. I knew who she was. I'd seen her plenty of times myself, spoken to her too. She was nice, I thought: didn't seem out of the ordinary in any way, but there it was. Wendy had fallen for her.

Wendy told me that I had changed. That was one of the barbed weapons she used against me in that protracted and awful period when I still thought we could talk our way through it. I saw a different side to her then. A harder side. Or -put it this way- I could see her guarding against any of the softer emotions I knew she was feeling underneath, especially when it came to Phoebe. She didn't want to be the person she was being. But she was tough enough to stick it out. In the end, she left with Phoebe and moved in with Tanya. And that was that.

But it was true that I had changed.

Not in my affections -which were constant- but in what people sometimes call the work-life balance. Mine, I admit, had veered gradually but definitely in favour of work.

After Frank left the force – we'd been together in the team for two years – I applied for a role in the OCG team, specialising, as the initials say, in the investigation of Organised Crime Gangs in the West Yorkshire area. I was interviewed – four interviews actually - and eventually accepted. I was over the moon.

Some people said I was mad, and I soon found out what they meant, but to me it was real policing, out there in the wild, wild world and it was exciting. There were eight of us in the team. We were a tight-knit unit, and we made all our own operational decisions. The others were all lovely misfits in a way, people driven, thriving on caffeine, nicotine and adrenalin, prepared to go thirty-six hours without sleep, ready to throw themselves into harm's way if need be.

Like a chameleon, I took on their colours.

We were dealing with dangerous people: mafia networks embedded in local communities, trafficking drugs, exploiting poverty, using children, ruling through fear and intimidation with an iron grip; and with no qualms about doling out violence when they saw fit. People who thought they were above the law.

In the team, it was a passion -an obsession even- to prove that this wasn't the case, but it was touch-and-go. Compiling evidence was a long-term business. Hours of sitting in cars, sometimes well into the early hours, observing the comings and goings of targets, taking photographs; hundreds of hours of working through phone records, drawing patterns and spider diagrams of contacts. Occasional dawn raids that led to arrests, and, more often than not -soul-destroying as it was- to bail and release without charge. Threats too, of the *we-know-where-you-live* variety, not just to potential witnesses, but to members of the team as well.

So, yes, it was a passion, and it became my passion too, almost like an addiction.

When Wendy left, I drew a deep breath, faced the void and threw myself back into it. Just after that there was a teenage stabbing, not fatal but in plain daylight, on a street in town. The perpetrator was not difficult to track down but he wouldn't say a thing. His 'no comment' responses were feeble, a line someone had told him to say. He was trying to be streetwise. In reality, he was just a little boy.

Underneath, he was frightened. He knew he was going to go down. If he went down silently, he'd have an easy time inside. That's how it works. No come-back. Easy drugs on the inside to help the time pass by.

That was what we were up against.

We went to interview his mother. She was in a flat with two younger kids, seven and twelve, and, by all the signs, with a habit. She wouldn't say a word. I looked round the flat. It was filthy, with beds that couldn't have been changed for weeks, if not months. I was sure that if social services weren't so hard pressed, those kids would be in care. One side of you says, just leave them to it. Let them just get on with destroying each other. But of course, you can't do that.

But then came the break-through.

The mother came in of her own accord. She made statements naming names of the people who had been controlling her son.

Under cross-examination, the son broke down and confirmed the names and gave us a run-down of the whole operation.

It went to the CPS. Three months later, we had convictions for sixteen members of the gang.

Needless to say, it was a big night in the pub.

But it was also an ending. The team had achieved its goal. It was to be disbanded and its members reassigned. We were all commended and given additional leave. In our professional discussions afterwards, were asked to think about what direction we wanted to pursue next.

CHAPTER 2

I decided to take a break. I had been working 24/7 for six months and I was owed bucketfuls of leave. I took two weeks.

Two weeks! You imagine it will be lovely. Stay in bed until noon. Binge on movies. Drink wine. Luxury!

But that rosy phase lasted no more than two days.

After that I became restless, agitated.

My system didn't know how to let go.

I took Phoebe out for the day on Saturday. She called me Aunty Nula. If I'd been thinking she'd be upset when I disappeared from the scene, I was wrong. She said she'd enjoyed it but declined the offer of a sleepover. The child's mind contains brilliant repair apparatus.

I decided to have a drive out along the valley to Milthwaite, which was where I'd done one of my last cases with Frank. It brought back a curious mixture of memories. There was nostalgia for the long hot spell we had had that summer, a nostalgia tinged with sadness because that was also the summer of Phoebe's birth. Now it was a crisp February day. I walked along by the canal and up through the lanes, wondering what had become of Natalie Anderson, the girl who'd found herself at the centre of the drama. Magda Bentley's studio had now become a welding shop for a firm producing wrought iron gates. This, I guessed, would not be much to the liking of Rob Jenkins, the carpet wholesaler with voyeuristic tendencies who had the premises opposite. It had been in the papers that Adam Mitchell, the writer, had died not long after the case. The cottage where he lived, where we'd interviewed him twice, had had a two-storey extension built. Probably a family, I thought.

Everything moves on!

I was glad to get back into work, back to my old desk. Well, not my actual old desk, as it had found a new occupant in the meantime, but it was nice to be back in the squad room. There were a few of my old colleagues still around, Geoff Stone, Simon Pooley and others, along with quite a few faces I didn't recognise. I located the desk I'd been allocated, logged on, and started to get up to speed with what was happening. Twenty minutes later, I got a call from Inspector Renwick inviting me along to have a chat in his office.

'Welcome back, Nula,' he said, affably. 'I hear great things.'

I shrugged my shoulders. It wasn't false modesty. I knew I'd been part of a team.

I found myself noticing his desk. It was a little bit like a home-from-home, with photographs, turned away from me, but obviously there to remind him, in moments of stress, perhaps, of cosy family things. I'd had a little picture of Phoebe on my old desk, and one of the three of us together, but I'd put them away somewhere. They would not have seemed right in the little room, reeking of sweat which we had called an office in the OCG group.

'I'd like you to have a look at these, Nula,' he said.

He pushed towards me, over the desk, NCA and WHO reports on Modern Slavery and Sex Trafficking.

'You'll be familiar with these?'

'Yes, guv,' I replied. Documents like these were standard background in the Unit I'd been working with.

'How many brothels would you say we've got in this division, Nula?'

I shrugged my shoulders. 'A few,' I said, which was as accurate as I could be.

'And how many massage parlours, and how many of them are legit?'

Again, I shrugged my shoulders. 'I've dealt with a few incidents of the sex worker meets drunk and disorderly variety, but I'm not a specialist.'

'I want you to become one,' he said, very directly, 'a specialist, that is,' he added, as if belatedly aware that what he had said could be taken the wrong way. 'With the experience you've gained with the OCG team, I want to set you up to collate all the information you can get hold of and report back to me on it. How do you feel about taking that on?'

'What are we talking about exactly?'

'Sex worker coercion,' he said. 'Enforced prostitution.' I could tell he wasn't entirely sure of his own terminology.'

'Haven't Human Trafficking got that covered?'

'They've got a big brief, Nula. They have to cast a very wide net. I want something focused, local. We can feed into Human Trafficking with what we find, if we find anything significant.'

I like Renwick. He's a decent boss, one who will stick up for you if need be, but I knew, as he spoke to me, that what he really wanted was some paperwork in place, some praiseworthy evidence that we were taking it seriously.

'Can I give it some thought, sir?'

He nodded, and I could tell from the way he nodded that he had expected me to jump at it, and that he was slightly inclined to take a dim view of my reticence.

'All right, Nula,' he said, running a pencil up and down between his fingers and the desk, 'have a think. Come and see me when you've made your mind up.'

There was a distinct headmasterly tone to this *see me* and I felt like the ungrateful sixth former being given leave to depart from his study.

I had a word with Geoff Stone, in the pub, later.

'Sounds like a lot of desk work to me, Geoff,' I said. 'A lot of report writing.'

He could see where I was coming from.

'And what about Human Trafficking?' I asked. 'I don't want to be treading on anybody's toes.'

'It's a potential can of worms,' said Geoff, 'make no mistake about it. But the big story has been sexual exploitation of girls locally, like in Rochdale. Maybe there could be another angle.'

'You're not reassuring me, Geoff,' I said, with a laugh.

'Set up a meeting with Angela in Leeds. Talk it through. Have you met her?'

'A couple of times. Yes, she came in on some of the OCG stuff.'

'She's reasonable. Not up her own backside.'

'Yeah, that was my impression.'

'Or why not just do it?' he said. 'Do yourself a favour. You've been out there in the trenches for a year. Give yourself a break. If it's cushty, so what? Do a good report. Get some more brownie points. Go for promotion. Go for a transfer.'

A year ago, I would have gone home to Wendy and we would have thrashed it out over a bottle of Sauvignon Blanc. Now the flat seemed to echo with the hollowness of my solitary thoughts. A year ago, a transfer would have been utterly out of the question. Now, it was different. Going for transfers, progressing on the back of your successes - or failures if you could spray them with a bit of glitter - was one of the ways upwards. Inspector? Chief Inspector? Superintendent? Was I really interested in those things?

Floating freely in my own loose orbit, and with a bottle of Sauvignon Blanc consumed but not shared, I was prepared to let my thoughts roam anywhere.

Printed in Great Britain
by Amazon